Birds of a Feather

A NOVEL

DANIELLE MORRIS

Birds

OF A

Feather

This book is a work of fiction. Any names, businesses, characters, places and events are products of the author's imagination. Any resemblance to actual events, or places, or persons, living or dead is entirely coincidental.

Copyright © 2023 by Danielle Morris

All rights reserved.

No portion of this book may be reproduced, or stored in a retrieval system, or transmitted in any form or by any means, electronic, mechanical, photocopying, recording, or otherwise, without express written permission of the author except for the use of brief quotations in a book review.

ISBN 979-8-9876836-0-6

Editing by Brenda Patience

Developmental Edits by Esther Godoy Montanez & Haley Warren

Cover Photo/Author Photo by Zachary Morris

Follow me on Instagram @daniellemorriswrites for more updates on future books!

To all the dark and twisty souls who find beauty hidden amongst the tragedy.

CONTENT WARNINGS

Dear reader,
Thank you so much for picking up my book. I truly hope when you read this book that you find something that resonates with you. That being said, I know this book deals with some very heavy topics that might be triggering for some of you. There's only one of you in this world and I am a firm believer in taking care of yourself first. Forever and always. I've listed some content warnings below for those of you who might need them.

Late-term pregnancy loss
Domestic assault/domestic violence
Dubious consent
Suicidal thoughts
Injury with knife and gun
Death scenes
Mild alcohol abuse

Prologue

"Hello, Miss? Can you hear me? Please, please wake up. Please open your eyes, please come back to me."

My eyes fly open when I hear the unfamiliar voice.

The morning sun is blinding, peaking through the forest of lush evergreens. My entire body feels heavy and my mind is in a fog.

Where am I?

What happened to me?

No–to us.

I try to move my hand to my swollen stomach; the effort alone feels almost impossible, like I'm wading through quicksand. Every inch I make towards my goal is in slow motion.

Suddenly, I realize how frozen I am. My body feels as though I've been submerged in ice water, and I can't stop shaking. It's making my movements jerky and uncoordinated.

After what feels like hours, I finally reach my stomach and feel something wet, something cold...

"Please try not to move. Help is on the way and should be here any minute. I am here for you, and I'm not going to let anything else happen to you. They'll be here soon, just please stay with me." says the stranger's pleading voice.

I hear him step closer to me and feel his hand on mine moments later. His hands are so warm on my frigid skin. I feel my eyes getting heavy again. The stranger touches my forehead with a feather-light caress. The feeling is so startling that I jerk myself back to consciousness.

I look up and into this stranger's eyes. They are the brightest blue I've ever seen, and I feel myself getting lost in them as if being pulled in by a riptide. The sunlight coming in from above him makes him look like someone out of a dream.

Is this real?

I feel something moist touch my cheek. It feels like something is sniffing me all over. I look over to see a large dog laying down next to me, almost as if he is guarding me.

The stranger's voice pulls me out of my head again. "Hello there, my name is Silas, and this is my dog, Duke. He's the one that found you this morning. Can you tell me your name? Can you tell me what happened to you, or who did this to you?"

I open my mouth and try to say my name, my throat is painfully dry as I try to swallow. I am fighting against sandpaper, and I cannot force a single noise out.

I hear sirens in the distance, and I remember that I'm not alone. I look down at my hand and see that it is covered in a dark red liquid. In the blink of an eye, the pain washes over my entire body as I see the knife that is protruding out of my stomach and into my unborn child.

I open my mouth to finally say something, anything, and all that comes out is a scream...

Chapter One

One Year Later

THIS IS THE PLACE of my nightmares. The place that has haunted me every night for the last year. The place where my entire life fell apart. And I haven't been able to piece it back together. Months of therapy and I still feel like the same woman who woke up in this forest, covered in our blood. Still unable to process the nightmare that happened to both of us.

It's been an entire year since I lost my child, and not a single day has gone by that I haven't thought of him.

My son.

My hands come up automatically to touch my scar, the scar where the knife was plunged into both of us. A few inches lower is the scar the doctors had to make to get him out of me.

—

All I can hear is the sound of my own screaming. He can't be gone. He cannot be gone.

"Please save him instead!" I scream and plead as several different people are trying to wrap blood pressure cuffs on me and trying to hold me down on the gurney.

"Ma'am, can you tell us your name?"

My name? Who gives a fuck about my name when I know my child is dying inside of my body right now?!

This cannot be happening. We were supposed to be happy. A happy family. I fought so hard to keep us all together. My baby cannot be gone. Our story cannot be over.

"Mr. Hale, do you happen to know her name?" *I hear the blood pressure cuff nurse ask someone. I assume it's the stranger named Silas who found me in the forest.*

"No, she wasn't able to tell me before she blacked out again. All I know is that she had to have been out there for less than 48 hours because I walk the forest trail every couple of days with my dog. He found her, and she wasn't there two days ago. I've never met her before today. " *I hear him take a deep breath next to me, and I feel his hand again as he reaches to hold mine. His hand is still so warm.* "Can you tell me if they are going to be okay?"

Two days.

He left me for dead for two days.

The love of my life tried to kill me.

My head is spinning. The blackness is returning to take me away again. But before I pass out again, I hear the four words that completely and utterly destroy me.

The four words that no mother should ever have to hear.

"There's no fetal heartbeat."

I swear I hear my heart crack in two before I pass out again.

—

We have all sorts of words for people who have been fundamentally changed by loss and grief.

If you lose your parents, they call you an orphan.

If you lose a spouse, they call you a widow.

But nobody has come up with a word to label a childless mother. That type of loss is so abhorrent that we shy away from it like it's a plague...as if we can somehow catch it like a disease if we talk openly about it.

No one should have to go through the pain of having a child that they've never really met, because that type of pain is unbearable in every single way. There isn't a word strong enough to describe this type of loss.

I stare into the entrance of the forest, my body unwilling to take another step forward. I haven't been back here since it happened. My therapist Dr. Lee has this fun idea that I should come back to face my demons, and she has been urging me to go ever since I started seeing her after the *accident*.

Because I *accidently* forced my husband to take me to the spot where we fell in love...the spot that has been a catalyst in the forming of our entire life together. And then I *accidentally* asked him to stab me, resulting in the *accidental* murder of our unborn child.

I want to scream every time she uses that word in our sessions.

According to her, calling it an accident is supposed to trick my own brain into easing the guilt I feel over not being able to protect my child or myself. Personally, I think that's a load of shit. As far as I can tell, I still feel the same weight of guilt and anguish over my own shortcomings.

There is no tricking my brain when I know that this is my fault. I caused this. If I would have listened to my gut when I knew something felt off, then I would be carrying my son in my arms today. But I thought I knew the man that loved me, and I chose not to run.

Instead, I'm carrying a bouquet of sunflowers and forget-me-nots in one arm, a teddy bear in the other, and my son's ashes tucked away in a bag over my shoulder.

"I can do this. I can do this." I mutter under my breath while trying to force myself to take the first step onto the clearly marked walking trail.

DANIELLE MORRIS

I must look like a total whack job to the few hikers that have walked past me in the last two hours, standing here by myself in my bright yellow crocs and arms full of flowers and a fluffy brown teddy bear. If my appearance wasn't concerning enough, then I know the whole "talking to myself" thing must be.

This forest used to be a place of solace. I came here so many times over the years. I used to walk these paths with my father when I was a young girl. He would hold my hand the entire time, nervous that I would somehow run too far ahead of him and end up lost to him forever. We used to walk these paths until the sun went down, hand-in-hand talking about everything and anything. My father was a quiet, pensive man, who didn't talk much. But he came to life in those moments we shared together in this forest. He loved pointing out things that reminded him of his own childhood, and never passed up an opportunity to give me some of the most important life lessons as we strolled down the familiar path together.

My mother took me here when I was old enough to experience my first heartbreak. I was 10, and the boy I liked told everyone that my wild red hair and incredibly pale skin was due to me being part demon. When I argued with him and told him I wasn't a demon, he told everyone that I *had* to be a vampire then. He convinced my entire 5th grade class to bring garlic to school to throw at me during recess. That evening, my mother held my hand as we walked the trails. She helped me get over my bitterness and resentment towards the people who had hurt me out by throwing rocks into the creek near our favorite spot. Each rock I threw made me feel invincible. The next day, I wore a necklace made of garlic knots and fake vampire teeth that my dad found in the attic with all the old Halloween costumes. That boy who broke my heart didn't mess with me too much after that.

These were the trails I ran through while screaming and yelling at God for taking them both from me in a careless car accident when I was only 14. I became an orphan and left the only home I had ever known to live with my grandparents a few towns over.

I used to cherish this place. Growing up I believed that this forest had a piece of my heart rooted into each tree that surrounds it. This place was the only place that felt like home after my parents died. Walking into this forest felt like walking into their outstretched arms and into their loving embrace. Each rustle of leaves sounded like a whispered "I love you" from them.

These were the trails where the first boy I fell in love with brought me for my first kiss when we were 15. He asked me to marry him in the same spot just a few years later.

But when that boy ripped my heart out with his bare hands and left me here to die, he made sure that this place would no longer hold the magic of my childhood or the loving memories of my parents.

Today it holds nothing but the tragedy of my life, and I don't know how to take the first step back into it.

I could always come back tomorrow. Dr. Lee doesn't need to know that I didn't come today. It's not like I can get graded in therapy, and if I did, then this would be the first failure I'd be happy to walk away with.

But I know I can't walk away, not today, not when I need to spread my son's ashes here so he can rest with my parents. He deserves more than sitting in a ceramic jar on my nightstand while watching me cry every night. I will stand here and grapple with my conflicted emotions until I have the courage to take that first step.

On one hand, I desperately want to go visit my parents' resting place. I'm holding onto that sliver of hope that coming here will help me feel close to them again and maybe even bring me a moment of comfort on this awful day. On the other hand, I know that this visit is going to bring even more shame onto myself. I don't know if I'm ready to face that yet.

My constant self-loathing makes me feel like I'm being torn apart from the inside by razor-sharp talons. Coming here, where they are, I don't know if I can handle this. Even though they don't walk this Earth anymore, I know they saw what happened.

They saw my first failure as a parent.

They saw me fail to protect my own child.

They would never forgive me if they were alive today, and that eats at my soul every single day.

I know *he* brought me here to this place for a reason. He knew what this place meant to me, how special it had always been for me. Part of me has always wondered if he brought me here to try and end my life because he loved me more than he had ever loved anyone. It was his last declaration of love to me. A promise that even though my life was possibly going to end, that at least I would never be alone.

Even though he failed at ending my life, he succeeded in making sure that I was more alone than ever. But I would rather be alone than tied to a monster. Everyday I am plagued with the knowledge that he will return to fulfill his second promise of taking me back...

If he couldn't have me, then nobody could.

That's it, time to stop feeling sorry for myself and self-sabotaging with my dark and twisty thoughts. I need to just hurry up and get this over with. If I don't go now, I know I'll never have the courage.

I take a deep breath and I take my first step forward into the place that was once my favorite in the world, to go face the demons that have invaded it.

Chapter Two

THE FOREST SEEMS DARKER than it used to. The trees are thicker with foliage and the sunlight doesn't penetrate through the treetops like I remember.

One step, two steps, three steps. My chest feels heavy, my breaths coming out in pants of slight panic. I shouldn't have come here, I tell myself as I focus on the path ahead of me and keep walking, hoping that the dizziness will fade before I run into someone.

Breathe in, breathe out. One step, two steps, three steps.

I make my way down the trail one step at a time, clutching the flowers and teddy bear tightly against my chest as if they are my only lifeline in this graveyard of evergreens and pine needles.

I gasp loudly as the memories I have of this place start rushing in.

—

"This is one of my favorite spots in this place," I say as I go to my knees at the edge of the creek.

"Why is that?" he asks me while he kneels next to me.

"Because this is where my parents are going to be," I say, pulling my backpack from across my back and hugging it to my chest.

"I'm not sure I understand what you mean..." he says, dipping his fingers into the cold water.

"When they died a year ago, I stole their urns from my grandparents' fireplace mantle and swapped them with the dust from the vacuum. I saw someone do it on TV, and I knew they would hate to be stuck in that house, just as much as I hate it there."

"Wait, you've had your parents' ashes in your backpack for an entire year, just waiting to meet some strange boy with a car that would bring you here, no questions asked?" He raises an eyebrow and looks at me.

"Yes. My grandma refused to bring me back here, and my grandpa can't drive anymore after his stroke."

"No fucking way. I swear to God if you pull ashes out of that backpack of yours then I'm going to fall in love with you." He huffs out a loud laugh and runs his fingers through his hair. "So unless you're ready to meet your soulmate at 15, you had better not pull any fucking Ziplock baggies of ashes out of that bag." He continues laughing as he stands and wipes his hands on his dark jeans.

I stand up and look at him. He's tall, dark brown hair curls at the nape of his neck, and hazel eyes that I swear can see right into the darkest depths of my own soul. He has a lip ring that he can't seem to stop playing with and I'd be lying if I said that kissing him and playing with that ring myself didn't intrigue me.

But this moment wasn't about me. It was about my parents and I needed to do this, no distractions.

Slowly, I reach into my backpack, watching his eyes follow every single movement, and pull out a Ziplock bag. His eyes widen, and he looks up at me before he smiles the most striking smile I've ever seen.

"I hope you know what this means?" *he says, running his fingers across his lips again while taking a step towards me.*

I look up at him and feel a small smile tugging at my lips. I bring my Ziplock ashes to my chest and hold them tightly. "Actually, you said if I pulled 'baggies' out of my bag. As you can see, I only have one bag."

His mouth drops open in confusion as he looks down at the bag I'm clutching against my chest. "So then, which parent are we freeing from the dusty mantle today?"

I look down at the bag in my arms and then look back up into his hazel eyes. "Both," I tell him. "I knew they'd hate being apart more than they'd hate spending eternity on that fireplace mantle, so I combined them into one bag, just in case it took me longer to find my way back to this place."

His eyes widen slightly as he takes in my answer. "I think I might have just fallen in love with you, and I don't even know your name," he says while taking another step closer to me.

"My name is Florence," I say. "Florence Renee Taylor."

"Hello, Florence Renee Taylor. I'm Ronan Scott Samuels, and I think I'd like to kiss you now."

"I think I'd really like that, Ronan Scott Samuels..." I respond quietly as I lean in towards his lips. His lips touch mine softly, and I kiss him back, as I hug my parents' ashes even closer to my chest.

—

Tears spring in my eyes as my knees give out underneath me. Those memories only serve to crush me now. Being back in this place has destroyed all my mental barriers. I usually don't allow myself to remember those moments unless I am locked away in my bedroom where not a soul can hear me scream.

How is this my life now?

Huge, body crippling sobs escape my lips as I throw the flowers across the trail in front of me, watching as bits and pieces of the yellow and blue scatter along the path. I hug the teddy bear even tighter, gripping it as if it can fill the giant empty space in my chest.

This was a stupid idea. I've accomplished nothing except cause myself yet another panic attack. I can't even walk the aisles in the grocery store without turning into a giant mess of emotions and forcing myself to leave to have my mental breakdown in the car.

What made me think I could climb this mountain without ending up in the same damn place?

The only thing I know for certain is that I don't want to do this.

I slowly pick myself up and get on my feet. I'm covered in dirt, and my flowers are ruined. My teddy bear seems to be the only one of us that made it out in one piece, even if it seems a little lopsided now. I shake myself out, trying to wipe as much of the dirt off of my black leggings as I can before taking a few steps to pick up the massacre of flowers.

God I am a mess. Definitely time to go.

As I turn around to walk back to my car, I hear a noise above my head. I look up and see a possum walking across a tree branch above me and let out an angry laugh towards the sky.

Dammit, Dad. If I didn't think he was already watching me, I know he's watching me now.

—

"Dad, what kind of rat is that? I've never seen one that looks like that," I ask while pointing at a big, hairy gray thing scurrying across the forest ahead of us.

It's getting dark in the forest now, but this is always the best time to go animal hunting...not that we would ever hunt animals. My dad has always enforced the "do no harm" rule in our house ever since I was old enough to realize that the eight-legged dust bunny in the corner of my bathroom could actually move. It was completely and utterly terrifying.

"That's an opossum, not a rat, Florence," he answers me with a little smile tugging at his cheeks. "They like to sleep during the day and are mostly active at night. They look big, and when they get scared they open their mouths and hiss like an alligator, but they won't hurt you. Possums are smart little creatures though. If they know they can't outrun you or win

in a fight, they'll play dead to predators and won't get up until they know the area is safe again."

"WHAT?! They can play dead?! Do you think it will let me pet it if we get closer and just scare him a little bit?" I ask him, already getting ready to take my shot at petting a new animal.

My dad lets out a big belly laugh and steps forward to put his arm around me.

"No, you cannot go over there just to scare him so you can pet him, but I do admire your quick thinking, Flore." He ruffles my hair with his giant hand and I laugh up at him. "He's just trying to get home to his family to get himself some dinner. We should do the same before your mother starts calling my cell phone to yell at us."

"...Or when she calls, we can just play dead, and maybe we'll be able to stay out longer," I say, reaching up to hold his hand for our walk back home.

"That's my girl," he chuckles while squeezing my hand.

—

Ever since that day, I've never been able to see a possum without immediately thinking of my dad, so I know he's looking down on me right this moment as I stare up at this damn possum hanging out above my head. Thanks, dad. Now I really can't chicken out...and really, actually have to do this.

I look back towards the trail that will lead me out of this forest and to the safety of my car, and take my next step in the opposite direction.

I can do this.

I am doing this.

I'm doing a fantastic job at giving myself emotional whiplash today.

The sun is slowly starting to set, so there has been little to no foot traffic from anyone else on the trail in the last hour. Thank God. I don't need witnesses for this. I already have my own ghosts watching me today as it is.

As I get closer to our spot, I listen carefully and can hear the water flowing from the creek. It used to be one of my favorite sounds in the world. So much so that when my parents died, I used to play river sounds every night through my headphones just to sleep.

As soon as I can hear the water, a sort of calm washes over me, and even though I do not want to be here for these particular reasons , I find myself quickening my pace just to get to our spot faster.

Not much further now, and then I can get this over with. Dr. Lee would be proud. She's constantly reminding me that I need to stop quitting everything before I can get even close to the hard part. And even though I have almost quit a couple, or ten, times today, I'm proud of myself for finally making it here. I hold the teddy bear and flowers even closer and square my shoulders.

I. Can. Do. This.

I cut off the marked trail and through the trees. These trees are much thicker with vines and leaves, obvious signs from not being disturbed often. They used to not be like this. We used to come here so often that we swore the trees would make way for us like the trees in that scene from The Little Mermaid.

These trees don't recognize me anymore, which is unsurprising since I hardly recognize myself anymore. I fight through the foliage until I can see the end of the tree line. Holding my breath and closing my eyes, I take the last step into the small open clearing that holds so many different pieces of my heart.

I breathe in deep, the smells of the dirt and the water that are as familiar as an old friend. As I open my eyes, I notice two things out of place immediately.

First, there is a small wooden bench near the edge of the creek that was never here before.

Second, I am not alone.

Chapter Three

I STAND HERE, SHOCKED and completely paralyzed, as I stare at the stranger. I recognize this person, but I can't recall where I've seen him before..

Why is he here?

Who would come to this spot on today of all days?

I immediately start to panic with the fear that Ronan has sent this person to finish the job he started one year ago. I strike that thought quickly. That wouldn't make any sense. He hoped that I would survive so that I'd come back to him one day. Ronan is not the type of man to let others do his dirty work. When he does come back for me, he will do it himself.

Part of me looks forward to that day, just so I can beg him to finish the job, so I can finally stop walking around in fear. It would be a blessing to finally shed this giant emptiness that plagues my every moment. But an even bigger part of me knows that he has to pay for what he did to our son. I can't wait to be the one who is standing over him with the knife this time.

While I'm lost in my own dark fantasy of revenge, I catch movement from the corner of my eyes. Before I can turn my head to see what it is, I'm being tackled to the ground by a giant mass of fur. Both my flowers and teddy bear go flying, and I fall painfully onto the wet forest ground.

"What the hell!" I scream while I try desperately to crawl away from my attacker. It is much harder than it should be because I'm being pinned flat on my back while being licked all over by a giant dog.

"DUKE! STOP! GET OFF OF HER! DAMMIT, DUKE!" yells an angry voice from nearby. Abruptly, the dog jumps off of me, ends up knocking the air out of my lungs, and leaves me alone again on the forest floor.

What in the ever-loving hell just happened?

Here I am again, laying on this damp ground, but instead of being here with my son, I'm here with a dirty teddy bear and broken flowers. I reach up and feel my bag still strapped across my shoulder. At least his ashes are safe.

I look to the sky, and I break open completely. The tears I've been trying my hardest to hold back finally hit, and they come crashing with no intention of ever stopping. This wasn't supposed to be my life. The loneliness and unfairness of it all is crushing me from every angle. I can't breathe, and I just want to bury myself in this forest and never come out again.

Why couldn't I have just died too?

I'm crying harder now, and my whole body is shaking from grief and anger.

"Ma'am, are you okay?"

Oh shit. I forgot that I'm not alone, because of course I can't be left to drown in my own misery in peace. First, the fucking possum, then I get plowed down by a flower-killing dog, and now, I have this stranger watching me have a full blown psychotic break.

I cover my face with my hands and can't stop myself from hysterically laughing in between my fit of sobs.

How is this my life now?

I hear footsteps coming closer to me, and I pull my hands away from my face to finally get a full look at who I'm sharing this miserably embarrassing moment with. I look up at him, and I'm met with the brightest blue eyes I've ever seen. Before I can say a word to him and apologize for my insane behavior, he stops dead in his tracks, eyes widening in surprise. He takes a few steps back as though I've physically pushed him.

"It's...*you*." he says.

Now I know I must look like a total idiot because I'm staring up at this man and I have no idea who he is. All while he's staring down at me like he knows exactly who I am. I can't tell if he's upset to see me or if he's surprised based on his initial reaction.

"I'm sorry?" I try to say but my voice comes out broken. I clear my throat and try to wipe some of the mess of tears off of my face. "But I don't think I know you."

My voice seems to break the weird spell, and he shakes his head and walks towards me, reaching his hand out to help me up. "I'm so sorry about Duke. I hope you aren't hurt." He says quickly.

"He gets overly excited sometimes. I knew as soon as I heard someone moving around the trees that he was going to investigate." He chuckles nervously and continues to explain, "I wasn't able to grab his harness fast enough before he bolted. As soon as I saw the teddy bear, I knew you were a goner."

I reach up and take his hand. I'm surprised to find it so warm compared to my own.

"Thanks for the help," I say before pulling myself to my feet and taking a few steps back. "I could literally die of embarrassment right now, so let's just say your dog knocking me on my ass makes us even and we never ever have to talk about you watching me have my meltdown. Deal?"

"I don't really see how that makes us even, since my dog is the reason you got so upset in the first place." He looks away, embarrassed.

"Plus, he ruined your flowers and teddy bear," he says while pointing over my shoulder.

I turn to look and see the dog licking the teddy bear in between his paws.

"It's probably better that he has it anyway. At least it'll get more love with him than it would have here," I say while huffing a joyless laugh. I turn around and look back up again. I find the stranger looking right back into my eyes with a concern and intensity that I don't fully understand.

Why does he seem so familiar?

I study him some more. He's tall. Taller than I originally thought when I first looked up at him from the forest floor. His red flannel fits tightly across his chest, and his thick arms fill out the sleeves to a snug perfection. He has dark hair that's long enough for him to run his hands through as he talks. I can't really tell if it's more brown or black since it's getting darker outside now that the sun has fallen under the tree line. I already noticed his gorgeously bright blue eyes. The more I continue to stare at him, the more I see something vaguely familiar about them.

I finally step towards him again and reach my hand out. "By the way, my name is Florence, and I'm not usually this big of a mess. It's just been a rough day for me."

He takes my hand in his with a firm shake and a friendly smile reaches his lips. "It's so nice to finally meet you, Florence. My name is Silas."

Silas.

Oh my god. It can't be him. Can it? Why else would he be here on today of all days?

"Silas..." I whisper, hand still clutched in his. "I think I know you..." I stare up at him and everything clicks into place as the memories of this day rush to the surface. "You were here. That day. It was you." He nods his head and gazes down at me. The concern and pity in his eyes is reflected back at me so clearly. It *is* him.

"Yeah, it was me. Or I guess it was us." He looks sadly over at Duke. "We were on our morning walk when Duke ran off the trail and found you."

I follow his gaze and see Duke sitting a few paces from me, staring up at me, like he remembers me. Memories resurface again as I'm thrown back to that day, and I remember Duke in vivid detail. "He stayed there and laid next to me, licking my hand and my face. I remember him too." How could I forget one of the small gestures of warmth and comfort I had during that day?

I pull my hand out of Silas's and turn to walk towards Duke. I don't make it more than a few steps before my legs give out and I am falling to my knees and crying all over again. I let myself drown in grief as I sit here in this place again. I bring my hands up to hide my face, but I'm interrupted by Duke coming up and nudging my chin with his nose. I look into his sweet puppy eyes and that just makes me cry even harder. This is way more than I bargained for today, and I don't know how to stop the giant tidal wave of emotions that has crashed into me so furiously.

I throw my arms around Duke and sob even harder into his fur. He is so soft and warm. A comfort I didn't know that I needed until this very minute.

Safe. Loved. And most importantly, not alone.

I hug Duke tighter and say a silent prayer to Sky Daddy for bringing them back here today.

Chapter Four

I HONESTLY WANTED TO get through this day without any type of human interaction. I didn't want to see anyone. I didn't want to talk to anyone. I hoped I wouldn't run into a single soul during this emotionally draining mission. But between the possum that I know was sent by my father, and literally being run over by the happiest of German Shepherds who was witness to the worst day of my life, I know that there was no way that I was going to make it through this mission without these small nudges of love from above.

"Florence, are you okay?" Silas says while kneeling down next to Duke and I. He looks at my ruined flowers and groans a moment later. "Okay...now I want to kick myself because I know that is literally the stupidest question I could have asked you on a day like today. I guess what I'm asking is if there's anything I can do to make this day a little less heavy?" His hand starts to reach out towards me, almost as if he thought about putting his hand on my shoulder to comfort me. I flinch, and instead, he pulls it back and reaches out to pet Duke instead. It's a nice middle ground since I still don't know how to process what I'm feeling about everything that's going on right now...especially about this handsome, somewhat-stranger that has magically come back into my life.

I can tell that Silas is completely out of his comfort zone. And why wouldn't he be? I'm sure he didn't come here today expecting to run into this crazy, emotional mess of a person that I've turned into over the last year.

My eyes linger on him and I can't help but wonder why he is here. I don't remember him sticking around once I got to the hospital. All I can really remember is that I think he was with me in the ambulance. I remember the sound of his voice and I remember the warmth and squeeze of his hand when I heard that my son had no heartbeat.

I don't remember ever seeing Silas again until today.

That's weird, right? Or is it my lack of trust after everything I've been through that's making me feel a little uneasy at this whole situation?

I look over at him and find him staring right back into my eyes, looking so concerned for me that it makes my lack of trust in him waver a little bit.

"Silas," I say. I'm hesitant and nervous to ask him this question because I'm not sure if I really want to know the answer. "Why are you here?"

He looks at me like he can see down into the darkest reaches of my own twisted dark soul. There isn't any pity in his stare like I see from almost every single person I've been forced to talk to over this last year. Instead, there's a strange type of admiration in his eyes as he continues to gaze at me. I watch as he takes a deep breath, opening and closing his fist like he's just as nervous to give me his answer as I am to hear it.

"To be honest, Duke and I come down here pretty often and just hang out by the creek for a bit before walking the rest of the trail back. I like to come by and clean off the bench every once in a while because birds love to take it over when nobody's around." He motions towards the bench. "At least that's what I'm guessing based on the piles of bird shit I find on it." He chuckles lightly before running his hand through his hair.

"Why would you bother with cleaning the bench off?" I say, narrowing my eyes at him. I'm still unsure how I feel about this entire situation.

He gives me a small shrug before putting his hands in his pockets. He seems nervous to tell me the truth. "I found myself coming out here a lot in the weeks after we met." His eyes reach mine for a brief moment before looking away again.

"I built this bench here a couple of months after what happened because I couldn't get it all out of my head. Standing here and staring at the creek for hours on end was turning into a weekly, sometimes daily routine for us. So, one day, I got some wood and my tools and spent the afternoon building the bench instead of just staring into the water. Afterwards, I was glad I did it because I'd hoped that one day you'd come back here. I wanted to make sure you had a place to sit for however long you needed."

He built the bench here? For me?

I'm literally speechless after hearing his confession. I'm not sure what I was expecting his answer to be, but that was definitely *not* it.

"Plus, I also like to come out here and sit by the creek to clear my head. My pants stay a lot drier when I have a place to sit that isn't the dirt. So, if we are being technical, then I clean the bench mostly for my own benefit," he tells me with a small smile tugging at his lips...as if he can read the thoughts flying through my head.

I stay quiet for a bit, then narrow my eyes at him. "So you're saying that you built this here?" I point towards the bench without breaking eye contact with him. "How is that even possible?"

I know that this "forest" is really a state park. The Evolit State Park to be exact. I grew up calling it *the woods* and *the forest* because that's what my parents always called it. But it's actually a state park located in Northern California. It has its own forest rangers and security to make sure the park stays clean and safe. Hunting here isn't allowed at all. You have to drive through a big gate and pay the $3.00 fee, or pay the yearly membership like I've always had, before you are allowed to even step foot in this park. There is absolutely *no freaking way* that they would let some random guy come in here and build a whole ass bench. It's just not possible.

Even though this man saved my miserable excuse for a life, I am choosing right now that trusting him and his cute, good guy act is a bad idea. I shouldn't even trust his cute dog, who's currently belly up looking at me with his big brown eyes.

"Look, Silas," I say a little too loudly. "I appreciate everything you did for me that day, I really do. But it's getting dark, and I need to get home."

And then I add in with a rush, just to make sure I don't actually almost get murdered here again, "Ivy, my roommate, is waiting for me with dinner and she'll start making all sorts of calls if I don't get home soon."

He probably thinks I'm lying about my roommate, but it's the truth. Ivy will literally bring out an entire firing squad if I don't come home. She was furious with me today for asking her to stay home and wait for me. But this was something that I knew I needed to do alone.

She's been my best friend for what feels like my entire life and most days, she knows me better than I know myself. So, as angry as she was at me this morning, she also understood that I needed this to be something that I could control. Silas may seem like a nice guy, but my gut is telling me something is off about him. My life would be so much more different if I had listened to my gut a year ago.

Sadness clouds his eyes. A sadness I don't quite understand. "Can I at least walk you back to your car?" he responds. "I'm sure we're walking back to the same parking lot, and my Nan would smite me from above if I left you to walk back alone." Shoving his hands in his pockets, he looks to the darkening sky and then back at me with a hopeful expression. "But I also totally understand if I've made you feel uncomfortable with anything I've said. I really just want to know that you'll get back safely."

I look to the sky and marvel at the darkness as it takes over the light. The stars are slowly starting to show their faces. I didn't plan on being here this late and of course, I don't have a flashlight with me. I could use my phone, but knowing my luck, the battery would die before I've even completed half of the trail back.

I have walked this path for what feels like my entire life, but today it felt like a stranger to me. I tripped over countless broken branches and fell into so many new ditches on the path that I would have never faltered on before.

I am still unsure about how I feel about Silas. On one hand, he did save my life, and I guess that should gain him a little favor in the "he's not going to murder me" category.

On the other hand, him showing up today of all days, at this spot, and having built a magic bench in the middle of a state park, that's kind of weird and iffy to me.

Logic wins out in the end, because I really don't want to walk this place alone once the moon fully rises. There are too many of my own ghosts here now. Far too many that I'd be happy to join. And that thought alone scares the hell out of me.

"Alright," I finally say. "But there is something I came here to do, and I can't leave until it's done. So please, take Duke and go wait on the trail for me. If that's okay?"

A smile tugs at his lips at my response. "Of course I'll wait for you. Take as long as you need."

Chapter Five

I WATCH SILAS AND Duke take off and disappear into the trees. I can hear the leaves crunching under their feet, and the tree branches being pushed aside while they make their way through the foliage and back to the trail.

I take a deep breath, tasting the chill that is creeping into the forest now that the sun is set.

I am finally alone again. A small part of me wishes that I had asked him to stay with me because I don't know how to do this. How to tell my son how much I miss him. Or how sorry I am for not being able to protect him. And how much I love him, a love so deep that his absence feels stronger and stronger every day that goes by. How I wish I could have held him to my chest, just once. So I could breathe in that small moment with him while forever committing it to memory, because I never got to hold him in my arms. I never even got to see his face.

—

I wake up as I'm being transferred from the ambulance and onto a gurney. I can hear the nurses yelling. Yelling at each other to get the doctor and to get an operating room booked immediately.

I can see the name of the hospital on the glass doors that lead to the emergency room, Saint Albert's Memorial Hospital.

All I can smell is the strong antiseptic of the hospital. I can still feel someone's hand holding my own, but my head feels too heavy to move to see who it is. My body feels like it is stuck in quicksand. Numb and heavy. I think I'd rather feel the pain so I would know for certain if I'm alive...or if all of this is something my subconscious has conjured up in order to help me process being attacked and left for dead by my husband. The father of my child.

I feel a strong squeeze on my hand, pulling me out of my own head again. A familiar voice that I can't put a face to pleads with the doctors.

"Please save her. Do whatever you can, just please save her."

Another man's voice answers back, "We are going to do everything we can to help her, but her injuries are extensive, and she's lost a lot of blood. Before we can do anything, we need to get the baby out before she turns septic. We don't know how long she was actually out there in this condition. Right now, that is our main focus. Afterwards, we will be able to reaccess her injuries and treat her accordingly. I promise you that we will do everything we can for her."

Get the baby out.

I'll never feel him move again or see him smile for the first time.

Because my son is gone.

The gurney is being pushed through two double doors, and the temperature of the room feels close to freezing. A mask is placed over my face, and the last thing I see is the kind eyes of another stranger before I am forced to close my own. I'm relieved to be forced into this form of unconsciousness, so that I can keep dreaming of the baby that I'll never get to meet.

—

I can't think of that moment without feeling like my insides are being pulverized, right before they are ripped out of my body. This is what a broken heart feels like. A true, honest to god broken heart. I thought I knew what pain was when I lost my parents, but losing the man that

DANIELLE MORRIS

I loved and then losing my son in the same breath, proved that feeling false. This is real pain, and when it sweeps over me in waves of anguish, it's unbearable.

I press my hands to my eyes and beg my tears to go away. I think back on that memory, and I slowly start putting more pieces of the puzzle together. The man that was pleading with the doctor to save me was Silas. I can recognize his voice now, and I know without a doubt that it was him. I don't know why I never saw him again after that. That fact nags at the back of my head, but it's going to have to wait another day for me to fully unpack. I have other things I need to focus on right now.

I walk over to the bench, picking up my destroyed flowers on the way. I sit down and silently thank Silas for its presence. Bringing the flowers to my face, I inhale deeply. These flowers don't really give out much of a smell, so all I smell is the sap that leaks out of the broken stems and the scents of the forest. I chose sunflowers because they have always reminded me of my mother, happy and radiant even on the hardest of days. She always knew what to say to make me feel better and always made me feel like I could conquer the world. I need that courage and strength from her today. My second flower choice was forget-me-nots, because they will forever remind me of my son. Together, the flowers made for a beautiful bouquet. The bright yellow of the sunflowers and the beautiful baby blues and lilac colors of the forget-me-nots.

Now that the moon has risen enough to let the light slowly peek through the treetops, I look down at the flowers that I'm holding to inspect them closer. Most are ruined now. They've been through the same type of hell I've been through today, just to get to this moment. But even though they are broken, and not as pretty as they were when I picked them up this morning, there is something pleasing about them being as imperfect and broken as I am.

An owl hoots from somewhere above and makes me jump, causing me to drop the flowers. The wildlife and the water running through the creek have always been louder at night. Tonight is no different, and it's a jolting reminder that while I know Silas is just up the path, I am still completely and entirely alone right here. I hear a tree branch snap to the right of me, the noise is so loud it makes me jump off the bench in pure panic and scream.

My instant thought is that it's Ronan, and that he has finally come back to finish the job of destroying me. In my darkest daydreams, I imagine him lying in wait here in this exact spot. Waiting for me to return so he can end my life with the same knife that the doctors pulled out of me; finally reuniting me with our son.

I hear movement coming closer to me. Something is running through the trees and coming at me fast. All I can feel is my heart about to beat completely out of my chest. I instinctively back away as far as I can until my feet are on the edge of the creek. My yellow crocs sink into the soft muddy bank, and I debate whether or not to just run into the creek and try to get to the other side before I hear Silas's voice.

"DUKE STOP! DUKE!" Silas yells through the forest before I see Duke running out from the tree line and right up to me. Sniffing me all over and pawing at my legs. My knees buckle with relief as Duke continues to lick my entire face as I pet him back.

"Holy shit Duke, you really are trying to kill me today." I chuckle while still trying to calm my breathing and get my heart to start beating normally again.

This damn dog. I laugh under my breath and continue to pet his soft coat of fur. Silas comes barreling out of the trees moments later, stopping short when he sees us.

"Thank God you're okay. When I heard you scream I don't know what I thought happened, I just started running." He says while trying to catch his own breath. "Obviously Duke is a much faster savior than I could ever be."

I watch him as he looks around the immediate area, deeming it safe and looking back at me. "What happened?" he asks me.

"Well..." I look away from him because I can feel the embarrassment flooding into my face. "I was sitting on the bench, and then an owl scared me. My mind got the best of me, and I started to think about how dark it was and how alone I was while sitting there."

I sneak a peek back up at him, and then quickly look away again. "I heard something in the trees over there, and I guess I got into my own head and screamed," I say sheepishly. "I'm usually not one of those girls."

At least I wasn't until what Ronan did to me. He changed me at my core and I don't know if that fear of being alone will ever go away.

"You know, the scaredy cat ones who need a man to hold their hand in the big dark forest. But today has been nothing but upside down for me," I add. "I think I really just need to get out of here." I finish my rant as I stand back up, and walk toward Silas with Duke following my footsteps closely.

There's a moment of pause between us, and then Silas asks quietly,. "Did you finish what you needed to do here?"

I sigh, looking over at the flowers thrown onto the ground by the bench. "No. No I did not," I say quietly between us before looking back at my feet and trying once again to keep the tears at bay.

Silas takes a step closer to me, close enough so I can see his own feet lined up with mine. I look up at him and into his impossibly bright blue eyes and feel a tear slipping out and leaving a wet trail down my cheek. Before I can wipe it away, Silas brings one hand up and hesitantly reaches out towards my cheek. I can see the question in his eyes...asking me if this is okay.

I close my eyes, and lean into his hand, letting him wipe the tear away for me before I step completely into his arms and let him hold me.

I've never realized how intimate a hug between two people could be, especially a hug shared between two strangers. But, are we really strangers? I feel like my body knows exactly who he is because this hug feels so unbelievably natural.

He lets me release him first, as if he knows the secret rule of a hug. Don't let go first. My parents always used to tell me that whoever initiated the hug is the one who needed it the most, so that person gets to say when the hug is over. The fact that he waited for me to let go first makes me smile.

I pull away and look up at him. "Thank you for that. It's been awhile since I've let myself be hugged by someone other than Ivy." I know I should feel a little embarrassed by that confession, but he makes it easy to open up without the fear of feeling judged.

Silas just nods like he understands that there isn't a need for words right now. He's giving me the space to sort through my own thoughts before choosing my next step.

Do I want to leave? Or do I want to let him sit next to me, offering me support, while I try to finish what I came here for?

I choose the latter and walk over to the bench, picking the flowers off of the forest floor yet again. I look over to Silas and notice that he hasn't moved a muscle since our hug.

"Do you think you can come and sit here with me for a while?" I ask him while patting the empty seat on the bench.

He smiles a crooked smile at me. "I'd like that."

Chapter Six

The bench isn't huge so naturally, our thighs are touching. I can feel his body heat and it makes me want to scoot even closer to him and envelope myself into the warmth of him. Right now, he makes me feel safe. Even though I know that, logically, I should be more wary of him, I find that I'm not.

Silas clears his throat, forcing me out of my own thoughts.

"I am so sorry for your loss, Florence. I'll live my entire life wishing I could have found you sooner, so that I could have saved him too. I would do anything to go back in time and walk just a bit faster or to have taken this trail the day before." I can hear the anguish and pain in his voice.

I reach out and grab his hand that is sitting on his lap, giving it a squeeze of support like all of the ones he's given me since the first time we met. It feels natural having him here with me. As natural as breathing.

"There isn't anything that anyone could have done. He was gone instantly," I whisper out while trying not to let my emotions take my voice away. "When I woke up in the hospital, it was three days later." I remember instantly looking around for my son and only finding Ivy sleeping in the chair next to my bed. I remember trying to call her name, but my throat was so dry I couldn't speak. I tried to sit up and find a pillow to throw at her, but she heard me move first and stood up, reaching for my face, hands, entire body to see if I was really okay. When she finally looked at me, I knew something was wrong.

Really, really wrong...something I didn't want to hear. But I knew it was something I couldn't escape.

—

"Ivy, what happened? Where is my baby?" I look at my best friend and see the devastation written all over her face.

"I'm so sorry, sweetheart. I'm so sorry." Full sobs rack her body as she tries her best to sit next to me on the bed while avoiding all the wires and tubes connected to my body.

"He's gone, Florence," she tells me as tears flood her eyes and fall down her sun-kissed cheeks.

He's gone. I knew that already. But part of me hoped it was all just a horrible nightmare that when I woke up, he'd be here waiting for me.

Ivy stares at me and waits for me to process the news, waiting for any type of reaction that I've heard and understood what she's just told me.

But I just stare at her. I'm unwilling to let the words sink in.

"He died when you were stabbed. The doctors said it was instant, so he didn't feel any pain," she chokes out as another sob escapes her lips.

That's the thought that finally hits me, and I finally let the words sink in.

He didn't feel any pain.

He didn't suffer.

He didn't sit in my belly in pain while we were waiting to be saved.

"Where is he, Ivy? Can I see him? Can I hold him?"

I just want to see his face once. He grew in my stomach for 27 weeks, nearly seven months. I felt him move. I sang to him. He knew my voice. I loved him more than anything, and I hadn't even truly met him yet.

Ivy looks into my eyes. Her gorgeous face is covered in red splotches from crying so hard, and her chestnut brown hair is pulled up into the messiest of buns.

I wonder how long she's been here. She looks more disheveled than I've ever seen before.

This time, I grab her hand knowing that she needs my support and strength just as much as I need hers right now.

"Florence, you suffered so much blood loss. The doctors were most concerned with saving you. By the time they got you in there, you were almost dead on the table. They...they got him out as fast as they could, so that they could figure out how to fix you." She takes a deep breath while trying to hold back the rush of tears I know are ready to burst out of her. "The baby, he wasn't, okay. He wasn't going to be able to be held. So they took him away. I don't know what happened after that, but he's gone. The doctors wouldn't give me any real specifics because I'm not a blood relative."

I feel my heart stop beating.

What does that mean?

How can he just be gone, without me ever getting to hold him?

"What do you mean they took him away?! THEY CAN'T DO THAT. THEY CAN'T JUST DO THAT, IVY!" I scream. I plead with her and hit her with my fists as she tries to hold me.

"I just need to see him once, Ivy. I just want to hold him once and tell him I'm sorry and that I will always love him." I cry out and finally let Ivy hold me as the finality of what has just happened washes over me.

I'll never get to see my son's face.

—

"I'm so sorry Florence. I had no idea what happened after they took you to the operating room." Silas says while he grips my hand and rubs his thumb over my own. "I stayed and waited, but the nurses refused to let me know anything because I wasn't family. I stayed for hours, begging

and praying that they'd save you, just so I could apologize to you for not being there sooner."

He continues. "I looked at the newspaper and watched the news everyday...just waiting to see if they ever mentioned you, but it was like you vanished without a trace. This whole time I had hoped that you had moved. Maybe to get away from this place. Maybe to be closer to family. I don't know. But I have prayed every single day for a year that you had made it and were somewhere in this world still. I couldn't bring myself to imagine you gone. When you stepped out of the trees today, and I saw you again for the first time in a year, I felt like I could finally breathe again. You were alive. You are alive."

I wipe the tears that are streaming down my face as I hear his confession and how much this stranger cared about what happened to me...wondering for an entire year what happened to me after only meeting me once. It breaks my heart and fills it all at the same time.

I stand up, then kneel beside the bench and start to dig a small hole. The ground here is soft because of the creek, so I'm able to dig at the ground easily. I dig a hole big enough for my flowers. I can feel Silas's eyes on me the entire time. Watching me. But he doesn't interrupt me.

When my flowers are finally in the ground, sticking up with the help of the hole I just dug, I sit on the ground, criss-cross applesauce style. I look down at these once perfect flowers, thinking about what a whirlwind of a day it's been just to get to this moment.

I pull my bag around and take the impossibly tiny jar out of it. I reach in and grab small handfuls of my son's ashes and start to spread them around the flowers while whispering softly.

I tell my son how much I love him. How much I miss him. How there isn't a day that goes by that I don't think of him. I tell him how lucky I was to be his mom, if only for a short time. I tell him about my parents and how much I know they must love him, and that I hope they're together and happy somewhere. I tell him how sorry I am for losing him, and how I wish, more than anything in the world, that I could have done more to save him.

Lastly, I tell him how much I will *always* love him.

My little bird.

Silas hasn't moved or said anything during all of this. He's just been a welcome and comforting presence. But after what feels like hours, he stands up and takes a seat on the ground next to me. I take his hand. It's almost a reflex now after the evening we've had together.

"What did you name him?" His words come out soft and full of emotion.

I smile and close my eyes and remember the day I chose his name. He was always fluttering around in my belly, like a little bird.

"His name is Wren."

Chapter Seven

WE SIT IN A comfortable silence after that and just listen to the sounds of the forest and the water flowing through the creek. Tonight has been heavy on my soul, but I feel so content as I sit here next to Silas.

I feel like he was meant to be here with me today. Tragedy brought us together a year ago and happenstance brought us back together again today. Though, I also feel like I should give that credit to Duke because if it weren't for him, we might not have ever crossed paths again... At least not long enough for us to actually recognize each other.

I know if I had walked through those trees and seen another person standing there, I would have bolted right back home. I reach over and give Duke some ear scratches which cause him to wag his tail excitedly. While I've never really been a dog person, Duke is making it very easy to fall in love with him.

My phone starts ringing loudly, interrupting the comfortable silence we've been sitting in together. I jump up and reach into my small bag to get it out and shut the ringer off quickly.

Ivy is calling me, and I send her call to voicemail before typing her a quick text letting her know that I'm okay and that I'll be heading home soon. She immediately calls me back. I shake my head and smile down at my phone. This is why she's my favorite person on the planet. Nothing deters this woman when she's on a mission, and her mission in life lately has been to be the most epic best friend in the world.

I answer the call and quickly say, "Ivy, I just texted you. I'm alive and I'll be home soon. Get your over-protective mother-henning panties out of a bunch please," I tease her. I don't let her get a word in before hanging up on her again.

A text comes in right away:

> Ivy: DON'T MAKE ME COME INTO THAT HAUNTED FOREST AND DRAG YOU OUT.

> Florence: Thank you for worrying but I'm okay. Today was a lot more than I expected and I'll tell you about it when I get home. Love you.

> Ivy: Just be safe please and come home when you are ready. You know I worry about you like a mother hen. I can't help it. Love you most.

I stand up, wipe my leggings off and put my phone back into my backpack. Then I hold my hand out to Silas to help him up. He's so much bigger than me that the help isn't much, but he thanks me anyways.

"Ready to get out of here?" he says, nodding towards the path.

"I am actually very, very ready to get out of here and into some dry pants," I laugh lightly. "I don't know why we sat on the wet ground for so long when there was a perfectly dry bench that someone was kind enough to build for me." I smirk and raise my eyebrow at him.

He raises his eyebrow right back at me. "I blame Duke. And maybe the flowers. I wanted to see them in their new home, and it's kind of hard to see how they look when you're towering over them. So, it's definitely the flowers fault," he jokes right back at me.

Silas pulls a small flashlight out of his jeans and signals the way out. We make our way back to the trail with Duke leading the way through the trees, his tail wagging and hitting every branch on our route.

Once we're back on the walking path, I know that there isn't much longer before we get to the parking lot yet I have so many questions I want to ask Silas.

We walk side by side, almost close enough to touch if either of us moves an inch closer to the other.

Why am I sort of hoping that he closes that small gap?

The last thing I need in my life is romance, but I can't stop thinking about how great it felt to be held by him. How safe his arms felt as they were wrapped around me. Especially today. I should want to get back to my car as fast as I can. I should want this to end in a quick 'thanks and goodbye' and drive away while hoping to never have to face him again, especially today after he watched me have too many breakdowns to count. I definitely should not be slowing down my pace trying to drag this walk out as slowly as I can.

Silas stops and looks at me like he's waiting on an answer to something. Oh no. Was he talking to me this whole time while I was fantasizing about him? Oh my god, did I say something out loud?

"Umm, did you say something? Sorry, I was kind of spacing out there for a minute," I ask him while completely unable to meet his eyes. I know if the sun was out he would see how bright red my cheeks turn when I get embarrassed...because honestly, I'm mortified right now.

He clears his throat, "I asked what you did for a living. I was telling you about my job, and then I asked what you did..." he responds. "But obviously you heard none of that, so I'll try again. What do you do during your normal non-forest adventure days?"

That isn't as bad as it could have been, and I sigh in relief under my breath. "Oh well, I used to be an art teacher. When I quit that job I spent a lot of my time painting, but I haven't done that in a long time. I'm actually sort of not doing anything at the moment. My therapist is constantly nagging me to find a new purpose in life. You know, something I can look forward to when I wake up in the mornings…"

Did I just bring up my therapist? Of course I did. I'm an oversharer when I get nervous.

"Alright, enough about me sharing all these personal things with a somewhat stranger." I pray that he'll let me steer this conversation in a less embarrassing direction. "What do you do? No, wait, my first question is– how exactly were you able to get away with building the bench here? I've been coming here since I was a kid, and these park rangers will fine the crap out of you if you even attempt to leave a bowl of food here for the wild animals."

My eyes widen in humiliation again as I realize what I just said. "Not that I ever tried to do that or anything."

Silas surprises me by laughing. A loud, belly deep, I can feel it in my bones, type of laugh.

I stop and just stare at him. He's laughing so hard he has to bend over and put his hands on his knees. Duke gets excited and comes running back from further up on the trail. He licks Silas's face and hands excitedly.

"Just to clarify," I finally say, "I was like seven years old and didn't fully understand why they had all the signs saying 'DO NOT FEED THE WILDLIFE.' I really thought they were trying to starve the animals."

Silas stands up straight again and brings both of his hands to his mouth, clearly to stifle another onslaught of laughter.

I start walking again feeling stupidly embarrassed and ready to be back in the comfort of my own car. I'm hoping to wipe this whole day away.

"So, what happened?" Silas says as he catches back up to me. "Please tell me. I'm dying of suspense here, Florence."

I narrow my eyes at him and laugh when I see how eager he is to hear my answer. "Okay, so one day, I packed a bowl from home and emptied an entire bag of Cheerios into my bag. When my parents weren't paying attention, I took the bowl out and filled it up with the cereal and left it by the creek. As we continued back to the trail I kept throwing little handfuls of them behind me. Basically making a path of breadcrumbs right to us. All the ranger had to do was follow it to find the Cheerio culprit." I pout and cross my arms across my chest.

"And then the park ranger gave you a fine?"

"No. But he did bring me into the ranger station, which is really just a fancy word for their break room, and he told me if I did it again then I had to help him clean up the park for a whole day, even the poop. As a seven-year-old that seemed like the worst type of fine ever. But of course, me being me...I totally tried to do it again."

"You didn't!" he gasps and brings both hands to his face to cover up the fact that he's still laughing at me.

"I did! The ranger, his name is Ted, explained to me why it's actually really bad to feed the wild animals. Not because the food is bad for them, which it actually really is, but because they get used to being fed and then they stop trying to hunt on their own. You can guess what might happen after that..." I shrug. "Ted actually still works here, mostly at the parking fee station now that he can't hike the park as well as he used to."

Silas continues to chuckle next to me as we come around the last bend on the trail. We can see the lights from the parking lot now. As hard as today was, it's been one of the best days I've had in the last year. I'm actually a little sad to find it almost over.

"I'm just over there," Silas says and points to a blue truck parked near the back of the lot. He *would* drive a truck. That is just so him. He's like a lumberjack without the fully burly beard. Instead he has a close-shaven sexy type of scruff going on. Can you even be classified as a lumberjack if you don't have a beard? I'm not entirely sure. But I know that's what Silas reminds me of. A tall, muscled, ruggedly sexy lumberjack with eyes that pierce my soul.

It's stupid that I'm feeling this way right now, but I'm going to let myself enjoy this giddy and happy feeling until he leaves. Then, I'll unpack all the emotional baggage I've been carrying today in the confines of my own bedroom.

I point at the small, orange Volkswagen Beetle parked on the other side of the lot. "That one is me."

Silas walks towards my car and leaves me staring at him in confusion. He turns around when he notices I'm not walking with him and looks at me with a raised eyebrow. "I did say I'd walk you to your car. Did I not?"

I jog and catch up to him easily. I can't help but shake my head and smile.

I unlock my car as soon as we reach it, with Silas hot on my heels. He reaches over and grabs the door handle once we've heard the distinct click of the car being unlocked and opens the door for me.

I get in and leave one of my legs outside, essentially forcing him to keep the door open a little bit longer while I try to stretch this evening out.

"Thank you for today," I tell him, letting our eyes meet again. "Seriously, Silas. I don't know that I would have gotten through today without you. So thank you, for everything."

"No thanks necessary," he replies. "I'm glad to have been here, and I'm glad to have found you again. I actually really enjoyed today a lot more than I should have considering the circumstances, so thank *you*."

It feels weird to have to say goodbye to him after spending so much of the day together. I'm not ready to never see him again. As much as I hate to let myself admit it, I'm interested in learning more about this man.

"Get home safe, Florence," he smiles down at me, and lets go of my door. Then, he turns and starts to walk to his truck.

"Wait!" I yell loudly as I jump out of my car and chase after him.

He turns around. His hands are in his pockets as he waits for me to say something.

"Umm. Do you maybe want to have coffee with me tomorrow?" I ask him. I'm nervous as all get out to hear his answer.

He smiles a huge, megawatt smile, giving me his answer without actually saying anything. I smile back at him, feeling a blush spread across my cheeks again.

"I work until 3:00 tomorrow, want to meet at Monique's Coffee House on the corner of Ayla Way and Mila Avenue at 4:00?" he asks me.

"That sounds perfect to me," I respond back to him happily and turn to walk back to my car. "Wait," I turn around again and yell back at him "You never told me where you work!"

"I guess you'll just have to find out tomorrow," he shouts back with a laugh.

Chapter Eight

I DON'T EVEN MAKE it to the front door before Ivy is throwing it open and pulling me into her arms. "Dammit, Florence!" she whisper screams into my hair, "You scared me half to death! Do you know how long you've been gone?! Or how long it's been since you told me you were 'coming home soon'!"

"I'm fine. Not murdered. Back in one piece. At least I was, until my best friend tackled me at the door and attempted to murder me by hugging me to death!" I choke out. I'm tapping her arms repeatedly and begging her to let me go so that I can breathe normally again, while also basking in the comforting and familiar feeling of her embrace.

She releases me with a sigh and brings her hands to my face to get a better look at me. "You know I'd lose my shit if anything ever happened to you. I can't help it when my paranoia runs wild when you leave my sight."

"I know, and I'm sorry. But I'm okay, really," I promise her. "And I can't wait to tell you about the wild ass day today was. Let's go inside and open the good tequila." Just being around Ivy makes everything feel better, I'm able to laugh and joke again with her despite the heaviness.

"You're speaking my love language, woman."

Once we are settled inside and both a few tequila shots deep, we dig into the take out we ordered and I finally tell Ivy everything that happened.

She laughs, cries, and gasps with me at all the right parts. "I cannot believe you said you love his dog," she mumbles while petting her very fluffy white cat, Lola, who has squeezed herself right in between us on the small couch. "Lola, don't listen to her, darling. She's talking like a traitor right now."

I reach over to pet Lola and whisper sweet nothings in her ears while reminding her that I'll never love another animal the way I love her. After everything happened last year, Lola became my own little support cat. She never once let me sleep alone and somehow always knew when I was getting too deep into my dark emotions and would come and cuddle with me. I didn't talk to many people once I left the hospital, but Lola made the loneliness a little bit less lonely.

—

Ivy picked me up and drove me right to her house the moment I was discharged from the hospital. I didn't tell her that I wasn't ready to face the memories of the home I shared with Ronan, she just knew. Ivy just <u>knows</u> me like that. If I was allowed to have more than one soulmate in my life, then Ivy was definitely it.

I couldn't go back there. I didn't want to see all the photos that were lining the walls and sitting over the mantle. The photos where we were madly in love. Happy. All taken before I got pregnant with Wren. Before Ronan found out we were having a boy and not the little girl he had dreamed of having. Everything started to change after that.

I couldn't walk through our house knowing that the last door on the right was the nursery I had started to set up for Wren. I had painted a bunch of colorful little birds all over the sage green wall where his crib was going to go.

I am scared to envelope myself in the memories of better days, because I know how broken those times will always look to me now.

Not only am I scared of my own memories, but I'm terrified of Ronan coming back. I know he's still out there. The cops came and talked to me as soon as I woke up in the hospital. I told them what I could remember...which was that Ronan had asked me to meet him at our spot in the forest and of course, I went. I thought he was ready to come home. I thought we were going to leave those wickedly evil notes, full of lies in the past and move forward together. Towards our future.

But that isn't what happened when I stepped through the trees and into the small clearing.

I could smell the whiskey on his breath, and his eyes were bloodshot and wild looking.

He sounded insane, accusing me of things I would never do to him.

He wouldn't believe anything I said.

We argued.

He pulled the knife out.

After that, everything just went so wrong.

—

They haven't found him yet. He disappeared without a trace after he left me there to die. But I know he's out there, and I know that one day he's going to come and find me again.

Ivy made sure that all the locks on the house were changed. We added security cameras and alarms on all the doors and windows. Everyday I wait for them to go off, signaling that he's finally back to claim me.

—

The same cops who initially interviewed me escorted Ivy and her parents as they helped me move my stuff out of the house that I shared with Ronan. They left me alone for the first time since I left the hospital. Like really, really alone. It felt like the whole weight of the world was about to crush me, squeezing my heart until it finally gave out. I walked into the kitchen, and my gaze stopped at the knives in the butcher block. How much easier it would all be if I had been killed too. I wished for just a moment that I had died too.

I force myself to turn away from the knives and try to shake myself of such cynical and intrusive thoughts. I couldn't leave Ivy. She's the only family I have left in this world now, and I could never do that to her...even if some days, the thought plagues my mind repeatedly.

I walk over to the fridge to grab some water and stop when I reach for the door handle. There are photos of me and Ivy all over the fridge doors, a few of Lola, and some of Ivy and her parents. I look at each and every photo. An empty laugh escapes my lips as I stare at some of the horrible ones...and then I see the ultrasound in the corner.

I remember showing up here the day I got that first scan. I had begged the doctor to print me a copy for Ivy, and I was so excited to give it to her. I hadn't told her I was pregnant yet, which was the longest month of my life. I had written on the ultrasound, "Hi Aunt Ivy, I can't wait to meet you!" I shoved it in her face as soon as she opened the door.

I wish so much I could go back to that day. The day where I thought my life couldn't get any better. I had a husband who loved me, a best friend who was going to be the best aunt to my unborn baby, and a baby who I couldn't wait to meet.

How wrong and naïve I was back then.

I grab the small black and white photo and hold it to my chest, then walk lifelessly to my bed. Lola followed right behind me and jumped onto the bed as soon as I buried myself in the covers. She laid there with me, letting me stroke her soft fur while I gripped the picture to my chest and cried, wishing with every stroke that I could go back in time.

—

After that, Lola became a frequent sleeper in my bed, never leaving my side for very long.

"Okay, wait," I say, clicking my chopsticks in Ivy's face. "That's the first thing you have to say after the whole whirlwind of a story I just gave?! His DOG. Are you kidding me?!"

"Well, I wasn't sure if you were drunk enough to let me tease you about the fact that the man who literally saved your life also built you a whole ass freaking bench. All while never knowing if you were even alive to use it...because that is the literal definition of romantic. If you don't marry the guy, then I might just have to swoop him up for myself."

"Is it though? Romantic?" Now that I'm home and really thinking about it, am I an idiot to let this stranger spin my whole emotional compass around? Five seconds before I decided to trust him, I was making excuses to get as far away from him as I could... because something felt *off* to me.

"... he never explained the bench." My appetite disappeared completely, and I'm left with this unsettling feeling in my stomach. "Just because he saved my life a year ago and basically kept me from having a complete and total breakdown today, doesn't mean he's not a bad guy–another bad guy just waiting to hurt me."

I can't let myself forget that.

Ivy puts her own food down, moves Lola from in between us, and scoops me into a hug. "Flo, I can't even fathom how hard today has to be for you. But you are allowed to hold onto the belief that good is still out there. He's not Ronan. From what you've told me about your accidental day with Silas, it sounds like through some type of crazy universal kismet, you found each other again. Let yourself enjoy this."

"And if he turns out to be another psychopath? What then? What if I fall for him and let my guard down and then he hurts me? I don't think I'd survive another heartbreak, Ivy. I know I won't."

"I know, hun, I know." Ivy sighs and releases me from our hug to grab my hands with her own. "But you deserve to find your own piece of happiness after all the bullshit this life has thrown at you. Grief isn't something you just get over. You won't ever escape it, and you can't hide from it. It will always have its own piece inside you waiting to flare up on the hard days. But you can try to fit in some love and happiness right on next to it, so that the hard days aren't as hard. You are allowed to do that." Squeezing my hands, she continues, "This Silas guy might not be your happily ever after, but he could be your 'right now.' And I think you owe it to yourself to give it a chance. So, no, you aren't allowed to bail on the coffee date that you asked him on. I swear to Sky Daddy, Flo, I'll drag you there myself...kicking and screaming."

I roll my eyes at her and wipe away the tears that linger on my cheeks. "I expect nothing less from you, you mother hen. But if this all ends badly, then I'm blaming you and stealing Lola and we're running away together," I tell her jokingly as I reach down to pick Lola up from off the floor to pull her into my lap. I love the contented purrs I get as soon as I touch her.

"Deal. Let's shake on it. You aren't allowed to wimp out of your date tomorrow. You have to promise to give it a real shot." She holds her hand up, like she's about to give a girl scout oath. "I, Ivy Elizabeth Hunter, promise you, Florence Renee Samuels, that if it ends badly, you can take my Lola as far away from me as possible...not that I wouldn't hunt you down just to steal her back," Ivy replies and shoves her hand towards me. We shake on it, and then both reach towards Lola to pet her.

Ivy stands up and grabs our empty shot glasses and take-out containers to take to the kitchen. She pauses to give me an extra serious look before she disappears, but not before saying, "Plus, if he hurts you, then Lola and I will just have to kill him."

DANIELLE MORRIS

I look down at the fluffy ball of white, making biscuits into my sweater.

"Lola does have some pretty sharp claws and definitely gives off some serious 'don't mess with my people or I'll murder you in your sleep' vibes."

Chapter Nine

I stare at myself in the full length mirror in my bedroom for the hundredth time and give my head a firm shake. No. This form-fitting red dress looks better on the hanger than it will ever look on me. Plus, it's a coffee date. Not a date to the club. I scoff at myself because I know that I'd never have the confidence to wear something like this to a club even if I got invited to one.

Even though I only made it to six and a half months, my body changed so much while I was pregnant. My hips widened, and they never really shrank back to the size they were before...not that I'm really complaining because the extra curves help fill my jeans out and that's one gift horse I won't look in the mouth. My stomach is softer, pudgier, and lined with stretch marks that I've grown to love. I know most women hate their stretch marks, but when I look at mine, I can't help but feel grateful that I didn't lose those too. They are my body's proof that Wren existed and that I survived as best as I could. I guess the two scars that also sit horizontally across my stomach are also proof. But I'll never love those the way that I love my stretch marks. Those scars happened to me when my son was taken away, and my stretch marks happened to me while he was growing inside of me. I look at them with nothing but fondness.

I'm just not the biggest fan of the way I look now, especially when I'm wearing over-revealing, tight clothes...like this dress that I'm now trying to force over my head to throw into the "nope" pile. I've changed my outfit at least a dozen times this morning even though I know we aren't supposed to meet up until 4:00. I'm a nervous mess and I wish Ivy were home to help me pick out what to wear. She always looks flawless, and her confidence tends to rub off on me when I'm feeling low about myself. I could definitely use that boost of confidence right now.

I sigh and hunt for my phone, hidden in my bed sheets, and text her:

> Florence: I'm bailing on the deal. I have nothing to wear.

> Ivy: Failure is unacceptable. Go raid my closet. That one scoop neck leopard print sweater looks fantastic on you.

> Florence: The one that hangs off of one shoulder?

> Ivy: Yep. Pair it with those tight black jeans that make your booty go pop.

I huff a laugh under my breath and shake my head at her text. *Oh my gosh Ivy. My booty does not pop.*

> Florence: My booty will never "pop". Shoes?

> Ivy: Wear those cute tan wedges that we got at Target a couple weeks ago.

> Florence: What would I do without you?

> Ivy: You'd show up in an oversized sweater that does nothing to help show off that amazing body you have.

Lola rubs against my legs and I lean down to pet her. "Amazing body my ass, Lola."

> Ivy: And you'd probably wear leggings and those obnoxious yellow crocs. GAG. GTG. Love you!

> Florence: Hey, don't knock the crocs. I love them almost as much as I love you. Almost. I'll see you tonight. Love you most!

Outfit crisis averted. I knew Ivy would save the day with her fashion sense and her "we do not quit" attitude. I throw myself onto my bed and look over at the clock hanging on my wall. 11:45. I have way too much free time to kill before I need to leave. Which means…I have way too much time to talk myself out of this. Lola saunters into my room and jumps onto the bed to lay right next to me. I start to pet her as I look around the room aimlessly. What am I supposed to do for the next few hours? I could read, but nothing I've read lately has been able to catch my interest. I could watch TV, but that sounds even worse than reading right now. Plus, I'm so nervous that I wouldn't be able to fully concentrate on either.

My eyes sweep around my room and land on my box of paint supplies. I sit up quickly, inciting an angry meow from Lola. How long has it been since I last painted? Talking to Silas about how I used to paint sparked something in me that I didn't expect to ever feel again. I'm sad that I gave up something I once loved so much.

Another thing Ronan took away from me.

I stand up and walk over to the paint supplies. I had angrily thrown them into a corner when Ivy brought them in after moving my stuff out of Ronan's house. I run my fingers along the dusty box and let myself remember the things I loved most about painting…

The smell of the oil paints and the paint speckled clothes I was always wearing. I craved the feeling of stroking my brush over a brand new canvas with the possibilities of creating something messy and beautiful with my own hands. Most of all, though, I loved that I could get so lost in the world while I was painting. I would start painting when the sun came up and would stop when the moon took its place in the sky, never realizing how fast the hours would fly by because I was living and thriving in the magic of it all.

It's a gorgeous day outside. Sunny and a perfect 78 degrees with a slight breeze kissing the tree leaves outside my window. I change into a pair of black leggings and an oversized tee while laughing to myself because I know Ivy is dead-on when it comes to knowing what makes me comfortable. I quickly throw my hair up into a messy bun and grab my easel. Then, I head to the covered patio in the backyard. It takes me several trips, but eventually, I have everything I need sitting in front of me. I sit on the bar stool I brought out from the kitchen and stare at the blank canvas sitting in front of me. I put my Air Pods into my ears and scroll my phone for today's music inspiration. I don't want anything that's going to make me cry, lord knows I've done enough of that in the last couple of days to last a lifetime. But I also don't want anything overly cheery because that just doesn't feel right either. I've scrolled all the way to the bottom of my music list now and still haven't found anything that fits the mood. So, I let fate decide instead. I put my songs on shuffle. Whatever plays first is the artist I'll let sing to me.

I instantly smile because I know that trusting fate with this one was the correct choice. I dip my brush into the forest green paint and let The All American Rejects serenade me with one of my all time favorite songs by them: *Swing, Swing*.

I get lost in my art. I know what I want the end result to be, so I let the paintbrush guide my hand with each stroke of color, bringing life to the canvas in front of me. I continue to layer on different colors until I have a background of dark green trees resting under a violet sky. I dip my brush in the silver paint so I can start on the stars when I see headlights pull into the driveway.

I pop my air pods out and stand up to stretch and shake out the pins and needles I feel all over my body from sitting for so long. I go to stretch my back out by leaning towards the sky when I finally notice that the sun has slowly started setting. The sky is painted with oranges and pinks layering the darkening blue.

It's in that exact moment that I remember why I came outside to kill time in the first place.

Silas.

And our date.

Oh, crap.

I grab my phone from the table, and look at the time. It's 4:15. I slip my crocs back on from underneath the bar stool and sprint inside. I run to my room and grab my purse before bolting back down the hall to grab my car keys. As I'm throwing the front door open, I pass Ivy on the steps, almost tackling her on my sprint to my car.

"Sorry! I'm late! I lost track of time while I was painting. I'll see you later!" I yell to her as I get into my car and shove the key into the ignition. I throw my car into reverse while trying to put my seat belt on as fast as I can.

When I look over at Ivy before I slam my foot onto the gas, I see she's bent over hysterically laughing at me. That asshole. I fly down the streets, praying that Silas is still there waiting for me.

And of course, I don't even have his number, so I can't call to tell him I'm running late.

·········

Fifteen minutes later, I'm finally pulling my orange slug-bug into the parking lot of the coffee shop. I hastily park like an asshole and run towards the entrance and do a quick scan of all the cars on the way. No blue truck. My heart is thumping out of my chest as I open the door. I'm still hoping that he has a second car that he drove here. As soon as I'm inside, I'm enveloped in the delicious aroma of freshly ground coffee, a smell that usually incites all kinds of happy thoughts for me. But right now, all I feel is crippling disappointment.

Silas isn't here. And why would he be? In his mind, I totally stood him up. And I'm so angry at myself I could spit. I should have set an alarm on my stupid phone before I got lost in my own little world while painting. I should have gotten his number before we parted ways the night before. I'm so fucking stupid.

"I have an order for Florence." the barista says from behind the counter. There's only two other people in the shop right now, both men. One of them looks vaguely familiar, but I can't be certain where I might have seen him.

I walk hesitantly over to the barista. "I'm Florence...but I haven't ordered anything."

"A guy that was here about 10 minutes ago ordered it and told me that if a red head walked in, to call the name out and give it to her. He left a great tip, so I said sure," he shrugs while handing me the coffee.

I take the cup from him and lift it to my face. I look at it and turn it in circles to read if there's anything written on it. To my immediate, but pleasant surprise and intense relief, there's a rolled up post-it note stuck to the side of the cup. I pull it off and unroll it.

"Florence, if you get this, and still want to see me again, even after this sort of creepy stalker move, then meet me at the bench. - Silas
P.S: I hope you like hot chocolate."

·•·••·••··

I haven't stopped smiling since I left the coffee shop. I stuck the post-it note to my dashboard before leaving the parking lot and every time I look at it, I can feel another goofy smile plaster my face again. I pull into the state park parking lot, and my body fills with excitement when I see Silas's blue truck parked in the same spot it was last night. I pull my car into the empty spot next to him and text Ivy to let her know where I am since I'm obviously no longer at the coffee shop…I don't want her going all mother hen on me and calling me five million times. She responds with the thumbs up emoji, quickly followed by an emoji of two people kissing. I roll my eyes at her response and chuckle to myself before putting my phone in my purse.

I'm so focused on my phone, I don't notice when someone moves to stand right in front of my car. When I look up and see someone there, I almost jump out of my own skin. I let out a startled shriek before I realize that it's Silas, and he's carrying an *actual* picnic basket…like the type of basket you see in fairy tales, but never in real life.

He throws up a hand in apology for scaring the hell out of me before walking over to my door and opening it. He offers me his hand to help me out of my seat. Such a gentleman. I grab it and instantly want to melt into the warmth of him. But instead, I nod a thank you to him and then cross my arms across my chest.

He takes a swift step back and runs his hand through his hair. "I am so sorry! I thought you saw me sitting in my truck when you pulled in."

"I guess this is a small wake up call to be more aware of my surroundings…because I *definitely* did not see you."

I give him a once over and admire the way his flannel shirt fits snug and perfectly across his chest and how great his arms look. Again, I can't help but think that he looks like a total lumberjack without the full-on beard.

As soon as I remember why we're both here, I burst out in a billion apologies. "Oh my god I'm so sorry! I swear I wasn't standing you up! I was in the backyard painting and then lost track of time. It wasn't even until Ivy got home that I realized hours had passed. I swear I've never ran, or driven so fast in my life," I blurt out in a rush. "When I got to Monique's and didn't see your truck, I knew I had blown it... And I didn't even have your phone number to reschedule!"

I look up at him and see a smile tugging at the edge of his lips, which makes a full on blush spread across my cheeks. "...And the hot chocolate was a genius move. Not stalker-like at all," I say as I grin up at him.

A real smile finally lights up his face, and it makes his eyes crinkle. If I was a swooner, I'd totally be swooning right now.

I clear my throat loudly and force myself to stop ogling him. "So what's with the picnic basket?"

"I thought we could have dinner together. In my spot this time."

"Sounds a little ominous," I say. "How do I know you aren't trying to lure me to the woods so you can murder me?"

I see all his thoughts fly across his features. Playfulness turns to panic as he opens his mouth to say something before closing it again.

"I'm joking, Silas. If anyone is allowed to joke about almost getting murdered in the woods, it's me." I bop his nose playfully then grab his hand, and steer us both to the entrance of the park.

"You are going to kill me, woman," he finally says. Laughter clearly rings in his voice. "Let's go."

Chapter Ten

WE START DOWN THE same path that I usually take when heading towards my spot, but instead of taking the left trail, Silas guides us to the trail on the right. The sun is almost completely gone, leaving the sky a dark gray, with some stars starting to peak out.

This forest is so beautiful at night. I love the different sounds of wildlife creatures that come to life once the sun goes down. The hoots of the owls, the sounds of the crunching leaves under the tiny feet of the foxes, the tree branches bristling back and forth from the crossing opossums.

Being back here for the second night in a row brings back all the magic of this place, and I never want to leave again. I can't believe I let Ronan take this place away from me for an entire year. He knew how much it meant, and he chose to ruin every good memory we had together here.

—

I walk hand in hand with Ronan as we make our way through the forest. I already know we're heading to the creek. Every time we come here, it's the only place we go to, and we both love to sit there for hours just talking and listening to the sounds of the creek.

He loves this place almost as much as I do. He's loved this park ever since that fateful day where I convinced him, a complete stranger, to drive me a few towns over. I was all of 15 and he was only two years older; we could have never guessed that we were twin flames destined to meet...

We step into the clearing together, always together.

We shared our first kiss here.

We shared our deepest hopes and our darkest desires while dipping our feet into the icy cold waters of the creek.

We fell in love here.

"Every time we come here I fall in love with this place even more," I say, leaning against his warm body, letting his arms wrap around me. He's the first person since the death of my parents to make me feel loved again...and not just a burden of responsibility for my grandparents when they got stuck with me. I know they love me, but I also know they weren't prepared to step back into the role of parents once their own children grew up. They basically let me come and go as I please, never asking where I'm going or when I'll be back. Sometimes I feel more like a roommate than their actual granddaughter.

"I love you," Ronan whispers into my hair while holding me tighter against him.

"And I love you. Always," I answer back before turning in his arms to kiss him.

"Do you feel any different today?" he asks in between kisses.

"Not really. I know it's supposed to feel like this life changing moment, but I don't feel any differently than I did yesterday."

"That's exactly how I felt afterwards too. I really thought this thing that was going to be such an important stepping stone in my life was going to make more of an impact."

"Right? Instead, it just felt rushed and anti-climatic."

He laughs into my hair again. "It's like you just get me, babe."

I take a step back so I can look at his face. "That's because we were made for each other."

"Damn right we are," he agrees and holds up a hand, waiting for me to high-five him.

"You are absolutely ridiculous." I giggle up at him before returning his high-five.

He wraps his hand around my own before I'm able to pull it back.

"Can you do something for me, Florence?" he asks, all laughter suddenly gone from his voice, replaced by a serious tone.

"I'll do anything for you. You know that."

"Marry me."

My eyes never leave his face, seeing the seriousness of his proposal written all over it.

I step into his arms, letting his warmth melt into my body. Placing my head against his, I listen to the strong beats of his heart before finally giving him my answer. The only answer my heart knows.

"Yes," I promise him.

I can't believe that just two hours ago I was walking across my graduation stage, getting my high school diploma, and now, I'm engaged.

—

I shake my head, trying to erase the emotions I feel when I think back to the wonderful times with him. As much as I hate what he did to me, and to our son, I know a part of me will always love him. He wasn't always this evil monster that everyone sees now. That darkness only started to come out of him after we were married and the struggles of life started to really weigh down on him. Before that, he loved me harder than anyone ever had, aside from my parents. He was my first everything and there wasn't a single thing I wouldn't have given him. He owned every piece of me. But now, I refuse to let him keep that power over me after what he did to us.

I let my hand brush against Silas's before I grab his hand with my own. I find him smiling down at me when I look up at him.

"So, you said you were painting again?" he says with pride in his voice. "I remember you saying you hadn't painted in awhile when we talked about it last night."

"I did," I respond. "I think maybe it's time that I try to let myself enjoy the little things again. I let Ronan take so much away from me, and it's not fair to keep giving him that sort of power over me."

As soon as I say the words out loud, I realize how much I really believe them. Being around Silas seems to bring down all the walls I've built around myself over the last year…leaving me with no choice but to want to be my most honest and vulnerable self with him.

Maybe it's because this man has seen me at my actual worst. He witnessed me at my lowest and hardest point in life and *still* chose to be here with me. I've let a whole year pass and lost myself in the fog of it, letting Ronan's actions turn me into a shell of who I used to be. I have spent an entire year scared to let my guard down because I was waiting for him to come back for me. I've become a panic-riddled ghost, and I'm tired of feeling empty.

"You make me feel brave," I confess to him. "And you make me want to feel alive again."

He steps closer to me. Bringing his hand to my face, he runs his thumb lightly across my cheek. "You are the strongest person I've ever met, Florence."

My confidence wavers, and I have to look away. I wish I could see what he seems to see in me.

Clearing my throat, I take a step back and look around to where we've stopped. "So, where is this place of yours?" All I can see is trees and the small ranger station that's just up the path.

"Well, if I seem to remember correctly, you wanted to know how I was able to smuggle the bench into the park, but you *also* wanted to know what I did for a living. Am I right?"

"Yes...?"

He holds his hand out, and I grab it without any hesitation. I choose to trust him as he pulls me towards the small ranger station door. He lets go of my hand so he can grab his keys from his pocket, and I watch as he puts a key in the door and unlocks it.

"I guess you could say this is my answer to both questions," he says with a wicked grin on his lips before he pulls the door, holding it open so I can enter first.

I step through the frame, fully expecting to be hit with the smell of stale air and decay. I know this building has been here forever, but I've never seen anyone come in or out of it. I've never seen a light on either, so I've always assumed it was just used for storage.

Instead, I'm hit with scents of coffee and something that smells a lot like apples. Silas closes the door behind us, leaving us in total darkness. I hear his footsteps coming closer to me, then I feel him walk right past me and brush my arm with his own. I'm about to ask him what he's doing when I'm blinded by the light that floods the small space.

Chapter Eleven

I BLINK RAPIDLY AS my eyes adjust to the light. I look around and finally take in the whole room. From the outside of the building, I always assumed it would be small and cramped on the inside. But I'm pleasantly surprised to find that it's so much more.

From the looks of it, it's basically a small apartment. I can see a small kitchen with a coffee maker sitting in the corner next to the stove. I guess that explains the coffee smell. To the left of the kitchen is an open door, and through it, I can see two neatly made bunk beds with a night stand sitting snugly between them. Turning around, I see that I'm standing in a living room-type area fitted with a loveseat and a television mounted on the opposite wall. I walk towards the kitchen, seeing a breakfast table with two chairs in the corner. Directly across from the bedroom door is another open door, revealing a small bathroom.

"So, do you live here or something?" I finally ask Silas, earning a chuckle in return.

"No, but I do stay here when I have the overnight shift."

I raise my eyebrow at him. "What do you mean 'overnight shift'? Do you work here? In the park?" He gives me a quick nod. My own confusion finally turns to understanding.

"You're a park ranger," I laugh. "That's how you got permission to build the damn bench! It makes so much sense now."

"I told you that this would answer both of your questions," he grins back at me.

We both look at each other from across the room, and then burst into fits of laughter. This is absolutely ridiculous. Of course, this seemingly perfect man would be a ranger.

"Okay, okay," I finally chuckle out. "What is hidden in that fairy-tale picnic basket that you've been toting around all night? I'm secretly hoping it's full of food because I'm freaking starving."

"Why don't you come take a seat here at the bar, and I'll show you everything I brought in my little 'fairytale' basket." He walks over the counter where he placed it and smirks over his shoulder at me. I watch him as he pulls out a bag of crackers along with a pre-made charcuterie board that's filled with an assortment of cheeses, olives, nuts, berries, and cured meats. My mouth is already watering, reminding me that I haven't eaten at all today. I was too nervous to eat breakfast, so I chugged down three cups of coffee instead and then went outside to paint, completely forgetting to eat in the chaos.

"Alright, you had me at the cheese," I respond while walking over to the bar stool. "What else are we having, besides this? I'll be eating the cheese all by myself, so, hands off."

He hands me the plate, then backs away with his hands in the air. "The cheese is all yours. You can snack on that while I cook for you."

"Wait, you're cooking for me?" I say, shocked. I know I left him waiting at Monique's for at least a half hour, maybe even longer. "Did you already have this basket ready to go before I almost stood you up by accident?"

He runs his hands through his dark hair, looking a little nervous. "I had hoped that maybe after coffee, you'd let me take you to dinner...but in case you said no, I was going to come here tonight anyway because I'm on shift at 10:00. So, I had the food for both reasons." He shrugs, then continues to pull various items out of the basket.

"That's a solid excuse," I say, plopping another piece of cheese into my mouth. "But what's with the picnic basket?" I know I should be a little ashamed that I'm talking with my mouth full, but somehow I know that Silas doesn't care if I act like a proper date. I smile at him and toss a slice of peppered salami into my mouth.

"The picnic basket is because of my grandmother." I watch him as he pulls a pot out of one of the cabinets near the sink. "She used to always send my grandpa to work with this same basket, filled to the brim with his favorite foods. He's a ranger here too," he continues while filling the pot with water. He puts it on the stove top to boil, adding a dash of salt to the water before turning back to me. Next, I watch him grab pasta noodles from the basket, adding them to the other items on the countertop. So far, we have noodles, eggs, bacon, chopped onions and mushrooms, and what looks like grated parmesan cheese. He puts the bacon onto a baking sheet and throws it in the oven, then adds the noodles to the water as soon as it's boiling.

I stay quiet, watching him go through each step with ease...the type of ease that only comes with years and practice. I can tell that he's a man that knows how to cook and that he's *also* a man that seems to really enjoy cooking. Someone that doesn't enjoy cooking wouldn't come prepared with such a time-consuming meal to cook just for himself.

"My parents had no interest in being parents, and they dumped me with my grandparents when I was still in diapers. They raised me and loved me the way parents are supposed to, you know?" I nod my head, understanding exactly what he means.

"Well, anyways, my Nan passed away when I was 13. Which left just me and my grandpa." I continue to watch him work as he sautés the onions and mushrooms. The aroma from the caramelization is heavenly.

"After she died, my grandpa used to bring me to work with him everyday when I got out of school. Every day, he packed this same basket full of my favorite foods and snacks. Sometimes, I'd find little gifts from him hiding at the bottom, a new comic book, or my favorite candy bar. Just little things that made me smile every time I found them." I see him smiling at the memory while draining the pasta noodles. I feel my heart growing even fonder for him by the minute. Who knew that this mysterious lumberjack of a man could be even more handsome when he talked about his grandparents?

"Once I got older and started working here, we decided to take turns using the picnic basket. Sometimes, I like to hide his favorite chocolate at the bottom during his turn with it. He's a sucker for a York peppermint patty," he says while pulling an empty York wrapper from the bottom of the basket as proof. I laugh as he tosses it across the bar top at me, earning himself a cheese curd to the head in return. He dodges it easily since my aim has always been tremendously awful.

He turns back to the stove and adds the noodles to the skillet with the onions and mushrooms and starts to work on a sauce. I can't stop staring at the way his hands work as he cracks a couple of eggs into a bowl. He is mesmerizing as he adds parmesan cheese into the bowl and whisks it all together.

What would those hands feel like on my body?

I nearly jump out of my skin when the oven timer goes off loudly. Silas looks up at me with a wicked smirk on his lips, like he knows what I was thinking as I was hyper-focused on his quick and skilled fingers.

He pulls the bacon out of the oven and uses those dexterous hands to crush it into the skillet, before adding the sauce over the top of everything. Finally after a few moments of blending everything together, he scoops the finished pasta onto plates.

"I hope you like spaghetti carbonara," he says excitedly while handing me my plate.

"Actually..." I whisper, refusing to grab the plate that is waiting for me. "I'm vegan."

The pure shock on his face is totally worth the stupid joke, and I start hysterically laughing. The big ugly snorts in between breaths, type of laughing.

His eyes narrow at me before they shift to the empty cheese plate I devoured during our conversation. Then he starts shaking his head and joins in my laughter. "Glad to see that all those cheese curds didn't dull down any of that sass that I'm learning to like so much. Now let's eat Little Miss Vegan."

Grabbing my plate, I flash him a smile and then go to sit at the breakfast table before digging in. I can't stop the moan of pleasure that comes out as I take my first bite. Holy balls, this is delicious. This man could open his own restaurant and fill the place everyday with this meal. I'm going in for my second bite when Silas starts to laugh.

"I take it you like it?" he says, raising his eyebrows at me.

I put down my fork and grab the napkin next to my plate and wipe my face, knowing full well that I have sauce all over my lips from inhaling that first bite so fast.

"Silas, I would marry this pasta and let it have its way with me just so I could have it for breakfast, lunch, and dinner every single night."

"So, you're saying you like it?" his eyes crinkle as he smiles at me from across the small table.

"I freaking love it," I promise him, before diving back in. "I fully intend on eating and enjoying every single bite. To waste such a masterpiece would be sacrilege."

"Alright, alright, it's just pasta. Nothing fancy to freak out about," he says sheepishly. I can see the tips of his ears turning a deep shade of red. He's obviously not used to having compliments thrown his way.

··········

Once we are both finished with dinner, I opt to do the dishes. He cooked this amazing meal for me, even after I was late for our originally planned date. The least I could do is wash the dishes. I start to clear the table, scrapping the few leftover bites into the garbage can, and then head to fill the sink up with soapy water. I've always loved doing the dishes. There is something cathartic about it. I love the feeling of the warm water cascading over my hands as I run the sponge over each dish, meticulously getting every nook and cranny. I love the smell of the dish soap as it fills each pot and pan to let them soak. The routine has always been relaxing to me, letting my mind drift and wander as I clean. It reminds me a lot of how I feel when I'm painting, but instead of adding color to a clean canvas, I'm cleaning the mess away on each dish.

I don't know when Silas came to stand next to me but suddenly, his hand is there and reaching for the clean plate before I can place it into the drying rack. We share a knowing smile, like washing and drying dishes together is something we've done for our whole lives.

As I hand him the next plate, he grabs my hand, rubbing his thumb across my palm. I feel his touch throughout my entire body. When I look up at him this time, his eyes are lidded with desire. I know they match my own. The air in the cozy kitchen has changed. It's filled with an electric sort of tension. Like one more stroke of his thumb across my own, will cause sparks to explode from every part of my body. It's been so long since I've let myself feel any sort of longing for a man, and I've never before wanted someone who isn't Ronan.

And holy hell I really, really want this man.

I place the plate into the drying rack and then turn the sink off, my eyes never leaving Silas's. His eyes still burn with desire as he stares down at me. Finding a courage I didn't know I had in me, I step closer to him. I bring my hands to his chest and then start to slowly unbutton his shirt. Our eyes never leaving one another's. Each button is a slow, but heady process. I'm only three buttons down when there's a loud knock on the door, startling us both.

"Oh, shit," Silas says while trying to refasten the few buttons I had managed to undo on his flannel. "I forgot my Paw was supposed to come and drop Duke off."

"Your Paw?"

"Yeah, my grandpa," he answers while heading towards the door.

"Umm, I'm just going to use the restroom real quick," I say, darting into the cramped bathroom and shutting the door loudly behind me.

I take one look at myself in the mirror and start silently laughing. My hair looks like a bird attempted to make its nest inside of the bun. I have paint everywhere since I forgot to change when I realized I was late to meet Silas.

So much for Ivy's fashion advice. In typical 'me' fashion, I am in my oversized tee and leggings. Both of which have different shades of green paint all over them. I try to fix my hair as much as I can. But I know there is no saving the outfit. I'm nervous to meet Silas's grandpa, but I know the longer I stay in here, the more awkward it's going to be.

So, I take a deep, calming breath and open the bathroom door. I step out of the bathroom expecting to come face to face with Silas and his Paw. Instead, I'm tackled to the floor by a giant ball of fur.

Freaking Duke.

Chapter Twelve

Silas is staring down at me with the most dazzling smile on his face. "I can't believe I let Duke do you dirty again," he chuckles.

We are standing right outside of the ranger bunkhouse. Duke is on the other side of the door whining and scratching at it, begging us to let him out.

I had no reason to be nervous before leaving the bathroom. Silas's grandpa didn't stick around long enough for me to meet him, claiming he didn't want to interrupt whatever we were up to. He did, however, tell Silas that he better bring me over for dinner at their place soon. Hearing that definitely made me smile.

"To be fair, if I had seen how horrendous I looked, I would have tackled me too. This is no way to dress for a first date," I groan, hiding my face in my hands. I still can't get over how embarrassed I am about my paint-covered clothes.

Silas pulls my hands away and then places his hands on both sides of my face, tugging me to look up at him. "You are beautiful, Florence. I don't care if you get all fancied up for me. I don't care if you show up in pajamas. I just want you to show up. Always."

He presses his forehead to mine. I close my eyes, breathing in the earthy scents of him and the forest surrounding us. "Thank you for tonight," I whisper. "Everything feels so much lighter when I'm with you...like the weight of my life isn't about to crush me–even if in exchange I get tackled by your dog every once in a while."

The joke breaks the moment between us, both of us laughing and pulling away from each other. He reaches down and grabs my hand before leaning in to kiss my cheek. "Are you sure I can't walk you back to your car?"

"I'll be okay. I've lived in this park for almost my entire life. I trust it more than I trust most people," I reassure him.

"Will you at least call me when you get to your car?" We made sure to exchange numbers tonight so that the next time I get lost in my own world I can call him. Watching him type his number into my phone made me feel all sorts of giddy emotions.

"I promise. Then I'll text you so many pictures of Lola that you'll wish you'd never left me the hot chocolate note," I tell him while forcing myself to walk away from him.

"That, Florence, is something I will never regret, no matter how many cat photos you send me on an hourly basis," he tells me. He lingers for a minute, then finally goes back inside and shuts the door behind him, leaving me alone to walk back.

It's strange. Part of me didn't really think he'd let me walk on my own. Ronan used to get so angry if I tried to go anywhere on my own. He had it in his head that something would happen to me. Funny that he ended up being that *something*.

To this day, I still have no idea why he couldn't just choose to believe me instead of doing what he did to us…why he chose to murder his unborn son, without an ounce of remorse. He stabbed me and walked away, leaving me alone to pick up the broken pieces of the life we once shared. I can't fathom what drove him to do what he did. He had to have known I would never be able to look at him again. Aside from the stupid papers full of lies, we were mostly happy. Sure, he had his struggles with hard liquor when he was overly stressed out from work, and I knew he could get violent when he was angry. But, I can't fathom why he chose to do what he did to our son.

What drove him to make *that* decision instead of just leaving us like he had originally done?

Why did he have to murder our child?

I know he wasn't thrilled right away to find out that we were having a boy. He had always said that he didn't want to have a son, because he didn't want his son to turn out just like him. Back then I didn't understand what he meant, but now that I've seen the evil side that Ronan had kept hidden away from me for so long...

I get why he didn't want to pass that type of anger and malice onto his son.

Which is why he had always talked about having a little girl of his own one day. The day I agreed to finally stop taking my birth control and start trying to have a baby with him, he went out and bought a tiny pink onesie that had "Daddy's Girl" written on it.

I look up at the night sky as I start to remember one of the happier times with him, before he ruined everything.

—

"Will you stop shaking!" I say while slamming my hand onto Ronan's knee. He has been a nervous, anxious mess ever since we sat down in the waiting room ten minutes ago.

"I can't help it, babe. Do you realize that when we walk out of that room we will finally know what this baby is going to be?!"

He reaches over to rub my belly, something he's done from the moment the two lines appeared on the stick. Being a dad is something he's dreamed of since we said "I Do" almost 5 years ago. But he has been mostly patient while he waited for me to catch up to the dream of being a parent.

DANIELLE MORRIS

We got engaged when I was 18, but we waited to get married until we both finished college. Now, I'm pushing 30 years old and finally bringing his dream to life after trying for several years.

"I don't know why I'm nervous, we both know you're a girl." he whispers to the belly.

"I'm telling you right now, it's a boy." I smirk down at him as he intertwines his fingers with my own, placing them both over my stomach. "And he's going to be perfect just like his daddy."

"Mrs. Samuels, we are ready for you." The nurse smiles at us while we follow her into the room.

"Ready to be proved wrong?" Ronan says as I struggle to get my growing body onto the table and into a comfortable position.

The nurse squeezes the warm gel onto my stomach before asking us what we think the baby is going to be. I immediately say boy, and Ronan immediately says girl.

She laughs at both of us and then places the ultrasound wand onto my stomach. We hear the baby's heartbeat right away, which always makes me cry happy tears. Ronan is still holding my hand, but he reaches up with his other hand to wipe my tears away. We share a smile before looking back at the screen.

We are both eagerly waiting for her to tell us, when she looks at me and winks.

"How upset is he going to be to be wrong? She asks me.

I'm crying all over again, full sobs escaping my lips.

It's a boy. I'm going to have a son.

I look over at Ronan and find him wide eyed and shocked.

"It's not a girl?"

"No, sir, not a girl. But you both have a very healthy baby boy."

He looks up at me and I see a quick flash of hesitancy before he finally smiles. I can see the acceptance and excitement lighting his face up again.

"I guess we'll just have to try again for a girl next." I reassure him. I still hope he gets his little girl even though we haven't talked about having more kids after this.

He leans in to kiss me, then says, "I already can't wait."

And just like that, I know one day I'll have a daughter too.

—

I know he was slowly growing into the idea of having a little boy to teach all about fishing and baseball once our son was older. I know he was happy about our baby growing inside of me. Every morning, before he left for work, he would rub my belly and give it a kiss, always saying, "Be nice to Mommy today, my little man." I know he loved his son, I know it. *Right?*

Why did he have to destroy it all over a lie conjured up by a stranger?

I'm little more than halfway up the trail to the parking lot when I notice that it's quiet, it's too quiet. These woods are never this silent, especially at night. There's always the sounds of wildlife filling the air with their music. The crickets chirping, the hoots from the owls, the frogs croaking. But right now, all the music has stopped, making it eerily quiet.

I stop to let myself completely focus on listening to the world around me. Nothing. No noises. I trust that the animals know to stay quiet when they know there is a predator nearby. For the first time in months, I feel real fear coursing through my veins.

The hair on the back of my neck stands up, a cold sweat coming over my body.

Somebody is out here with me.

Somebody is watching me.

I turn in circles to look around as full panic claws at my throat. I hear a branch snap behind me, and I turn around quickly to follow the noise. That's when I see someone standing there. Hiding in the trees. I can see the outline of their white shirt glowing faintly in the moonlight. I can't see who it is, but my heart knows it's him.

Ronan.

I refuse to let him have me again. I pull the pepper spray that Ivy gave me out of my purse, for once glad that she is insanely overprotective of me, and point it towards him.

"Don't come closer to me, Ronan." I snap at him, full fury igniting under my skin. "I will fucking KILL you!"

He doesn't respond, making me second guess myself. He would have never let me speak this way to him without lashing back out at me. Maybe it's not him. I watch him take slow steps backwards into the cover of the trees until he has completely disappeared from sight.

This person might be Ronan, or it might just be some innocent stranger. Either way, I'm not going to sit around and wait to find out.

I'm closer to my car than I am to the ranger cabin, so I take off in a full sprint towards the parking lot. The adrenaline rush makes me run faster than I've ever ran before, and within a minute I'm flying up to the last turn of the trail. I refuse to look behind me. I know if I see him I'll freeze up in terror. I run straight to my car while pulling desperately at my purse to find my keys. When I finally find them, I put them into the lock, only to realize...my car is already unlocked.

I throw myself into the driver's seat and slam the door behind me, locking it and then making sure every other door is locked. My hands are shaking as I try to get the key into the ignition. I curse as I drop them at my feet twice before I manage to calm down enough to start the car. I pull out of the parking lot as fast as I can. My only focus is getting away from him.

I scream as my phone rings, and I slam on the brakes as hard as I can before checking to see who it is.

"Silas! I think he's back. Someone was following me, and I forgot to call you when I got to my car. I saw somebody standing there watching me," I blurt out all at once. My heart is pounding still, and my hands are shaking so hard I drop the phone.

"Florence, what are you talking about? Are you okay? Please tell me you've left the parking lot. Florence?!" I hear him yell my name as the phone is in my lap. I'm trying to get myself to calm down enough to pick it back up.

Deep breath in.

Deep breath out.

I'm okay.

"Silas, I'm okay," I finally answer him. "I'm sorry. I dropped the phone and couldn't catch my breath. But I'm okay now. I'm okay."

"Where are you?"

"I'm already out of the park. Let me put you on speaker, so I can drive home."

"I'm not hanging up until you're inside your house and safe. Now, tell me what happened, please." I can hear the panic in his voice that he's trying desperately to hide from me.

I replay everything that I heard and saw while I was in the forest, letting the familiar drive home calm my nerves, while the sound of his voice makes me feel safe again.

It isn't until I pull into our driveway and say good-night to Silas, that I realize the hot chocolate post-it note is missing from where I stuck it on my dashboard.

He was in my car.

Chapter Thirteen

Ivy is sitting with me in the small interview room at the police station, waiting for the detective to come in and take my statement.

When I got home last night and realized that the note was missing, I ran inside and locked every door. Then, I checked and rechecked every window, before waking Ivy up to tell her what had happened.

She immediately wanted to call the police, but what could they have done? It was 11:00pm and we had cameras and alarms set up. Plus, I wasn't even 100% sure that the note was missing. I was a mess last night when I got into my car, dropping my keys and my phone multiple times. Maybe I knocked the note off the dash? I didn't want to run to the cops and look like an idiot for being paranoid. I also wasn't ready for the questions and judgements I knew I would get after being with Silas.

Ivy and I agreed to wait until morning before making any drastic decisions. Then, we could both search the car together once the sun was out. I was too wired to sleep, so I stayed in the living room all night watching reruns of The Walking Dead and texting Silas.

Silas: I have Duke to protect me, I'm more worried about you and Ivy being in that house by yourselves tonight. I wish I could be there with you.

Florence: Please be careful out there tonight. My stomach is in knots from the idea of him being that close to you.

Silas: I'm not sure what you mean…

Florence: Having you here would be the opposite of "on guard". Wouldn't it?

Silas: And now I really, really wish I was there.

Florence: Well, I just know that if you were here, sitting right next to me, that I would definitely be more than a little distracted…

Silas: Are you seriously watching TWD after everything that happened tonight…

Florence: I guess I'll just have to settle for Lola and Rick Grimes to keep me company tonight.

Silas: You are one strange lady, Florence. But please try to get some sleep for me.

Florence: Shut up. It's a comfort show for me. Don't judge me.

Florence: You don't even know the half of it, Silas. Only if you try to get some sleep for me too.

Silas: Goodnight, Florence.

Florence: Goodnight, Silas.

I fell asleep after that. A very restless sleep that was full of nightmares. Many of which had Ronan coming after me as a zombie in the forest. Maybe watching The Walking Dead before falling asleep wasn't the brightest idea.

When we both woke up, Ivy and I searched my car from top to bottom and didn't find the note…

Which is why we are sitting here waiting as the door opens and the detective finally walks in. He hasn't changed much in the year I've known him. He's still startlingly handsome; tall with dark skin, deep brown eyes and black hair that he keeps short with a close cut beard that covers most of his face. He looks like he's in his mid-thirties, and has a stare that can pin you to the seat without ever saying a word.

"Good morning ladies, how can I help you today?"

"Hello again, Detective Olsen. I don't know if you remember, but this is my friend Ivy Hunter," I say as he takes a seat in the metal chair across from us. He nods a quick hello to her before turning back to me.

"What brings you both in?"

"I think Ronan is back," I blurt out quickly.

He raises an eyebrow at me as he picks up his pen and small notepad. "I see. What makes you think that Ms. Samuels?"

"I was at the state park last night visiting a friend." I shift in my seat at the mention of Silas. "When I was walking back to my car, there was someone following me."

"What time was this?" He asks while making notes. The sound of the pen scratching across the pad of paper is calming.

"Around 9:45pm."

"That's pretty late to be visiting a friend in the forest, Ms. Samuels." He puts his pen down and cocks an eyebrow at me again, and I know I've already lost him. Just another "she's crying wolf" moment.

I let out an exasperated sigh. "He's a park ranger. I was having dinner with him before he went on shift," I say. "But I know I was being followed. I saw somebody watching me from the trees, and when I got to my car it was unlocked and there was something missing." Even as I say it, I know it sounds unbelievable.

"Could you see this person's face?"

"No. It was dark. All I could see was the outline of his shirt, but I'm pretty sure it was Ronan."

Detective Olsen eyes me skeptically. "What was missing from your vehicle?"

"...a post-it note."

"A post-it note?"

"Yes. It was sticking to my dashboard when I got to the park, and when I got into my car later, it was missing."

I already know he doesn't believe me. After I got out of the hospital last year, I swore I saw Ronan everywhere. The grocery store, the pharmacy, behind me in the McDonald's drive-thru. I know how this looks after all those sightings I reported but couldn't prove. It got so bad that I ended up in mandated therapy because I couldn't differentiate fantasy from my reality.

"Look, I know how this sounds, but I swear I saw someone last night," I say, my voice breaking. Ivy reaches out from under the table and grabs my hand. She knows he doesn't believe me either.

"Ms. Samuels, I can't imagine how you must feel after everything you've been through, but this doesn't sound to me like he's back. I've read your reports, and read the notes from Ms. Lee. I know you believe you saw your husband..."

"He is not her husband anymore," Ivy seethes. "If she says he's back, then you need to do everything in your power to keep her safe."

I can't take this. I can't listen to him try to talk me into believing that I made all of this up again. I *know* what I saw.

"Let's go, Ivy, he doesn't believe me. This is a waste of fucking time." I stand up. "Let's just go."

Ivy stands up and follows me out of the room. Before we make it to the front door, I hear the metal chair being scraped back and hear his footsteps rushing down the hall.

"Wait!" Detective Olsen comes around the corner, walking straight towards us. He motions for us to go outside and sit at the small picnic table in front of the station.

"Look, I can't spend resources on this until we have concrete proof that he's back. We've been keeping tabs on all his accounts, credit cards, cell phone, looking for his car, the whole works for over a year now. We haven't found anything. It's like he disappeared the same day he tried to kill you." This time he looks at me with something other than disbelief in his eyes. It looks a lot like pity.

I know all of this already. "But what if it is really him this time? It's been a whole year. Maybe he wanted to come back and see what my life looks like now."

"I believe you, Ms. Samuels. But I can't spend the resources on it. Not yet."

"So, are we supposed to just fucking wait around until he comes and hurts her again?!" Ivy whispers angrily at him.

"No. No, I'm not going to let that happen. I would like to personally help you with this," he says discreetly, looking at me as he speaks.

"You're going to help me?" I ask him. Color me completely shocked because this is the first time a cop has actually offered to help me instead of just blowing me off.

"Yes, but we are going to be doing this off the record, at least until I get the evidence I need to prove that he's back."

"How exactly are you planning on helping her? All on your own?" Ivy says, her tone much less hostile now that she sees that he's on my side.

"I'll stake out your house when I'm not on duty, and if you decide to go back to the park, I can escort you. You shouldn't be alone there."

"I won't go back there alone again. I can ask Silas to go with me. He knows those woods, I promise."

I refuse to let the forest become a crime scene again, surrounded by cops and yellow tape. I know Detective Olsen is only trying to help me, but I can't let him follow me into the forest after last night. Even if I can't see Ronan, I'll know he's there watching me. The thought gives me goosebumps, and a nervous energy starts soaring through my body.

"If you feel like you can trust this Silas guy, then I'll just have to believe you. But you need to call my cell right away if something else happens. I need to catch this asshole."

"Thank you, Detective. I really, really appreciate it." Just knowing that I have someone here who believes me lifts a giant weight off of my shoulders.

"You're welcome, Ms. Samuels." He reaches out and shakes my hand, then shakes Ivy's. "But also, for appearances sake, I'm going to write in the file from today that I've recommended you go back to see Dr. Lee. Whether you go again or not is up to you. I don't want my boss to know that I'm going against his orders by helping you with all of this." He nods his goodbye.

We watch in silence as Detective Olsen makes his way back inside the station.

"I guess I should call Dr. Lee," I sigh. Ivy looks at me, her eyes flashing in anger again.

"You aren't crazy, Flo. If you saw him, then I believe you. You don't have to go back to Dr. Lee unless you really want to."

Leave it to my best friend to make me want to cry while also sort of yelling at me.

"I know, but I think it might be good for me to talk to her again. Especially with everything else that's been going on since I went back to the park."

Maybe she can help me figure out why my life has suddenly turned upside down. And why, even though I know I very well could be in real danger again, all I can think about is seeing Silas again.

Chapter Fourteen

Two weeks later, I'm sitting in a familiar cozy yellow armchair in Dr. Lee's office. She's been patiently waiting for me to start talking for the last 10 minutes. This has always been our routine ever since I met her last year. I have always been a very closed off person, not wanting to burden people with my true feelings. Talking to Dr. Lee is no different, but she has been one of the only people in my life to not push me to open up. I really love that about her.

"Okay, so obviously, you know that I saw Ronan again," I finally mumble to her.

"Yes, Detective Olsen gave me a call after you met with him. He seems to be under the impression that you might have been incorrect."

A sudden flash of anger hits my body at the mention of me making this up again, before remembering that Detective Olsen is supposed to say that. We don't want word getting back that he's helping me under the radar.

"I know what I saw. I know it was him. It was Ronan, and he stole the post-it note from Silas out of my car."

"Silas?"

Right. I haven't told her about him yet. I bite my lip anxiously as I try to look anywhere but at her. Why am I this nervous to talk about him?

"Silas is the man that saved my life that day," I say quietly, still avoiding eye contact with her. I feel my face flush as I remember the kiss we shared in the kitchen.

"And this Silas, he's back in your life now?"

I finally look at her and can't help the rush of relief that I feel when I see that she is smiling about this news.

"He is. We ran into each other again on the day I went back to the forest. His dog totally tried to murder me," I laugh at the memory as I tuck a wayward piece of hair behind my ear. "We spent hours talking and while sitting there with Wren. We went on our first date the next night, which was amazing. But afterwards I saw Ronan, and now I'm not sure what's going on with us. All I know is that I feel safer when he's around, and I'm not exactly sure how I feel about that yet."

"You two went through something very traumatic together when he found you that day last year. It's only natural that the two of you might share a trauma-bond. You feel safe around him because he brought you to safety that day. There's absolutely nothing wrong with feeling the way you are feeling about him. I know a lot of people who meet their best friends through a shared trauma bond," she says matter-of-factly with a small smile.

I feel a weight lift off of my chest at her explanation. Maybe I'm not the biggest fool ever to feel like I can trust Silas after just meeting him. The thought makes me smile again.

"Now, let's say you are right about Ronan being back. Why do you think he would come back after being in hiding for over a year?" Dr. Lee asks while writing in her notepad. I love listening to the sound of the pen scratching at the paper.

"Honestly, I have no idea. And not knowing why he's back scares me more than knowing he *is* back. But I know it was him. I just know it, Dr.

Lee." I tell her, grabbing tissues off the small end table next to the chair to dab at my eyes.

I've thought about this at length during the few times I've been allowed to be alone over the last couple of weeks, and haven't come any closer to finding the answer. Between meeting Silas for random lunches and quick coffee dates, and having Ivy mother-henning the hell out of me, I haven't had a minute to myself except to use the bathroom and shower. We've even had Detective Olsen watching the house during random times of the day and night when I'm home alone. I know they all mean well and that they both just want to keep me safe in their own ways, but I have felt so smothered.

The only times I've seen Silas over the last two weeks is the couple of times we've met up, but it's always in public now...which has been so sweet, but also a major hit to my ego. He doesn't seem to want to be alone with me anymore, and honestly, why would he? The last time we were alone my psychotic ex-husband followed me, and I turned into an anxiety riddled mess all over again.

Now that I've involved Detective Olsen, I wouldn't want to date me either. I should just walk around with a flashing caution sign taped to my forehead to warn everyone away.

"Florence, did you hear me?" Dr. Lee asks, bringing me back to the present.

"I'm sorry no. I totally zoned out. It's been a really rough couple of weeks for me."

"That is understandable. You've had a lot of emotional triggers lately."

"What do you mean?" I ask, really wanting to know what she thinks.

"Well, let's go back to the anniversary of your son's death. That's when you met Silas, again, correct?"

I flinch involuntarily at the mention of Wren, suddenly feeling guilty that I haven't given him as much thought as I usually do with everything else going on around me. I've been so swamped in my own woes that I forgot to grieve for him. I press my hands to my face as I try to reign in my emotions because I know that I'm moments away from losing my shit.

Dr. Lee's voice comes out softly. "Finding a small slice of happiness in midst of the chaos surrounding you doesn't mean you love him any less, Florence. I could see the guilt written all over your face the moment I mentioned him and Silas in the same sentence. You can let yourself feel both grief and hope at the same time."

I nod at her in understanding before I dab at my eyes again. I do feel both emotions, sometimes more of one than the other, but they both sit there in my heart at all times. Nestled right next to them, is overwhelming fear.

"When I went back to the spot where Ronan killed Wren," I say, sucking down a breath so I don't cry again, "Silas was there already."

"How did that make you feel? Seeing him in the place that has been so personal for you throughout your life?"

"At first I thought it was Ronan, and I was terrified," I admit. "But then I realized it wasn't him, and it was Silas instead. A lot happened that night, and Silas stayed there with me the whole time, lending me the support I couldn't muster up myself. I swear I don't think I could have made it through that day without him. It felt like fate that he was there, and even now, thinking about him makes me feel safe. The last couple of weeks we haven't seen each other very much, and I miss him. I miss the strength he gives me. Now I'm worried that maybe all of this is too good to be true, and that I blew it with all of my baggage before it even had a chance to begin. The thought of Silas walking away from me makes me feel like my heart is being crushed all over again. And I know that sounds absurd since we just met. But it's how I feel," I shrug, trying to hide my embarrassment about the situation.

"Do you think maybe it wasn't Ronan in the woods following you, and that maybe, just *maybe* it's your conscious feeling guilty for wanting to move on with Silas?"

Her question gives me pause, because as much as I don't want to admit it, it does make a little sense. I know I saw someone, but maybe I didn't see Ronan. But then that doesn't explain the note being missing. Unless it somehow flew out of my car when I was rushing to leave the park.

Maybe I really am going fucking crazy.

"I don't know," I tell her. "I don't know what I believe or think anymore. I feel like no matter what, Ronan will always have this upper hand over me. This power over me that I'll never be able to shake off. I live every moment of every day just waiting for the hammer to drop on my head and I'm so damn sick of it. I'm tired of feeling this way. Not being able to trust what I see, what I feel, constantly living in fear. I just know that I'm tired of letting him win. I'm tired of one minute wanting to rip Silas's clothes off, sorry I know, TMI...and the next wondering if he's going to hurt me too and that maybe I should be the one running as far away from him as I can. But I know that I want to give this a shot. A real shot. I don't want to let Ronan ruin this too," I confess, anger and defiance filling my veins.

"Then, don't you dare let him. Give yourself a chance to find out who you are without Ronan's influence guiding your every move. I'm not saying to throw all caution to the wind. We do know that he's out there somewhere, but you don't know that he's back and you don't know that he will ever come back. But living each day in fear is no way to live. You are too young and too beautiful to allow this world to do that to you."

Dr. Lee stands up and crosses the room to the office door, this is always her cue to let me know that our hour is up. I stand up and cross the room to give her a quick hug.

"Thanks, Dr. Lee, for everything."

"I am so proud of the progress you've made, Florence. When I met you last year, you were a shell of a woman, being haunted by ghosts. Today I see courage lighting up behind those beautiful eyes of yours. Let yourself enjoy this life of yours, you only get one." She smiles at me and squeezes my shoulders. "I'm always here if you ever want to talk about anything. You know where to find me," she winks.

I'm leaving Dr. Lee's office and heading towards my car when my phone starts ringing from my purse. I'm fumbling for it, looking for it amongst the clutter of chapsticks, candy wrappers and old receipts that have taken over my purse, when I look up and see him.

He's standing there across the busy street watching me. His body disappears when a car passes between us, and reappears moments later.

Ronan.

I'm frozen in place as I watch him take a trance-like step closer to me, as if he is being pulled towards me by an invisible string. All rational thoughts clear my head, replaced by a loud buzzing in my skull.

I feel dizzy.

I can't breathe.

He stops at the edge of the sidewalk. One more step forward would lead him into the busy traffic of this street between us. I see his lips moving. He's trying to say something to me, but the cars passing between us make it impossible for me to decipher the words on his lips.

Then, I watch as he brings his hand to his lips and blows me a kiss.

I can feel his phantom lips caress my cheek, causing my entire body to shudder.

After that, I see nothing but darkness as the world swallows me whole.

Chapter Fifteen

I WAKE UP IN the same parking lot. I can see my orange Volkswagen to my right, and Dr. Lee kneeling next to me on my left, talking to someone I can't see. I hear different voices shouting from somewhere close by.

When I try to get up, Dr. Lee places her hand on my shoulder, then reaches up to stroke my face. The small gesture reminds me so much of my mother.

"Shh, don't get up yet, hun. The ambulance is on the way to make sure you don't have a concussion."

What? Why would I have a concussion? Then I remember. Ronan.

I sit up fast, startling Dr. Lee and making her fall backwards.

"Where is he?! Where did he go?!" I yell, panic lacing my words.

I try standing up before losing my balance again, only to be caught by Detective Olsen.

"He was here. I swear to God Ronan was here! You have to believe me! He was standing on that side of the street when I got out of my therapy session and he blew me a kiss and then…" I plead with Detective Olsen to believe me. "I can't remember what happened next, but he was here. He was here. I SAW him. He wasn't a shadow or a ghost in the trees. He was HERE!" I scream.

Detective Olsen pulls me closer to him, just enough so he can whisper in my ear.

"Florence, you need to stop talking right now and listen to me." I stop talking and listen. "I will pull the security tapes from the street cameras and the local businesses, but if you keep screaming that you saw him, you are going to scare him into running again, and we won't be able to catch him. So. Stop. Talking. Nod if you understand."

I nod stoically. He releases his grasp on me and I walk over to my car and lean against the small hood of it. I feel like my entire world just got out from under me. One minute, I was talking to Dr. Lee, and finally feeling like I had some type of say in my life. The next minute, I'm watching Ronan prove that he still has complete power over me. He'll always have this power, and I was a fool to think I could escape him.

―

"Hi honey, I'm home!" I shout out, giggling to myself as I come through the front door. Even after years of living together, I still always come home from work and say the same thing. Every time I come home I can't help but wonder what this place will feel like once we have a couple of babies.

Maybe I should tell Ronan that I think I'm finally ready to start trying for a family. He's been so patient with me as I've tried to catch up to the idea of being a mother, but I think I'm ready now.

The house is quieter than usual today. I wonder if Ronan hasn't made it home from the office yet. He just got promoted to Head of Sales at the car dealership where he works, so it's not unusual for me to beat him home most nights.

I head to the kitchen to get started on dinner when the lights flick on. I jump back, startled since I didn't hit the switch, and see Ronan sitting at the table.

"Jesus, babe, you scared me half to death!" I tease while walking over to him to give him a kiss before I start cooking.

He still hasn't said anything to me, and once I cross the room, I see that he has a bottle of whiskey at the table with him. Half of it has already been drunk.

Now I'm feeling a little nervous. He doesn't typically drink, and when he does, it's a glass of champagne like at our wedding, or a glass of wine at a fancy dinner. He doesn't really drink the hard stuff anymore. Unless he's really upset at me for something...

"Hey, babe," I say nervously while placing a hand on his shoulder. "Are you okay?"

He finally looks up at me, and his expression is one I've never seen before. His usual handsome features are twisted into something monstrous. His eyes are lined with fury.

"That's all you have to say, Florence?" His tone is angry and hateful. He only speaks to me like this when he's been drinking. He slams his hand down onto the table, making me jump. Real fear takes over my body. "Why the fuck would I be okay after what you've done?"

"Ronan, I have no idea what you are talking about, but whatever it is we can fix it together. Please just tell me what's going on," I tell him. I've never seen my husband like this before. We've been together since we were teenagers, and he's never once raised his voice at me like this...let alone hit anything out of anger around me.

He stands up suddenly, knocking the chair over from underneath him and grabs me roughly by my throat. He squeezes the air out of my lungs as I slap against his hands in a desperate attempt to get him to let me go.

"I saw you with him, Florence. *I FUCKING SAW YOU WITH THAT MAN!*" He screams at me. Spit and whiskey fly out of his mouth and onto my face as he pushes me into the table. The wood presses so hard into my back that I know I'll have bruises tomorrow. He finally releases his tight grip on my throat, and I suck in as many breaths as I can...not knowing if he'll choke me again.

"What man? What are you talking about?!" I gasp out. "What man?!"

He steps away from me and flips the chair back to its normal position before sitting down. He seems calm again, like none of this just happened. But I know it happened. I can still feel the imprints of his hands around my throat.

He fixes his tie before he looks at me again.

"The man I know you're fucking at that school you insisted on working at."

His words come out so calmly that it takes me a second to register what he just said.

"What? What man?! I would never cheat on you. How could you even think that?!" I yell sharply at him. All traces of fear have left my body, leaving only disbelief and anger. "You know you're my entire world, Ronan. I would never betray you like that. Never."

He continues to stare at me, completely void of emotion. "Then, who is the man you had lunch with today?"

"Tyler?!" I let out a shaky laugh because this is ridiculous. "Tyler is my student aide. And he's 17! And a student! He asked me for a recommendation for a college he's applying to. We had lunch together with a couple of other staff members and their aides to discuss their college plans. That was it. I swear I would never do anything to hurt you like that. I can't even believe that's what your first thought was. Have I not earned your full trust by now? We've been together for nearly a decade!"

His chilling stare continues to pierce my heart, until I watch the fury behind his eyes dissipate. He jumps out of his chair and rushes up to me, sweeping me into a hug and holding me tight against him.

"I'm so sorry, babe. I don't know what I was thinking. I saw you leave the school with him and watched you walk across to the sushi restaurant. I don't know what came over me. I trust you. Always. I have never trusted anyone more in my life."

He is kissing me now, all over my face, shoulders, arms, and whispering "sorry" after each kiss.

"I'm that one that's sorry. I didn't even think that it could be misconstrued as that. Walking alone with him was foolish, and we should have all just walked as a group." I kiss him back in earnest. "I'll do anything if it means you never look at me with hate like that in your eyes again. Please tell me what I can do?" I ask.

"I need you to quit that job. I think it's finally time we try for a baby and you know that being a stay at home mom would be easier on all of us."

I nod in agreement against his lips. His kisses turn more forceful as he tugs my shirt over my head. He pushes me back against the table. This time I don't mind the bruises that he'll leave on me. He kisses his way down to my breast, grazing my nipple over my bra with his teeth.

I gasp, my back arching into him, begging him to take more of me. I already know that I'll agree to anything this man wants.

"Okay," I moan. "I'll turn in my resignation tomorrow morning."

He lifts up my skirt, tugging aside my underwear and presses his thumb to my most sensitive place, teasing me and turning me to liquid the way only he can.

"Throw your birth control away after this," he continues, his torturous fingers dragging out the orgasm he knows I yearn for. "You are mine. And only mine. I will kill any man that thinks he can have you. You belong to me," he growls, then slams himself into me, making me scream out his name.

"I'm yours. Only yours," I promise him, and he then finally allows the waves of pleasure to crash over me again and again.

—

I'm caught in his cat and mouse trap, and I can't escape it. In his eyes, I'll always belong to him.

I hear the ambulance sirens before I can see them and wish I could just get in my car and run away. No part of me wants to talk to them about Ronan, or I guess *not* talk to them about Ronan.

Because he wasn't here.

I desperately want this day to be over. But I let them take my blood pressure, check my reflexes and examine my eyes to see if my pupils dilate with their flashlight. They give me a thumbs up and tell me to come in if I start feeling faint or dizzy again.

Dr. Lee walks over to me and wraps an arm around my shoulder Another gesture that makes me miss my mom so much. "What happened, Florence?"

"I honestly have no idea," I know I can't tell her the whole truth. In order to help Detective Olsen catch Ronan, I can't let anyone know that I really saw him, but it doesn't make lying to her any easier. "I think maybe you were right about everything you said today in our session."

"What part do you think I was right about? We talked about many different things."

"I think..." I take a deep breath to stave off the tears forming in my eyes. "I think maybe I do feel guilty about wanting to move on with Silas. I was reaching into my purse to get my phone and call him, and when I looked up, I saw Ronan. Or *thought* I saw him. Both times I thought I saw him, it was when I was thinking about Silas. You might be right about my conscious feeling some sort of guilt about it." I look over at her, letting my own embarrassment help sell the lie. "I swear he looked so real, my imagination hasn't forgotten a single thing about him even if I haven't seen him for a year. The next thing I know I was waking up on the asphalt feeling like a real jackass."

"It'll get easier. One day, you won't let yourself feel so guilty about wanting to be happy again. I'm just glad you fainted instead of daydreaming into traffic!" She lets out a husky laugh, and then gives my shoulders another squeeze. "I think she's going to be okay, James!"

I look around confused. Who is James?

Detective Olsen walks over and gives her a hand shake, "Thanks, Angelica. I'll make sure she gets home safe. Thanks for your help today." She smiles at him and nods before telling me a quick goodbye and goes back into her office.

"Your name is James?" I say incredulously. "I totally pictured you as something like a Chad or Mike. Never would have thought James though," I laugh.

He shakes his head at me and chuckles. "Let's go, I'll follow you home and then we can talk about what you actually saw today. Deal?"

"Deal."

Chapter Sixteen

When I got home, Ivy was in the kitchen dancing to Selena Quintanilla and making tacos. As soon as she saw the distress written all over my face, she immediately stopped the music, ran up to me, and gently embraced me. Then she saw Detective Olsen standing behind me; the seriousness in her face told me she knew it had something to do with Ronan.

Now, the three of us are sitting together, picking at our tacos, and each nursing a beer. Silas is supposed to come over as soon as he gets off of work, but that's not for another hour.

"I can't believe he's actually back," Ivy says. The look of shock has been plastered all over her face from the moment I told her that I actually saw Ronan.

"We *are* going to catch him. He isn't going to hurt either of you," James promises us as he takes a swig of his drink. I'm still having a hard time wrapping my head around the fact that I sort of see him as enough of an ally to stop calling him Detective Olsen.

"Look guys, I know you mean well, but I can't be followed by either of you 24/7. I'll go insane if I spend another day cooped up in this house. Like literally, more insane than I feel already," I finish the last of my beer and get up to throw my bottle away. "I can't let him run my life anymore."

I watch as Ivy and James shoot each other a look. I know both of them are secretly agreeing to never let me out of their sight. "I saw that," I say, shooting them daggers from my eyes. "You can't lock me in this house."

"I just need you to stay safe. I would lose my shit if anything ever happened to you again," Ivy explains. James nods along with her in agreement.

"I know, Ivy, I know," I sigh. "I just want my life back. I really, really do." I lean my head against the wall and close my eyes...praying and hoping that life will give me a break, even if it's just for a minute.

"Hey, why don't we all go out and do something fun tonight?" James offers.

Ivy and I look over at him, then look at each other, and both burst into fits of laughter.

"What did I say? he asks. "Is there something on my face?" I laugh harder as he wipes his cheeks in quick motions and then looks at his hands.

"No, your face is perfect. I just didn't think cops were capable of having fun," Ivy quips out. "I thought you just had to stay this serious, stick up your ass at all times, type guy."

"You both wound me!" James yells as he grabs his chest dramatically with a shocked look on his face. "Oh, I know how to have fun. Ladies, go get dressed in your best survival clothes and meet me out front," he orders. We both look at each other again and shrug before heading to change.

"Oh, and Florence, tell Silas to meet us at the arcade," he smirks.

·····•·····

We're all being suited up with heavy, electronic vests by a teenager who goes by the name of Adrian. Once we're strapped into our armor, Adrian hands each of us a laser gun and shows us where the aiming laser and the trigger button are.

I've never in my life played laser tag before, but I'd be lying if I said I wasn't stupidly excited right now. I literally can't sit still. I've already jumped into multiple crazy stances and poses while pointing my laser gun at each of my different friends. Ivy has taken a thousand photos, and we haven't even started the game yet. This is exactly what I needed. Some good, classic fun with my best friend. Having Silas and James tag along has been a nice bonus. I think I've laughed more in the last thirty minutes than I have in the last year.

"Alright, you guys get 20 minutes to shoot at each other and try to get as many points as possible," Adrian explains to us. "Once you get hit, you can't get hit again for 10 seconds, so no trying to get points that way, okay?"

We all nod our heads in understanding before he continues.

"How do you want to play? Teams of two or every man, or woman, for themselves?" he asks us as he steps behind the desk and starts typing into the computer.

Ivy gives me her sassy smirk, and I already know what she's thinking.

"We are going to play boys versus girls," I answer back. Ivy gives me a high five as the lights in our vests turn pink. We watch as Silas's and James's vests turn blue. "Oh no. Boys get pink. Girls get green."

Silas and James both roll their eyes when their vests turn pink. Ivy and I fist pump as we flash evil smiles their way.

"And losers buy us pie!" Ivy hollers as the doors finally open up in front of us, revealing a large arena filled with tons of random walls and ramps.

Silas comes over to me, looking insanely gorgeous in his faded jeans and blue flannel. I've missed him so much.

"I'll bake you a pie even when I win," he whispers into my ear, giving me goosebumps that spread across my whole body. I look up at him and smile.

"So you bake too? I may never let you go if you keep telling me all these fantastic qualities you have," I joke back.

"I don't want you to let me go," he says, now very, very serious.

I'm speechless when I look back up at him. The way he's staring at me makes my body feel on fire. Hot waves of desire are making their way through my bones. I lean into him, our faces only inches apart when a loud buzzer rings through the air.

"Your 20 minutes starts...NOW!" Adrian yells from his spot behind the desk.

Silas grabs my hand as we all run into the laser tag maze. Both of us are laughing our asses off. He squeezes my hand once before letting go, then we all go separate ways into the arena.

So much for Ivy being on my team. I don't even know which way she went because I was too focused on Silas's hand on mine.

"IVY!" I yell loudly. "IVY!" The music in here is so loud I know there's no possible way she'll hear me. My best chance is to sneak from wall to wall and try to find her without being caught by the guys. I step from place to place, slowly checking around each corner before stepping out. No way am I letting these boys beat me at this game.

I'm climbing up a small ramp that leads to a castle-like fortress. It has windows cut out on all sides. It's the perfect place to make my base camp. I'll be able to see out from all sides, and there's only one way up here. I climb up as fast as I can without fully standing up and giving my position away. When I reach the top, I kneel down and try to spot Ivy, hoping to see her from this higher ground.

THERE!

I see her squatting behind a stack of tires, gun pointed and ready to shoot anyone that comes near here. My girl.

I start to make my way back across the ramp when I feel my entire vest vibrate and light up red. Crap. I've been hit. There's a small screen on the front of my vest counting down from 10. I look around furiously, trying to find where the culprit came from, but I don't see anyone. I look down at my vest, seeing that I still have 5 seconds until I can be hit again. Then I run as fast as I can through the maze towards where I last spotted Ivy.

She's not here. But Silas is. A Cheshire cat-like smile spreads across my face as I lift my gun up and shoot him in the back, laughing as I watch his vest flash red. He turns around, wide eyed until he sees me. He stands up and saunters over to me, a wicked grin on his lips.

"Does this count as a win?" I tease him, only to feel my vest vibrate again. Silas doesn't have his gun pointed at me, and we both looked around confused.

Then I spot his pink vest, laughing from my castle with his gun pointed at me.

James.

I don't give Silas a second thought before I'm running through the course again towards the castle. That's when I see Ivy running just ahead of me, her green vest lighting up like a beacon. Suddenly she's turning around and running towards me.

"RUN, FLORENCE, RUN!" She screams at me while grabbing my arm and pulling me behind her. I risk a peek behind us and see both Silas and James gaining on us. Silas must have gone around the other way after I ran away from him. Both of them have their guns pointed at us and are pulling their trigger buttons nonstop. I laugh loudly as they continue to miss us.

Ivy and I are running at top speed, ducking and dodging as best as we can to make it harder for them to hit us. That's when I see it. A small space carved into the walls, big enough to hide two smaller people. I yank Ivy into the small space with me, and we watch as both Silas and James run right past us, not seeing us at all.

"Holy shit, this is intense!" Ivy yells into my ear. We're both laughing and trying to catch our breaths while being wedged together into the tight space.

"Okay, plan time," I say, back into serious mode. "I think the best way for us to win is if we can get back to the castle. We can see them from all sides, and once we shoot them we'll still be able to see where they go to hide after the 10 second timer resets. Then we shoot them again. Rinse and repeat!"

Ivy smiles that sassy ass smile I love so much before yelling, "Let's freaking end them!" and takes off into the direction of the castle.

She is so much faster than me and quickly turns a corner, cutting her off from my sight completely. I stop and put my hands on my knees, trying to catch my breath. I know she has to be at the castle by now, so at least I know she's safe.

I stand up, ready to head to the castle when I'm grabbed from behind. A hand makes its way to my mouth, covering it completely. Then, I'm being pulled backwards. I'm so shocked that I don't even try to fight right away. I'm dragged like a ragdoll into a dark corner.

That's when I hear his voice in my ear.

"Hello again, Florence. Oh how I've missed you."

Ronan.

My whole body freezes, and I feel my heart pounding ferociously in my chest.

"Now, I'm going to take my hand from your mouth, and you aren't going to scream. Nod if you understand me."

I nod.

He releases his hand and then moves so he's now in front of me, his body shielding me from view. If anyone runs past here, they won't see me at all. I stare at him in horror. This is not the same man I fell in love with so many years ago. Now that I can see him up close, he looks like he hasn't slept in weeks. His face looks haggard and his eyes have lost the light that always shone from them.

He looks like a man that's been eaten apart from the inside.

He reaches up and wipes away a tear from my face. His touch is gentle, almost loving.

"I have always loved you, Florence, and only you. I told you that you belong to me, and you can't escape me by getting yourself a new cop friend. He can't keep you safe like I can. I don't care how long it takes me, I will keep my promise to you," he says solemnly. His hands come up to cup my face, then they are squeezing my chin and he's pushing me hard against the wall. "One day you're going to come back to me. I will kill any man that thinks they can have you. You. Are. Mine."

His hands are squeezing harder now, and my jaw feels like it's moments away from snapping under the pressure. "Now, I need you to listen to me. You aren't safe and I'm going to find proof. I promise I'll keep you safe." He leans in and kisses me hard on my lips. His lips taste like whiskey and betrayal. A small sliver of my heart wants to give into this and kiss him back.

No. This man already took my son from me, I will not let him take anything else. He doesn't get to worm his way back into my life with his promises to keep me safe. He is the reason I'll never feel safe again, and I will not live with this fear any longer...not when he chose to destroy us. He chose our fate and he doesn't get to lay claim to me anymore.

I feel my body shaking in anticipation and fury. I look into his eyes once he releases his lips from mine, letting the hatred I have for him shine through, causing his face to contort into pure agony before he loosens his grip on me.

That's when I throw my knee into his groin as hard as I can. Screaming and pushing him away from me, I run as fast as I can towards the castle.

That's when the lights flicker on and Adrian's voice blares out from the loudspeaker.

"Game over, people. Come to the waiting room to see your scores."

I turn around, looking frantically for Ronan. But he's gone. There is an emergency exit next to where he held me and it's wide open.

I scream when I feel a hand touch my shoulder. When I turn and see that it's Silas, I lose it completely. My knees buckle, and I hit the ground hard as strangled and horrible noises escape my throat. Silas is there in an instant.

"I'm here, everything is okay," he whispers to me as he is picking me up. "You hear my heartbeat? Just focus on that. Breathe Florence, just breathe."

I listen to the steady thumps of his heart, letting them wash over me to help soothe my own racing heart. Now that he's holding me, I feel safe again. Ronan can't touch me anymore.

But now I know that in order to keep him safe and out of Ronan's clutches, I might have to let him go for good. The realization makes me cling to him even tighter.

Chapter Seventeen

WE ARE SITTING AT our small kitchen table in silence, waiting to hear from James. After I explained what happened with Ronan in the laser tag arena, James went full Detective mode again and yelled at Adrian to show him any and all surveillance camera footage from the entire place. Adrian had stared at all of us in shock before getting on the phone to call his boss. James yelled and pulled his badge out when the manager started to deny his request, but as soon as the man saw my face, he relented and took James back to the security room.

Soon after that, Silas, Ivy, and I left to go home and wait. I couldn't stay in that place any longer. I felt like Ronan's hands were still around me, squeezing the life slowly out of me. I couldn't shake the feeling that he was still watching me. Still following me. He had to have been following me ever since I saw him in the forest, because how else would he have found me at Dr. Lee's office and then at the arcade shortly afterwards?

Has he been following me since he tried to kill me last year? Or did he come back and somehow see me with Silas? Maybe he had been at the forest for the anniversary of our son's death as well...hiding in the shadows as he watched Silas and I spread the ashes of our son together.

So many "how's" and "what if's" have been circling my brain ever since we left the arcade. The thing I know for certain is that I'll never escape him. And he knows it.

"What's going on in that head of yours Flo-bear?" Ivy asks me. "I've seen your wheels turning nonstop ever since we sat down."

I look up at her. My beautiful and amazing best friend. I hate myself for bringing her into this. Because now that Ronan is back, she's in danger too. And if she somehow gets hurt because of me, then I'll never forgive myself.

I open my mouth to answer her when the security alarm in our house starts blaring. We all jump up from our spots on the couch...all three of us, startled and wide-eyed and searching around the entire room looking for the intruder. Silas runs over to the fireplace and grabs the poker, ready to use it to fight if necessary. I grab Ivy and throw her behind me, promising myself to protect her from my monster at all costs.

We all watch the front door open slowly. Silas has the poker over his head and tip-toes over to the door, ready to hit whoever is breaking into our house. That's when I watch him release his breath and bring the poker back down to his side.

"What the fuck, James! I literally almost knocked your head off!" Silas yells at James while closing the door behind both of them.

"I was just double checking that your security system is working because the one at the arcade was tampered with. From the minute we stepped into the laser maze, it had been turned off," he yells over the loud alarm, looking right at me as he says it.

Ivy walks over to the security box and types in our password, the loud alarm stopping and leaving us all in muted silence. All of us are taking in what James just said.

"So you didn't see him on the cameras at all," my voice comes out in a hushed whisper. "There's still no proof that he's really back."

"*We* don't even show up on the cameras. There's no proof that any of us were there either," he replies, shaking his head in disbelief. "The only proof of us being there is our names on the scoreboard. You girls won, by the way. Not that any of that matters right now," he sighs while running his hand down his face.

"Florence, the bruises on your face are the only proof we need!" Ivy exclaims while looking over at James. "You need to get the rest of the force involved! This is the third fucking time that this asshole has HURT her!" She comes over to stand next to me, wrapping her arms around my shoulders, her body seething in anger.

"What is he supposed to tell them, Ivy? Am I supposed to go and show them my face and hope that they believe me? You know they all think I'm already crazy. Seeing Ronan when he wasn't really there, or maybe he was but I couldn't prove it. Hell, they'll probably blame Silas for the bruises for all we know. How many times have I cried wolf over the last year? Too fucking many." I am furious that Ronan is still calling the shots, making me feel like this crazy person when he's the one who started all of this. "They won't believe me this time, either." My eyes meet with James's from across the living room. "And you know it's true."

—

It's been six weeks since I lost my son. Every day feels heavier than the last. They say time heals all wounds, but what if I'm too weak to allow it to?

What if I want to feel the stabbing pain of the knife for the rest of my life?

Will this open and festering wound in my soul close and heal on its own like the two incisions on my own body, slowly but surely?

What if I deserve to live with this pain after failing to protect my own child?

I live in a constant battle of "what if" with myself now. What if I had refused to meet up with Ronan at the creek? What if I had seen the knife sooner? What if I hadn't chosen to believe him or trust him against all my better judgment? What if. What if. What if.

There's a gentle knock on my door.

My voice is empty and lifeless as I call out to her. "It's open, Ivy. You don't have to knock in your own house."

"How many times do I need to remind you that this is your home too now?" She walks into the room with two steaming cups of coffee and holds one out for me. "I see Lola has gotten comfortable," she points to my lap where Lola has been sitting all morning.

"She likes me better than you," I shrug then take a small sip of the coffee she brought me.

"She only likes you better because you keep feeding her your food from under the table when you both think I can't see you."

I roll my eyes at her and stick my tongue out.

"Someone is feeling a little feisty today. Want to go to the grocery store with me? It might be good for you to get out of the house for a bit."

I know she's been worried about me. I haven't left the house except to go to the mandatory doctors appointments to check on the progress of my healing. Too bad my heart isn't healing as fast as everything else seems to be.

"Okay, let me take a shower and get dressed."

Ivy stands up excitedly and walks over to my chair and gives me a hug. "I'm so proud of you hun. Every day is another day closer to a new normal, but it's going to take as long as it takes. I'm proud of you for this small step."

I wipe the tears that threaten to fall. My best friend is my favorite person in the world sometimes.

A half hour later, Ivy and I are walking into our favorite local grocery store.

"Okay, you take the list for the veggies, meat, and fruit. I'll get the rest and we'll meet back up in the wine aisle. Deal?" Ivy holds my half of the list out to me and flashes me her famous sassy smile. She's up to no good and she knows that I know it.

I laugh and snatch the list out of her hand. "Deal, but don't forget the cheese or the hot Cheetos!"

I make my way over to the fruit, mindlessly grabbing the items on her list; grapes, strawberries, bananas, and mangos. Ivy knows how to make the best mango salsa. One of my favorite meals that she makes is tilapia topped with her mango salsa. I look down at the list she gave me and see that she has tilapia added on the meat section and smile while heading over to that section.

I'm walking past all the aisles, making my way to the meat and seafood department when I look up and see Ronan standing in the middle of the bread aisle staring back at me.

I drop the grocery basket at my feet as a blood curdling scream escapes my throat.

An employee is at my side in an instant, asking me if I'm okay or if I'm hurt, but all I can focus on is the monster standing 10 feet away and smiling at me.

Ivy is there a second later, grabbing me and pulling me to her in a fierce hug. "It's okay, it's okay. You're safe, hun. I've got you."

"No, Ivy, Ronan is here!" I yell, pushing her away and turning towards the aisle again where I last saw him. "He's here!" I point down the aisle, eyes scanning for him everywhere, but he's gone. "He's gone. He's just gone."

After that, everything happened in slow motion. The cops showed up and they took my statement in the small break room of the grocery store. I repeated word for word for the fourth time what happened, and that I had seen Ronan. But then he disappeared after he knew I had seen him.

The same detective, Detective Olsen, who had taken my statement at the hospital six weeks ago was there again. He just asked me to rehash everything for him, for the fifth time that day.

I couldn't understand why they were questioning me instead of looking for Ronan. He has been missing ever since the day he stabbed me and our son.

"Why aren't you out looking for him instead of sitting here asking me the same fucking questions that I've answered a hundred times now?!" I snap at Detective Olsen.

He takes a deep breath before answering me, and I know at that moment that something is wrong.

"Mrs. Samuels, we've checked the security footage three times and your husband doesn't show up on it."

"How is that possible? He was standing right there. He smiled at me!" *I shake my head in confusion at him.*

"Ma'am, when I got here and reviewed the footage, there was nobody in the aisle when you started screaming," *I'm shaking my head, trying to cover my ears because this isn't possible.* "I'm sorry. I know this is confusing for you, but you went through a major trauma not very long ago. It's entirely possible that you are seeing something that isn't really there. After everything you've been through, it's not unexpected either." *His voice is so kind and gentle as he's explaining that I've turned into a crazy person.*

I hear Ivy come into the room, her dangling bracelets making music of their own. She pulls me into a hug as she talks to Detective Olsen quietly.

"What can I do to help her?" *Her voice breaks as she asks him for help.*

"I can recommend a doctor who specializes in cases like this," *he answers.*

"What kind of doctor is this?"

"She's a therapist who caters to victims of abuse and severe trauma. I think she can really help Mrs. Samuels if you can get her there."

I sit up and glare at Detective Olsen. "It's Miss Samuels now," *I croak out. My voice feels raw from screaming.* "And I'll go see this doctor. I'll go for as many sessions as you say I need to." *I look over at Ivy as she grabs my hand from under the table.* "Because one day Ronan is going to come back.

And when that happens, I need you to believe me. My life might depend on it."

—

All four of us are sitting at the table now, with undrunk beers sitting in front of each of us. The house is silent as we're all lost in our own thoughts about this totally fucked up situation. I hate that I've dragged so many people into my mess, but I'm too selfish to ask any of them to leave tonight...even if admitting that makes me the worst type of person.

Silas is sitting next to me, rubbing his thumb up and down my thigh from under the table. Ivy and James are across from us, both of them look as exhausted as I feel.

I look at my phone and see that it's nearly midnight.

"Let's all go to bed, it's late, and we are all obviously exhausted. Sitting here and thinking about what to do next isn't getting us anywhere tonight." Ivy gives me a thumbs up before putting her head down on the table.

"I'd like to take a full look at your security system before I head home for the night. I'll feel better if I see that he hasn't somehow tampered with this one too." James rubs his hands over his face, exhaustion clearly eating at him too. "You girls should change the password too, just in case."

"Yeah, that's probably a good idea," Silas agrees. Ivy picks her head up and looks at me, a silent conversation going through our heads before I nod at her.

"I'll show you where everything is," she tells James.

Silas and I watch as Lola appears out of nowhere and follows them down the hallway, getting a small chuckle out of me.

"I love that stupid cat so much," I say out loud.

"Duke is going to hate me when I get home. She's been rubbing all over my legs under the table for the last hour."

"That traitor!" I gasp, then yawn dramatically. "God I'm so tired. Today has been the longest day of my life."

Silas brings his hand to my back, rubbing it up and down in heavenly strokes.

"Alright, everything looks good to go," James says as he walks back towards us, Ivy on his heels. "Ivy reset the password, and I couldn't see anything major that stood out. Everything is online and giving the green light."

"Fan-freaking-tastic," Ivy grumbles. "Now let's all go the fluff to sleep." She waves at Silas and James before disappearing down the hallway to her room.

"Thanks again for everything, James. It really means a lot that you're here, not just as a cop, but as a friend too," I tell him as I walk him out.

He smiles down at me, then gives me a quick hug before reaching out to shake Silas's hand. "Keep her safe, man." Silas gives him a quick nod, and then we both watch from the doorway as James makes his way to his car.

Silas takes a step out onto the porch. "I guess I should get going too. Please call me if you need me, and I'll be here as soon as possible."

"Stay with me tonight. Please."

His eyes gleam with emotion as he stares down at me. He takes a step back into the house, closes the door behind us and locks it firmly into place.

"Let's go to sleep," he whispers before giving me a soft kiss on my forehead.

Chapter Eighteen

WE REACH FOR EACH other's hands at the same time and then make our way to my bedroom in silence. I close the door quietly behind me and when I turn, I see him looking at the painting I brought back inside from the patio. I spent a lot of my free time painting over the last two weeks. It's been the only time I didn't feel like somebody was hovering over my shoulder. As soon as I picked up my paint brush and stuck my headphones in, I let the world disappear for a few hours. It was the best way to shut everyone out.

"I can't believe you painted this," Silas gestures to the painting as I lay my head against his shoulder. "It's beautiful."

When I started painting this, I started with dark hues and shades of greens, blending them to paint the trees of the forest. Over the last two weeks, I added the small wooden bench that Silas had built, using different shades of browns and coppers to bring it to life on the canvas. Leaning against the legs of the bench are my flowers for Wren. The bright yellows of the sunflowers and violets of the forget-me-nots together on the canvas look just like it did when I held them in my arms.

Accidently perfect together.

The colors contrast each other beautifully in the painting and stand out brightly against the darkness of the forest. The last thing I added to the painting before declaring it finished was Duke. I painted him laying on the other side of the bench, with the small teddy bear nestled between his paws.

"Thank you," I say nervously. "Umm, I actually painted it for you."

"For me?" He looks down at me incredulously before looking back at the painting. He clears his throat and steps sideways so he's standing in front of me. "I don't know how to thank you. This is the best gift I've ever been given."

He reaches up to stroke the hair out of my face, and then leans down and brushes his lips softly against mine. He pulls away and looks deep into my eyes, like he's searching for something in them. "Is this okay?" his voice coming out in a hoarse whisper. I lick my lips and bring my hands to his chest, grabbing onto his jacket before pulling his lips back down to mine.

This kiss isn't gentle like the first one. We are both grabbing at each other, trying to pull the other even closer. Each kiss is even rougher than the last as our lips crash together over and over. He pushes me hard against the wall. A photo falls and shatters at our feet, but neither of us make any effort to stop the desire that's coursing through the both of us. His hands are grabbing at my waist, making their way up my shirt in desperation. I can't get enough of him. I reach at him greedily to pull his own shirt off and over his head, forcing our mouths apart. He's breathing hard, staring down at me with lust filled eyes before I grab his face and bring his lips down harshly on my own again. I moan loudly into his mouth as I feel his fingers graze over my nipple.

There's a loud knock at my door. Both of us freeze in place and stare at each other before we hear Ivy's voice from the other side.

"Just tell me if you are getting murdered or if you and Silas are the ones breaking shit in the fiery throws of passion so I can go back to sleep."

"IVY GO AWAY AND STOP MOTHER-HENNING ME!" I shout at her while Silas is quietly laughing with his head against my shoulder.

"But also thank you for checking on me, and I promise I'm not being murdered. Ignore any noises you hear tonight, okay?"

"You got it dude," she answers back. "Lola, stay out of that room tonight. You are too young to see Mama Flo doing the nasty with her handsome boy toy."

"Ivy! I swear to Sky Daddy that I'm going to murder you myself tomorrow!"

Now, Silas and I are both hysterically laughing. The hot and heavy mood from moments earlier totally evaporated. I'm laughing so hard that I have tears coming out of my eyes, and Silas is grabbing his side while trying to catch his breath in between fits of laughter.

I finally compose myself and reach for Silas's hand, fully intending on pulling him into the bathroom with me. "Come on, let's go take a shower so we can go to sleep."

He lifts an eyebrow at me. "Just to sleep, eh?"

"There is no way I'm having sex with Lola listening at the door. It's almost as bad as when I was a kid and my parents had really, really loud sex in the room next to mine."

"Well now that you put it like that..." he shudders mockingly.

I crank on the shower and let the water heat up, then I grab two washcloths from under the sink and set them on the edge of the tub. Silas is leaning against the sink and watching me with amusement.

"What?" I ask him.

"You want to take a shower with me?"

"I mean, the scientists do say that you should share showers, to conserve, like water and stuff. I'm just trying to do my part," I explain to him. His blue eyes are molten lava as he watches me slowly take off each piece of clothing. "You can wait until I'm done though if you want to shower alone."

I let out another loud laugh as he undresses himself faster than I thought possible. He steps into the shower, holding his hand out to help me in after him.

I never thought I'd feel this way with another person. I feel completely and totally at ease as Silas pulls me into him and just holds me under the hot stream of water. The awkwardness I expected to have about being naked in front of him isn't there. It's like my soul knows him from another life, which I didn't think would be possible after Ronan.

The first and only guy to ever see me naked was Ronan. And every time we were together, I was nervous and self-conscious. I tried to hide my body from him as much as possible, insisting that the lights always be off. I would stay hidden under the blankets afterwards until I could get dressed again. The anxiety and insecurity I had with him didn't go away until we were much older. He never did anything to make me feel like I needed to hide, but I always had this nagging voice in the back of my head that told me I wasn't good enough for him, or pretty enough for him, or adventurous enough in bed for him.

Silas doesn't make me feel that way at all. Somehow my heart and brain are on the same page, both agreeing I'm safe with him, and that there isn't anything about my body that he would look away from. As if he can read my thoughts, he pulls away from me and really looks at me. I'm looking at him as well, and loving every single thing that my eyes are taking in about him.

"You're perfect," I tell him.

"So are you," he says softly. He grabs the washcloth and pours a generous amount of my lavender scented body wash on it before he starts rubbing it gently over every inch of me, turning me in slow circles to wash my entire body. He kneels down to wash my legs and when he does he sees my scars. He looks up at me and gives me a loving smile before leaning in and kissing each one so softly that it feels like a feather has just caressed them.

If I wasn't already falling for this man, those two kisses would have done the trick.

He stands back up and pulls me under the hot water, helping me rinse off before I grab the washcloth and return the favor for him. I rub the cloth over his strong shoulders and muscled back and shower him in soft kisses all over during each swipe of the cloth.

Then, I'm kissing his lips. This time our kiss is slow. We take our time and explore every part of each other before the hot water starts to run out, forcing us to dry off quickly and run into bed to warm up under the covers. Silas has me wrapped up in his arms as we fall asleep together.

Chapter Nineteen

I WAKE UP TO the sound of Lola scratching at my bedroom door. I glance at the clock and see that it's only 4:00am and groan in frustration. This cat is so lucky that I love her so much.

I fell asleep with Silas's arms wrapped tightly around me; luckily now, he only has one arm slung over my chest. I inhale the scent of him and smile because he smells like the forest mixed with my lavender body wash. I slowly wiggle out from under his arms, taking care not to wake him. I stand up and grab my robe from the hook on the backside of the bathroom door and shove my arms in the sleeves, shivering as I wrap it around my body. It's freezing in the house tonight. We must have forgotten to turn the heater back on before we all went to sleep.

I tip-toe back over to my bedroom door and open it quietly. Lola is staring up at me from the floor. I flash her the stink eye for waking me up, before reaching down to pick her up to cradle her in my arms. She instantly starts purring as I carry her with me to turn on the thermostat in the kitchen. Her fur is so warm, and I hold her tighter to my chest as her purrs vibrate through my chest. The sight of the full moon pulls my focus, and I spend a few minutes staring up at it in wonder. The sun might get all the credit for the bright and cheery moments of life, but I've always been a bigger fan of the moon and the quiet serenity that she casts down on all of us. There's something beautiful in the way she tries every night to cast some light into the darkness for us.

By the time we make it back to my bedroom I can tell that the heater has already started to warm up the room. Silas has thrown off the blanket, his muscled chest exposed with one arm thrown over his face. His other arm is thrown onto my side of the bed, as if he's been waiting for me to come back to him. I shed my robe quickly and climb over to him, enjoying the immediate warmth of his body as he wraps his arms back around me.

Lola curls up in her usual ball at the end of my bed, right between mine and Silas's feet. I could get used to this type of cuddle session every night. I snuggle deeper into Silas's chest, letting the steady rhythm of his breathing help lull me back to sleep. I sleepily gaze around my room, my eyes skimming across my window when I think I see a pair of familiar eyes looking at me.

When my eyes flick back to the window though, there is nobody there. I almost get up just to check, but then Silas pulls me in closer and all my thoughts drift away as I fall asleep with his strong and steady arms wrapped around me.

·········

I wake up in a cocoon of warmth. Silas is on one side of me with his arms wrapped around me, and Lola is laying spread out on the other side of me. For the first time in a long time I woke up with a smile on my face. This feels too good to be true after the last couple of weeks. I know Ronan is out there planning his next move, laying in wait to make me look even more crazy to everyone around me. But at this moment, right here in this bed, I can't help but feel so incredibly lucky that this is what I am waking up to on this bright and sunny morning.

Silas squeezes his arms tighter around me and pulls me closer. "Good morning, beautiful." He places a chaste kiss into my hair.

I smile and push my body even closer to him. "Good morning, handsome," I answer back. I know we've been asleep, but I missed him even while he was laying here right next to me all night.

"What's on your schedule for today?"

"I don't have any plans actually. Usually once Ivy leaves for work, I catch up on some housework. Sometimes I go to the store so she doesn't have to on the way home. Other times, I sit here and contemplate my life choices while Lola sits with me and begs for more food," I joke. "But today I don't have anything set in stone. What about you?"

"Would you like to come to lunch with me and my Paw?"

"Really?! I would love to," I answer back with a huge grin spreading over my face. "But first, I need to talk to Ivy." I jump out of bed and grab my robe from the floor. "You stay in bed, hang out with Lola, or do whatever you usually do in the mornings."

I turn around to look at him and find him with an amused expression on his face. His bright blue eyes shining with some sort of secret, "What? Do I have drool on my face?"

"Nope. You're perfect." He throws his arm across his face. "Actually you looked so perfect jumping out of bed without any clothes on, that instead of taking my usual hot shower in the morning, I'll be taking a much, much colder one."

I feel the blush spread across my face as I take in what he said. "Oh, umm. Well you have fun with that shower. I'll have coffee on the pot for you whenever you're finished." Then I'm running out of the door with Lola hot on my heels as my pillow comes flying in my direction. I hear Silas's deep laugh echoing down the hall as I knock on Ivy's door.

"Ivy! I'm having another fashion emergency, and I need your help." As soon as she hears this she throws the door open, standing in front of me in only a black pencil skirt and a bright lacy red bra.

"First off, your entire wardrobe is a fashion emergency, and I'm glad you are finally seeing that after so many years of horrid mistakes and paint stained sweatpants."

I scowl at her before I follow her into the room and shut the door behind us. Her room always looks the same. Her leopard print duvet tugged perfectly into place on her queen sized bed, with her bright red throw pillows piled neatly against the black tufted headboard. That's where the tidiness of the room ends. There are clothes strewn across the floor and on every available surface in her room. Her closet is thrown open and inside of it there is a large pile of unmatched shoes. The first time I slept in here I thought there was someone sitting in the closet staring at us the entire night.

"Alright, so where is Silas taking you today?" Ivy asks while sitting at her vanity and expertly applying her black winged eyeliner in one swipe.

"He asked me to go to lunch with him and his grandpa," I tell her, totally mesmerized by the way she goes through her entire makeup routine without making a single mistake. "I haven't met him before, so naturally I'm a nervous mess."

Ronan didn't have a family, at least not one that he cared enough about to introduce me to. He was given up at birth, and grew up in and out of foster homes until he was 12 years old. After that, he was adopted by a family who only wanted the government issued check that came along with him. The minute he turned 18, he got a job at the dealership and moved out. I know at some point he was really close to a couple of his foster siblings–he even invited one of them to our small wedding, but they couldn't make it, and he never brought them back up again.

I've never had to worry about getting that family seal of approval, or lack thereof, so Silas taking me to meet his grandfather is a much bigger deal to me than he realizes.

"You can never go wrong with a cute dress and some strappy sandals to go with it." Ivy is standing in her closet now, flipping through the many dresses she owns. "You don't want to show up with your tits out, so I'm thinking this cute, boho-maxi dress vibe is the way to go." She holds up a dress I haven't seen before. It's a pale pink, with an assortment of tribal-like patterns that cover the entire dress in mustard yellows, turquoise blues, and deep rich browns. The sleeves are flowy, stopping just at the elbows, and the neckline is high enough to cover my cleavage without making me look like I just walked out of the Victorian Era.

"I can tell by the way your eyes are lighting up that you love it! I knew it was perfect!" Ivy squeals while jumping up and down in excitement. "I saw this dress a few weeks ago and it just screamed 'Florence' to me! I was saving it for your birthday, but meeting your new beau's family is just a tad bit more important so I'll allow you to have it early. Now tell me you love me and go try it on so I can see you in it before I have to leave!" She tosses the dress at me and shoos me into her bathroom, closing the door loudly behind me.

I put the dress on and look at myself in her full length mirror. She's right, this dress really is perfect.

Chapter Twenty

SILAS HAS ONE HAND on the wheel of his blue truck and his other hand is clutched in mine and sitting on my lap as we listen to Old Dominion serenade us over the speakers. We are both singing at the top of our lungs as we drive down the highway towards his grandpa's house. They both live on the same property of land, but in separate houses, essentially making them the cutest grandpa/grandson duo I've ever heard of. My heart totally melted when Silas told me that he chose to stick around and help his grandpa out after he finished school because he didn't want him to be alone. The kindness and selflessness of this man's heart knows no bounds, and I am falling for him more and more with every moment I spend in his presence.

Silas brings my hand to his lips. I can feel him smile as he places a quick kiss on my knuckles. "You look so beautiful today." I feel the blush rushing to my cheeks as I look away from him. He reaches over with his hand, my hand still wrapped around it, and pulls my chin back towards him. "My wish is to one day say it enough times that you believe it...because you truly are the most beautiful woman I've ever seen, and I'll spend every day for the rest of my life reminding you of that." I feel the moisture starting to pool in my eyes. I try to blink it away, but it only causes the tears to fall down my cheeks. Silas slows down and pulls the truck over and stops on the side of the highway.

"What's wrong? What did I say to upset you?" He asks while pulling my body over to his and wrapping me in his arms.

"Nothing," I sniffle. "I'm just really happy being here with you, which makes me the worst type of person. I know the timing of everything is wrong, and if I wasn't a selfish piece of shit I'd tell you to run from me as fast as you can because we both know that you aren't safe with me until Ronan is caught...but I want to be selfish with you because I'm not ready to lose you yet."

Silas holds me tighter as I cry out all the emotions and unshed confessions that I've let bottle up inside of me.

"I'm not going anywhere, Florence. Now that I've found you again, I won't let you go. I've never felt this sure about anything in my entire life, and I know without a shadow of a doubt that you and I are meant to be. You are the other half that I've been searching for, nothing and no one is going to keep me away from you as long as you want me here." He reaches down and brings my face to his, placing gentle kisses on my cheeks. "I'm okay with being the selfish one if that's what it takes to be with you. But please, let me be with you."

I nod my head and pull his face closer. We both smile as his lips meet mine. "I'm all yours, Silas," I promise him. I give him one last kiss and then pull myself out of his arms and slide back over to my seat. I tug the sun-visor down, flip the mirror open, and grimace. "Now give me five minutes to put my face back together, so I can go meet your grandpa."

"Take all the time you need, but one, you are already beautiful," he looks over at me and flashes me a smug smile which makes me roll my eyes at him before turning back to the mirror to fix my makeup. "And two," he continues, "We're here already." I look away from the mirror and my gaze follows to where he's pointing. There's a small mailbox, and right past it is a small dirt road. I would have missed it completely if he wasn't here to point it out to me. The small road is almost completely covered by trees.

I quickly wipe away the small trails of mascara that my tears left. My heart is pounding as nervous butterflies have taken flight in my stomach and I feel the palms of my hands start to sweat.

"Are you okay?" Silas asks as he places his hand over my own. My pulse instantly starts to slow at the contact. I close my eyes and take a couple of slow and steady breaths.

"I'm just a little nervous to meet your grandpa. I've never met anyone's family before, well besides Ivy's, and I'm worried he's not going to like me."

He lets out a small chuckle and then slides over and brings my lips to his again. "I promise he's going to love you. In fact, I'm sure you both are going to have a lot to catch up on." I raise an eyebrow at him in confusion. Instead of elaborating, he flashes me a knowing smile before sliding back to his own seat. He then expertly navigates the truck into the small opening, following the dirt road until a small blue house emerges ahead of us.

The house is painted light blue, with white shutters and a bright red door. It's surrounded by a white picket fence, with a garden filled with wildflowers of every color planted in the front. It's magical, like a home pulled straight out of a fairy tale.

Silas gets out of the truck and walks around to open my door, holding his hand out for me. "Silas, this place is beautiful. I can see why you didn't want to move far from here. I would stay here forever." I look over at him, and he's looking at the house with a smile on his face.

"I have always loved it here. After my Nan died, this house always made me believe she was still around. There were months that me and Paw forgot to water the garden, but come spring time new flowers would still pop up out of the soil and bloom. She adored her garden, so we always knew the flowers were little gifts from her."

We are both admiring the flowers when we hear the front door open, and Duke comes flying out towards us. I immediately jump behind Silas. No way am I letting this dog knock me into the mud today. Silas opens his arms up wide and Duke runs straight into him, licking him all over his face with his tail wagging fiercely behind him.

"I know you aren't scared of that dog. No way is the little girl that tried to feed the wild animals cereal scared of a big teddy bear like Duke."

I look up and see Ted standing on the porch, leaning against the pillar with his arms crossed staring down at me with a big smile on his face.

"Ranger Ted is your grandpa?!" I look at Silas with shock on my face. "Why didn't you tell me when I was going on and on about him!" I smack Silas on the arm.

"All good things I hope," Ted laughs out. That huge amused smile still on his face.

I cross the rest of the way and head up to give him a hug. I've known Ted forever, so meeting him as Silas's grandpa is truly wonderful, and the nervousness I had about meeting him disappears entirely.

"Hi Ted. I cannot believe your grandson kept this gigantic secret from me! I would have begged him to bring me sooner." I let the familiar smell of tobacco that has always clung to him wrap around me as I hug him.

"And if I knew it was my sweet Florence hiding in the bathroom during Silas's date then I would have whooped his butt for letting you hide!" His husky laugh vibrates through my body as he hugs me back.

"What do you mean 'my sweet Florence,' old man?" Silas walks over and gives his Paw an evil glare, which only causes all three of us to laugh. Silas pulls me to him and throws his arm around my shoulders before planting a swift kiss on my head. "This one is all mine, Paw."

Ted laughs and heads towards the door. "Let's go eat before Florence comes to her senses and runs away from us both."

"What's for lunch?" I ask as we walk inside together. "It smells amazing."

"Pizza Casserole," Silas and Ted answer together.

"Casseroles are kind of our thing," Silas explains. "My Nan had this rule that the boys had to cook on the weekends. She said it was because she wanted me to learn how to cook so that I could impress that one special lady someday."

"But my wife knew that there was no way we were going to come up with anything edible. So she used to hide all these random casserole recipes in weird spots in the house. I swear I found one folded into a toilet paper roll one time," Ted says wistfully.

"I found one taped to the bottom of the inside of the trash can," Silas added. "So, casseroles just became our thing. Every weekend, we made different ones from the recipes we found. Nan always thanked us and said it was the best meal we'd ever made her. But she never once admitted that she left those recipes for us."

"That might be the sweetest and most diabolical story I've ever heard. Your Nan sounds like my type of lady. I wish I could have met her so I could thank her for raising such a great man, who loves to cook for that special lady in his life." I beam up at Silas and watch him blush.

"I wish you could have met her too. She would have loved you," he whispers to me before heading to the kitchen to help Ted bring the plates to the table.

We all sit at the table together and make small talk between bites. Ted and Silas talk about work and about projects they both want to get done around the house. I listen in grateful silence. I don't know what I would say if Ted asked me how life has been for me lately.

How do I tell the grandfather of the guy I'm dating that my husband is stalking me and has threatened to kill any man that I'm with if he can't have me? It's kind of a difficult thing to just throw out there during a casual lunch date.

I offer to clear the table and head to the kitchen to start the dishes while the guys head to the living room to catch the last half of the Braves game. There is a big bay window that overlooks the kitchen sink, and I watch Duke run back and forth in the yard while I meticulously clean and rinse each dish. This is the type of home I always dreamed of having one day. A big yard for the kids to play in, with a tire swing hanging from an old oak tree in the front yard...an herb garden that I actually keep alive and can go pick whatever I need for dinner that night. A home where you walk inside and you can instantly feel the love oozing out of the walls and wrapping you in a warm embrace.

A home like this.

Silas startles me when he grabs the next plate out of my hand as I'm transferring it to the drying rack. "You wash, I dry. Remember?"

It feels like forever ago that we had that date, but really it's only been a couple of weeks. The feelings I have for Silas have grown significantly in such a short amount of time. I look up at him and smile. He makes everywhere feel like the way this house makes me feel. Safe, loved, protected. *Cherished.*

I finish washing the last of the dishes and dry my hands off before putting both my arms around him and laying my head against his chest. His arms come around me and he holds me, letting the sound of his heartbeat soothe me once again. If I could stay right here, right in this moment forever, I would.

Ted clears his throat from behind us. "I'm leaving to go play cards with the buds. You guys good to lock up the house?"

"Of course, Paw. We are actually going to head home too, so we'll follow you out."

We all head back outside, and Duke runs right up to me for pets, luckily choosing not to knock me on my ass this time.

"That dog likes you. That dog doesn't like too many people," Ted grumbles out with a smile.

"I find that very hard to believe, Ted. He's the sweetest boy!" I protest while Duke continues wagging his tail in happy circles as I scratch behind his big floppy ears.

"Yeah, well, it's true. I always tell Silas that he chose a dog with the same temperament as him, loners those two."

"Duke just has great taste, and he doesn't like people that he doesn't trust." Silas chips in.

"Come on, Duke," Ted calls while walking to his old pickup truck. "He can run around with Phil's new pup while we play."

Silas and I wave goodbye to Ted and Duke as they get in the truck and drive off, disappearing down the small dirt road we took to get here.

"Come on." Silas grabs my hand and pulls me towards his blue truck. "Let's go find the perfect spot for the painting you gave me."

His smile is pure sunshine, and I can't help but answer him with one of my own as we hold hands during the short drive to his house.

Chapter Twenty-One

"What do you think?" Silas and I are both staring up at my painting hanging above the fireplace in his house. "Does it look better above the fireplace, or back in the bedroom above the dresser?"

Silas's house has a completely different vibe than his grandparents' house. Their house is so full of natural light and warmth. Silas's house is charming, but noticeably darker. The outside of his house looks like a small cabin that you would find in the woods. Walnut-wood panels cover the outer walls, and forest green shutters hug the windows. The inside is much of the same with its gray walls and leather furniture. The brightest part of his home is the walls of bookshelves lining the entire back wall of the living room. He has books of every color and genre, making his cozy home the perfect spot for a book lover to get lost in.

"I think I like it above the fireplace better," I finally say. "I love that the deep green shades of the trees in the painting match your cute velvet green chair." I wiggle my eyebrows at him. "Honestly the only thing missing to make it a perfect fit is an end table to put my coffee cup on while I'm reading with some fresh sunflowers placed on top in a glass vase. And of course a yellow throw blanket to keep me warm. If you had those, then you'd never get me out of here," I smirk over at him.

"Mentally adding a yellow blanket and sunflowers to my next Target run," Silas utters under his breath, making me giggle like an idiot. I know we've moved a little fast, but I love how open and honest he is about wanting me to stick around. It makes me feel just a little less insane for never wanting to leave his side.

As I look up at the painting hanging in its new home over Silas's fireplace, I get an overwhelming feeling of nostalgia. I miss the days when I looked at the forest and only saw love in the sway of the trees, and heard my parents encouraging voices in the flow and ebb of the creek. I miss wanting to go there for comfort and solace, and being able to let all the heaviness of life melt away for a few hours while sitting on the forest floor and looking up at the canopy of trees above me.

I miss loving the forest, instead of being afraid of it.

Silas comes up from behind me and wraps his arms around me in a hug. "What are you thinking about right now?"

I turn in his arms and wrap my arms around his waist and look up at him. His eyes are so blue, and he has a nice five o'clock shadow covering his face from not having a razor to use at my house this morning. A little scruff looks good on him. A smile is tugging on his lips, causing the cutest crinkles to appear around his eyes.

"Do you think we could go to the bench you built me?"

His eyes sparkle with pride as he looks down at me. "Really?" he asks earnestly and I shake my head yes at him. "Of course we can, Florence. I told you that you were the strongest person I've ever met."

I stand on my tip toes and give him a chaste kiss on his lips. "You make me want to be fearless again. I know I can face that place again as long as you are with me."

"I'm not going anywhere. As long as you want me, I'm here." He kisses my forehead gently and I love the way he lets his lips linger there for a moment before he pulls away and looks down at me.

I smile at him with happy tears glistening in my eyes and give him one last kiss before pulling him through the front door. Back to the forest

I go, only this time the dread I felt a few weeks ago doesn't plague me. This time, I'm overjoyed with the thought of going back. Because I know now that I'm strong enough to face anything, as long as I have him by my side.

·········

I gaze over at Silas as he drives, his hand resting on my thigh, intertwined with my own. I can't help but wonder how much differently my life would have turned out if I had met Silas first. Would we feel the same way we feel for each other without the traumatic introduction we first had? Would we be happy, married and in love, with a son or daughter of our own, alive and safe with us?

I would never trade those small moments of life I had with Wren. Those quiet nights when I would lay there and feel his little kicks and wiggles, smiling to myself as tears escaped down my cheeks because I was so in love with him already.

I wouldn't trade those memories for anything in the world.

But I do wish our lives had turned out differently. I wish his father loved him as much as I loved him, even though I hadn't truly met him yet. I wish I had been stronger. Strong enough to protect him and keep him safe. I wish that Ronan had chosen to believe me that day. Our lives would all be so much different now.

But he didn't.

And this is my life now.

It really isn't so bad when I have Silas's hand wrapped around my own. We found each other amidst the tragedy, and I'll always be thankful for that.

Silas pulls the truck into the familiar parking lot of the forest. There are only two other cars parked in the lot, and I know one of them must belong to whatever ranger is on shift tonight. The sun is setting just above the tree line, casting shadows of the evergreens throughout the parking lot, which means we only have about an hour of light left.

"Twilight was always my favorite time of day. It makes the world look a little sparkly," Silas says nonchalantly as he peeks over at me to see how I'm going to react to his confession.

"Did you just make a Twilight joke?" I look back at him while trying not to laugh because there's no way this grown ass man just made an actual Twilight joke out loud.

"Team Edward all the way." His eyes sparkle as he continues to stare at me. "Now my Nan was totally Team Jacob, and to this day, I know she's arguing with me from her grave over the fact that werewolves are way, way cooler than the 'dumb sparkly vampires.'"

I put my hand over my mouth to try to stifle the ugly laughs that are trying to escape my lips.

"So which team are you? Don't tell me you're a Team Jacob gal. I might actually have to kick you out of my truck if you say the werewolves are cooler."

This time I cannot contain the bubble of laughter that fills the space around us. I'm grabbing my sides and trying not to snort from laughing so hard. This is the most ridiculous conversation I think I've ever had in my entire life.

He is looking at me like whatever my answer is going to be is the most important thing in the world. "So...?"

I bring my hand to my face, making it look like I'm giving his question lots of thought before answering him. His eyes are looking at me eagerly, waiting to hear if this answer is our very own "make it or break it" move.

"Hmm..." I cock my eyebrow up at him. "While I do love both Edward and Jacob–"

He interrupts me before I can finish my sentence. "No, you aren't allowed to say both. You have to choose one."

The audacity of this man. I cross my arms and sit back against the window and glare at him. "Are you done getting your panties in a twist so I can answer now?"

He brings his hands up, surrendering in silence.

"As I was saying before someone so rudely interrupted me," I roll my eyes and jokingly glare at him some more before I continue, "I love Edward and Jacob both, but this gal will forever and always be Team Charlie. Team Daddy Swan. Chief Daddy."

"I—" Silas is shaking his head at me while trying not to laugh. "I don't even know why I asked. Only you would come up with something like 'Daddy Swan.'"

I beam over at him as he pulls himself over to my side of the truck.

"You never cease to amaze me...." He plants a kiss on my cheek. "Or cease to make me laugh with the ridiculous shit that comes out of this mouth." I smile as he places his lips on mine. "I wish I had met you sooner," he whispers against my lips, then kisses me fiercely, making me gasp. I kiss him back just as savagely. I let my teeth bite down on his bottom lip, which only makes him kiss me more forcefully, making both of us groan in response.

If I could stay tangled up with him like this for the rest of my life I would die a very happy woman. It's so easy to get lost in him, and the passion that is sparking between the two of us as we continue to tear at each other's clothes. I almost forgot that we were sitting in his truck and parked in the very visible parking lot at the state park...

Then we are both jumping apart and tugging our clothes back in place as we hear a dog bark, followed by a car door slamming somewhere near us. I look up and see the other car that was parked in the lot driving away, a small white dog barking in the back seat.

Silas and I look over at each other, each of us smiling, blushing, and slightly embarrassed that we let ourselves get that carried away in public. His lips are slightly swollen and red from kissing. I know that mine are identical without having to look.

I reach over and open my door before finally breaking the silence between us. "I think it's safe to say that we should probably get out of this parking lot before we get arrested for indecent exposure."

"Or worse..." Silas steps out of the truck and shuts the door behind him, then walks around to my side of the truck.

"What could be worse than getting arrested?"

"What's worse, is that my Paw could catch us."

We both look at each other in horror at the idea of being caught by Ted. I literally would die of embarrassment. Like completely melt into a puddle of shame.

"You're right. That would be much, much worse." I shudder at the thought and then take Silas's outstretched hand as I jump out of the truck.

He pulls me to him and puts his arm around my shoulders. "Let's go say hi to Wren."

I think it might be easy for me to love this man.

Chapter Twenty-Two

I PAUSE JUST BEFORE cutting off the path to where the bench is and force myself to take a deep breath. And then another.

Silas is rubbing gentle circles across my back in silence. His presence alone is a huge balm on all the feelings and memories rushing in. Being here always brings back memories, the worst ones and the best ones. But having him here by my side, I feel like I can survive living through them without letting them cripple me into nothing like they did last time I tried to come here.

I know I can do this, but his presence next to me makes the last few strides into the trees less daunting.

The bench is exactly how we left it all those weeks ago. The flowers are still there, but they are most certainly dead. All the petals have lost their colors and the leaves are wilted. The teddy bear I gave Duke is still here, albeit much dirtier.

I walk over and kneel into the dirt and place a hand on the ground near the wilted flowers, while my other hand comes up to my stomach. I feel a tear slide down my cheek before I'm able to say a single word. "I miss you so much my sweet boy. I hope that you are with grandma and grandpa up there." I bring my hand to my lips and kiss it, then gently place that same hand back onto the earth. "I love you always."

Silas comes and stands next to me, and I wrap my arms around him, letting the warmth of his body soothe me. Wearing this dress to the forest at night wasn't the smartest of ideas, and I'm freezing now that we are deeper into the woods and next to the creek. Silas feels me shiver as he goes to wrap his arms around me, so he takes a step back in order to take his flannel off. I almost start to protest, but then he's draping it around my body and wrapping me back into his arms. The flannel smells like him, a heady scent of pine and cologne that makes me want to wrap him even closer to me and bury myself in him.

In one swift motion that makes me yelp out in surprise, I'm being picked up off of my feet and then cradled in his arms. I wrap my arms around his neck as he sits us both down on the bench.

Being here with him, in this place that has always been so special to me, it feels a little like fate. It's like he was made right here in this forest just for me to find one day. I hold onto him tighter while trying to steal some more of the constant heat that his body gives off in waves.

Maybe I had to go through everything I went through in order to make it to this moment right here. Right here with this man, on this bench that he built for a stranger in hopes of seeing her again one day.

And beyond all hope and reason, he found me again. He found me while I was at my lowest, when being in my life is dangerous, especially for him, and yet he chooses to stay here with me. He keeps choosing me, over and over again. It's time I choose him too.

"Silas..." I look up as I say his name, my eyes reaching his and all the nervousness that was swelling up in my body dissipates as I gaze into his impossibly bright blue eyes. I place my hand on his face before I finally release all the words that I've bottled up inside, since the minute he came back into my life. "I wish I could put into words how thankful I am to have found you again, even after an entire year passed us by. I thought about you a lot during the hardest of days. I remembered your kindness, and your warmth during the worst day of my life. Anytime I started to lose complete faith in the world, you popped into my head and reminded me that there's still good out there. There had to be because I knew you still existed somewhere in this world."

I move so that both of my legs are on each side of his, then I grab his face with both of my hands and pull his lips down to mine. I pull back and continue to look into his eyes. I want him to know that I mean every single word. "You make me want to live again, not just survive, but really live. Finding each other again has woken me up to feelings that I buried on the day I lost my son. Feelings I never thought I could feel again. Feelings like I didn't think I would ever want to feel again. But Silas, I want to feel it all with you. I want to wake up every single day and remember that life is survivable, even when it feels impossible. Because you've made it possible, and I'll be thankful for the rest of my life that life gave us another chance when I stumbled into this spot, and found you waiting here for me."

He brings his hands up and places them gently on both sides of my own face, mirroring me completely. "Florence, I have loved you from the first moment I laid eyes on you. I fell in love with the fire inside you, and the resilience to not let life walk all over you. I have prayed everyday that one day you might possibly feel the same way towards me. But I was okay if you didn't, as long as I knew you were alive and safe somewhere in the world. All I've ever wanted in my life was to know that you were okay." He meets my lips with his before he continues. "This, what's happened between us ever since you came back into my life, this is all I've ever dreamed of. Hearing that you feel the same way that I've felt for so long, I don't know if there are enough words to describe how much it means to me that you want me too. But I do know that I've never been happier than I am right here at this moment. Here with you."

"I love you too, Silas."

DANIELLE MORRIS

I pull his face to mine and I kiss him with every feeling that I've bottled up over the last year, and let him help me forget about everything that's going on in our lives right now. This time we don't take our time getting to know each other's bodies. Our kisses are rough and full of heated passion, just like both of our hands are. We are ripping at each other's clothes with zero hesitation. He pulls his flannel from off of my shoulders, while leaving a trail of rough kisses from my throat all the way to the sensitive flesh behind my ears. His hands are pulling my dress up from around my thighs, as I am hastily trying to unbutton the tops of his jeans. We both hurry to adjust for each other, before he grabs the back of my neck and forces me to look at him. His eyes are alight with desire, making my insides melt and a fire blaze from within me. I move my hands lower to push aside the last clothing barrier between us.

Without ever breaking eye contact, I lower myself onto him, letting him stretch and fill me completely before throwing my head back, moaning in pure ecstasy. We both start to move, our movements fast and unrelenting as we surge towards each other. Our mouths are a brutal claim on each other. His teeth graze passionately at my lips, causing us both to moan loudly as we both move in tandem to reach our own pleasure. I grind myself harder against him as he wraps his hands around my legs to push me even closer to him. Stars explode around me as my body detonates around him, causing me to scream his name out to the sky as I dig my fingers into his back. He follows right after me, his fingers leaving bruises on my thighs as he squeezes them and rides out his own pleasure.

We are both panting hard as we both bring our foreheads together. I can't hear anything but the sounds of us breathing. My heart is trying to pound right out of my chest. I reach up and put my hand over his chest and feel that his heart is beating just as hard as my own. He reaches up and brushes my hair out of my face and tucks it gently behind my ear. I lean into his hand, and bring my hand up to cover his, closing my eyes against the warmth and bathing in the aftermath of happiness that I feel.

He leans in and places the softest of kisses on my lips, which feels even more intimate after everything that has just passed between us.

"I love you," He whispers against my lips.

"And I love you," I smile and whisper back against his lips.

·········

We walk hand in hand through the forest. Silas's flannel is wrapped around me again and I can't stop smiling at how perfect this day has been. I haven't felt this free and weightless in such a long time. Between coming back here to the forest, confessing my feelings and baring my heart and soul to Silas, and lastly, letting myself live in the moment with him...

Life just doesn't feel like it can get any more perfect than it is at this moment.

"What are you over there smiling about?"

I blush and look over at him sheepishly, "I was just thinking about how great today has been, and how much I've really loved being here with you."

"But mainly you're smiling about the fantastic bench I built, right?" He winks at me as he pulls his keys out of his pocket.

"If bench is code word for the mind blowing sex, then yes. I am thrilled about the bench you built me." I reach up and give him a quick kiss on his cheek before going to the passenger side of the truck and hopping in.

Once we're both in the truck he turns to me with a sly smile on his face. "Yeah, I don't think I can top the bench, but I'd like to try. A lot. I'd enjoy testing that theory out–maybe every single day that ends in a Y." He wiggles his eyebrows at me and I can't help but laugh.

I love this playful version of him. Tonight we broke down all of our walls, emotional and physical, and now I feel even more completely at ease and safe with him than I already did.

"I actually do have a gift for you." He turns the light on in the car and then reaches into the glove box and pulls out a small velvet box. My eyes widen in horror the moment I see it and my heart kicks into overdrive before he throws his hands up. "Wait, wait. Don't freak out. I promise it's not a ring."

"Okay..." My eyes narrow at him and I'm filled with about a thousand questions.

"Just, open it. Please." He hands me the small box...my hands are shaking even though I know it's not a ring.

I slowly open the box. I can't tell if my heart is pounding from excitement or nervousness. Perhaps a good dose of both. When the box is open, I stare down at the small piece of jewelry and gasp, bringing my hand to my mouth as I feel the tears welling up in my eyes. I look over at Silas and he's smiling, a soft smile.

"How? How did you make this?" I look back down at the necklace in the box. It's a dainty, thin gold chain, and the pendant has a small forget-me-not in the center of it, coated and protected by some kind of clear resin, with a gold border. It's beautiful and perfect in a million different ways. I run my fingers over the small flower and think only of my sweet Wren. The tears are falling down my cheeks and I look back up at Silas and throw myself into his arms. "Thank you. It's perfect. How did you find this?"

"The night you came with me to the cabin, after you left, I came back to the bench and picked one of the flowers. I took it to a jeweler in town the next day and picked it up on my way to meet you at the arcade. I wanted to give it to you then, but after everything that happened with

Ro-" He pauses, not wanting to say his name and ruin this moment. "It just didn't seem like the right time."

I look back down at the necklace, even more in love with it because I know it was a flower I left for Wren. I'll always have this small piece of him with me.

"Will you help me put it on?" I sit up and turn my back to him as he carefully places the necklace around my neck and fastens the clasp. I reach for it immediately, holding the small pendant between my fingers as I turn around to look at him. "Thank you, Silas. I can't even begin to explain how much this means to me. I'll cherish this forever."

He leans in and wipes the tears off of my cheeks and then places a kiss on my forehead before turning the car light off and putting his seat belt on. "Let's go get something to eat, and then let's go home."

I slide over and buckle my own seatbelt before grabbing my purse from the back seat. I take my phone out and see that I have 13 missed calls from Ivy and even more missed calls from James. I quickly scan the texts from Ivy and look over at Silas, dread pooling in my stomach.

"We need to get to my house now."

Chapter Twenty-Three

"She's still not answering!" I yell for the tenth time, before hitting redial immediately. Silas is driving as fast as he can while I'm sitting here feeling completely and utterly helpless in the passenger seat, praying and pleading that Ivy is okay and that Ronan hasn't hurt her.

I can't believe I thought for five fucking minutes that life was safe again. I used Silas to forget that I had actual real problems in my life. Ronan is never going to stop taunting me. He's never going to let me go. I can't believe I let myself forget that, even for one minute.

While I was out living in a fairy tale, Ronan was breaking into mine and Ivy's house. Now she's not answering her phone and every bone in my body is coated in razor sharp terror for my best friend. If anything happens to her, I'll never forgive myself.

"Try Olsen's cell instead." Silas says calmly, while taking a right turn so fast that the back end of the truck slides a bit before he is able to correct it.

I hit James's number, and it goes straight to voicemail. "He's not answering either. I don't even know if he made it to the house yet. The last text I had from Ivy was that she called James and that he was coming over. There isn't anything after that from either of them."

Please, please, please. Let them be okay.

My entire body is shaking as we turn on my street, and before Silas has fully parked I've thrown the door open and I'm running through the damp grass as fast as I can to the front door.

"Ivy! Ivy!" I'm screaming her name at the top of my lungs when the front door opens, and she's standing there with streaks of mascara leaving a trail down her beautiful face. I throw my arms around her, and we both slide to the floor. I'm still shaking as we both stay wrapped up together, sobbing and holding onto each other for dear life.

I feel a hand touch my shoulder, gently squeezing. I look up and see James kneeling down next to Ivy and me.

"You're okay?" I choke out at him.

"Yeah we're okay," he answers. "What about you? Are you okay?" His concern for me makes me want to cry even harder. I shake my head at him, knowing that if I open my mouth to talk again then I'll definitely start crying harder.

"Hey Ivy, Olsen." Silas finally makes it to the door after parking the truck. "Everybody okay?"

Ivy and I finally force ourselves apart and stand up. Neither of us let the other go far before we are reaching out to link arms and walk to the couch. One of the guys shuts the door behind us and locks it.

"Okay, what the fuck happened?!" I blurt out. The adrenaline in my body is finally starting to wear off, and I'm left with a raging headache.

Ivy finally speaks for the first time since I've tackled her at the door. "James, can you grab some aspirin from the bathroom cabinet and bring us all a beer?"

"Got it." He heads down the hall and into her bedroom.

"I'll get the beers, and I'll order us some pizza. I have a feeling it's going to be a long night for all of us." Silas leans down and kisses the top of my head before he heads to the kitchen.

"If you don't marry that man then move over so I can." Ivy says to me as she watches Silas walk into the kitchen. Her eyebrows lift in appreciation as she checks out his ass.

I slap her thigh before we both burst out laughing. I'm so relieved that she's okay. I feel like I can breathe again now that she's here with me, making jokes about marrying the guy I'm dating. Like nothing has changed. But I know Ivy better than I know 99% of the world, and I know that she doesn't scare easily. I know that something bad happened, and I know that it involves Ronan.

"Ivy. You need to tell me what happened. Please." I plead, bringing my hands to rest on hers. "Did he hurt you?"

Ivy looks up at me. A mask of calm on her face. "No. I wasn't here, and when I got here, the house was empty."

"I don't understand. What exactly happened? And don't leave anything out," I hiss through my teeth. I'm trying my best to stay calm, but these emotional mood swings are starting to catch up to me. I feel the irritation of the last hour starting to wreak havoc throughout my body, and I know it's only a matter of minutes before I completely lose my shit on everyone. Rationally, I know it's not fair to take my stress and anger out on them, because the only person deserving of it is Ronan. But he isn't here, and I wish somebody would tell me what the fuck is going on.

Ivy and I both glance up when we hear footsteps approaching from the hall. I breathe a small sigh of relief when I see that it's just James with the much needed pain relief and a bottle of water for me in his hands. I take it graciously and pop two pills in my mouth before taking several gulps of water, letting the cold liquid flow down my throat as I close my eyes and relish in the moment of silence.

Silas breaks the silence when he walks into the living room with two kitchen chairs in tow. He hands one to James before he puts his down and walks back into the kitchen to grab the drinks. It feels like a somber affair as we all try to get comfortable around the small coffee table, none of us speaking to one another.

How did such a perfect day turn into such a wretched evening?

Silas finally breaks the silence by popping his beer open and taking a long swig while we all stare at him with vacant expressions on our faces.

"This is ridiculous!" I stand up, throwing Ivy's arms away from mine as I glare at her. "If somebody doesn't start talking in the next two seconds then I'm going to start throwing things."

"Okay, okay. Just sit down and give her a minute," James glares up at me. "She's been through a hell of a day, especially since you couldn't be bothered to answer the damn phone!"

I feel as though he's slapped me, the anger in his voice catches me by surprise, and I sit right back down next to Ivy. I turn towards her and see that she's trying so hard not to cry, but there's a fresh trail of tears gliding down her cheeks.

"Oh my god, Ivy!" I lunge forward and pull her to me. Her body finally releases the sobs that she's been trying so hard to hold in. Suffering in silence right next to me as I let my emotions get the best of me and sat here acting like this only affected me. "I'm so sorry. I'm here now. I won't let him hurt you."

"It's not me I'm worried about!" She screams at me while angrily wiping the tears off of her face. "He wants YOU, Florence! He called me at work today, asking where you were, and that if I didn't tell him where you were that he would still find you."

"Wait, you spoke to him?!" I ask her immediately, terror and hope both sparking in me. If she spoke to him then we might finally have the proof we need to open an actual investigation again. I might finally be able to prove to James's colleagues once and for all that I'm not crazy.

She jumps to her feet and slams her phone down onto the coffee table, making the three of us jump. "When I refused to tell him, he promised me that when he did find you, that he was going to make it even worse for you, as a thank you for 'all my help.' Then he hung up and never called back. AND YOU DIDN'T ANSWER YOUR FUCKING PHONE!"

She is standing over me now screaming in my face. I've never in the span of our friendship seen her this furious with me. I'm completely frozen in shock as I stare into the angry hazel eyes of my best friend. She grabs my shoulders roughly and screams at me again, "WHY DIDN'T YOU ANSWER THE PHONE?! I THOUGHT YOU WERE DEAD, FLORENCE!"

James jumps up and pulls her off of me, leading her into the kitchen to calm her down. I can hear her crying, and I feel as though a knife has been shoved into my heart this time.

Silas stands up and kneels down in front of me, placing his hands on my knees. He doesn't say anything, but just knowing that he's here with me helps. I place my hands over his and he intertwines our fingers together. My eyes meet his, and I let his calm demeanor and strength flood through me. It's hard to believe just hours ago it was just me and him and our bench.

Ivy comes rushing out of the kitchen and beelines right to us. Silas stands up and backs away as she sweeps me into a soul crushing hug. We are okay and that's all that's important right now. I squeeze her tighter and whisper into her ear how sorry I am for everything I'm putting her through. Instead of answering me back, she pulls me away from her so she can look me in the eyes, and then flashes her favorite middle finger in my face.

I grab her hand and roll my eyes at her. "I love you, even when you're an asshole."

"No, you love me because I'm an asshole. Now where's the pizza?!"

We both watch as James walks out of the kitchen and leans against the wall. I can see the stress that today's toll has taken written all over his face. I grab his beer off of the coffee table and walk over to him.

"You look like you could use about ten of these," I say as I hand him his beer, "But you'll have to settle for one because I need your mind sharp while we figure out how we can use Ronan's calls to Ivy as proof that he's back."

He lets out a slow exhale and runs his hands over his face. "Trust me, I've been trying to rack my brain around this for hours. I don't know how we can prove it was him."

I reach out and grab the end of his beer bottle and bring it to his lips, essentially cutting him off from finishing any train of thought he had. "First we drink, then we eat. Once both of those are done, we can work on figuring the rest out."

I look at all three of them and raise an eyebrow. "Savvy?" I say in my best Jack Sparrow accent.

They stare at me like I've grown a second head instead of answering me back.

Chapter Twenty-Four

THE HEAVENLY AROMA OF garlic and breadsticks has drifted its way into the kitchen where we're all sitting around the dining table. Some people can't touch food when they are stressed out, but food will always be a source of comfort for me. There is nothing better than coming home after a hard day and biting into one of your favorite meals. After all the activities of today, I'm most definitely going to enjoy this fourth slice of pepperoni and pineapple pizza that I'm pulling out of the box.

James watches me bring the pizza to my mouth and chuckles. "You know, I feel like I'm watching Shaggy from Scooby Doo while watching you inhale that slice."

"Shaggy?" Ivy cocks an eyebrow at me and then back at James.

"Yeah, you know how he and Scooby are constantly eating without chewing. It's like a vacuum opens up and they just inhale all the food. I used to try to do it as a kid, but only ended up choking and looking like a dumbass." He gestures towards me again, "Florence has obviously mastered the skill."

They all turn to look at me as I shove the last bit of crust into my mouth. "I can't help it. I just really love pizza." I shrug in response as I reach to grab the last breadstick. Silas reaches out and grabs it first and eats half of it in one giant bite.

"You, swine!" I yell and attempt to wrestle away the rest of the breadstick from him before he eats it. He holds the breadstick high above his head and uses his other hand to tap his lips.

I roll my eyes at him and stand up and give him a quick kiss, then reach up and yank my breadstick out of his hand. He gives me the breadstick, but pulls me into his lap before I can sit back into my own seat. I wrap one of my arms around his neck while I eat the remainder of my crushed breadstick with a smile on my face.

"God, you guys are adorable and disgusting at the same time," Ivy coos, a happy grin spreading across her face. "Get a room!"

James starts laughing and goes to add his two cents in when we're all interrupted by a loud, gut-wrenching cry from the hallway. Ivy and I look across the table at each other as dread pools in my stomach.

"LOLA!" We both yell and jump out of our chairs and run down the hall. Ivy throws open the bathroom door, and we don't see her. I run to the office to see if she's somehow locked herself in the closet, but she isn't in there either.

We hear a loud crash coupled with a sound of breaking glass and both turn towards my bedroom door. Silas and James have joined us in the hallway. James holds up a finger to silence us as he reaches behind his back and pulls his gun out before motioning to Ivy and me to back up. Silas and him share a look and a silent conversation passes between them. Silas grabs hold of the door handle as James brings his gun up and points it towards the room.

Ivy and I are both standing at the end of the hallway, but both jump when Silas throws the door open and ducks out of the way as James enters the room. Lola comes barreling out of the bedroom. A streak of white and red flies by us, and we both chase after her. Seconds later we hear the sound of the gun going off and James screaming incoherently.

Ivy continues to run after Lola, and I run back to my bedroom, praying with every ounce of faith in me that James is okay.

I slide into the door frame and see Silas leaning out of one side of the window, glass shattered around his feet. "Go, James, don't let him get away!" Silas is yelling out the broken window. He starts to climb up onto the windowsill, and I lurch forward and grab his arm before he can jump.

"What happened?!" He looks back at me and then back out the open window, torn between two choices. Before he can answer, we hear Ivy let out a blood curdling scream. I let go of Silas and run towards her voice as fast as I can. I find her in the kitchen leaning over something next to the stove. She looks up at me with tears in her eyes and brings a hand up to brush her hair out of her face, leaving a bright red streak of blood across her cheek.

I take a step closer and see Lola laying down, covered in blood.

No. Not her. I take a step back, a rush of air escaping my lungs at the same time I feel the tears stinging my eyes. My entire body starts shaking as I cover my mouth and stand there looking at the two of them, unable to move.

Ivy reaches up and grabs my hand and then reaches down to pet Lola. The moment her hand hits Lola's body, Lola jumps up and hisses at her, then takes off down the hall again. We both stare at each other in confusion, and I pull her off of the kitchen floor before we go look for Lola again.

"What the hell is going on?" Ivy whispers as we walk into the living room.

I start to answer her, telling her that I have no idea either, when the front door opens and James and Silas walk inside. James's white shirt is covered in bright red blood and Ivy and I both run over to him in panic.

Ivy reaches him first and tells me to call 911, but James shakes his head no as I reach for my phone in my back pocket.

"It's not blood." He says, his voice is angry. "It's just red paint."

"Paint?" Ivy asks him, still reaching out and checking his shirt for a wound.

"Your room was covered in it when we went in." Silas says, reaching my side and grabbing my hand. "When we opened the door, somebody in a black hoodie was climbing out of the window. They got away before we could catch them."

The broken window.

The gun shot.

I squeeze Silas's hand hard. "Was it Ronan? Did you see his face?!" James looks up at me. Anger and defeat cloud his features, and I know the answer immediately. I know that it has to be Ronan, but again, there's no solid proof.

Again, he's ten steps ahead of us, taunting me while knowing it's just making me look crazy and making me feel like I'm slowly losing my mind.

I release Silas's hand and walk to my room. It's completely destroyed. One of the windows has been smashed in from the outside, which must be how Ronan got inside. The security system isn't going to alert us to a broken window. It only alerts us if the window is pried open and trips the censor at the top. Of course, he would make sure to keep the cops away while he did this. All of my drawers are pulled out and all the contents thrown all over the room. My mattress has been flipped over, along with my vanity chair. All of my paint supplies have been ruined. It looks like he used a knife to cut through all the canvases, and all of the paint has been dumped into the bathtub, leaving a runny rainbow of colors and overwhelming smell of acrylics. The only paint that made it was the red one, which he tossed all over my room, making it look like a murder scene from American Psycho. There are small, red cat prints scattered throughout the bedroom. I breathe a sigh of relief when I realize that Lola isn't covered in blood, it's just paint.

There are red handprints and marks all over the clothes in my closet, including all the small boxes of sentimental items I had stored on top. Everything is pulled out of the boxes, so the closet floor is littered with old notes and photos from different stages of my life.

He was searching for something. I close my eyes and picture him in his manic stage, ripping through all of my belongings. I've seen him do this before.

—

I wave goodbye to Ivy from the front door as she drives off. We spent all afternoon together shopping and catching up on life. I've hit that point in my pregnancy where I desperately needed new clothes. I'm only 25 weeks along, but I swear this baby gets bigger every day. I needed to get clothes that I could go out in, something other than Ronan's oversized t-shirts and gym shorts that I typically wear everyday at home.

Ivy jumped at the idea of shopping, and even though it isn't my favorite pastime, I loved being able to spend the day with my best friend. Ever since I quit my job at the school, I hardly ever get to see her. Our classrooms used to be just down the hall from each other, and I desperately miss being able to eat lunch with her on a daily basis.

Today was full of laughs and gossip, and it was exactly what I needed while Ronan was out of town on business. He has been so busy going to all these different leadership conferences since he got his big promotion. I know it's good for him and for his career, but I'd be lying if I said I wasn't lonely.

Most days, I wake up and mosey around the house, tidying things up and doing daily chores. Lately, I've been spending my days putting the nursery together. I've started to paint little birds behind his crib, and today, I was able to get more of the colors I needed to finish them.

I take a step up the stairs, and I hear a loud thud from above me, where our bedroom is. I freeze and realize that I left my phone in Ivy's car. I insisted on being in charge of the music because I couldn't think straight with the death metal that she was blasting when I got into the car.

I hear another loud thump and decide that I'll go to the neighbors house and call the cops. I turn to head back towards the front door when I hear Ronan's voice shouting from our bedroom.

"FUCK!" He screams. Then I hear another crash of something heavy.

I run up the stairs, open our bedroom door, and stop in my tracks. The whole room has been turned upside down. All the drawers have been pulled out and thrown across the room. Picture frames that hold photos of us that were on top of our dresser have been thrown in every corner of the room, leaving shattered glass everywhere.

Ronan walks out of our closet with an empty bottle of whiskey in his hand. He stops when he sees me standing in the doorway. His eyes are bloodshot and unfocused as he stares at me. His clothes are disheveled, and his hair looks as though he's been pulling at it like he does when he's stressed.

He takes a step towards me, and I take a step back instinctively and place my hands over my stomach. I don't trust him when he is this angry, and even less when he drinks this much.

He huffs an unamused laugh at me. "What, you're too good to let me touch you now? Too busy giving your body to another man while I'm gone?"

I resist the urge to roll my eyes as I reach my hand out and take a small step towards him. "Babe, what are you talking about?" We've been here before. This isn't the first time he's gotten overly drunk and accused me of being with another man. He needs to be reassured and reminded that I belong to him. And only to him.

He looks me up and down as I take slow steps towards him. His eyes flashing at me in resentment and distrust. I reach him and place one hand softly over his chest, while my other hand reaches down to take the bottle out of his hand. I notice he's clutching a piece of paper in the hand that's holding the empty whiskey bottle.

I try to gently pry it from his grip. "What's this, hun?" His hand tightens over the note and the bottle, and when I look up at him, I know this isn't one of his normal mood swings. There's real hatred in his eyes as he gazes down at me.

"You know what this is, Florence. Don't act fucking stupid." His face twists in disgust as he throws the bottle across the room. It shatters against the wall, making me flinch against him.

"Please, tell me what it is. Whatever it is, we can fix it." I lean my head against his chest, trying to stifle the tears that are threatening to come out. "We can fix it together. I love you so much." My body is quivering in fear as I feel our son moving between us. Every instinct of mine is screaming at me to run. To protect my child. But I can't walk away from Ronan, I'm tied to him in every way. He's my whole heart and soul, and I can't live without him.

I bring both my hands to his face and reach up to kiss him. I kiss his lips, and then move to kiss both of his cheeks. He closes his eyes and leans into me, bringing one arm around my body to pull me closer to his. I move one of my hands to the zipper of his jeans now that he's kissing me back in earnest. I feel the anger slowly leaving his body as his lust for me takes over and I smile against his lips.

We are past the worst of it now.

Then he's roughly pushing me back and only stops when my back is thrown into the wall. He brings his hand up and grabs my face forcefully. I can feel the paper he's holding against my skin. The air is charged again, but with his hatred instead of his lust as he stares down at me, both of us breathing hard against each other.

"This is your little love note I found in my suitcase this morning from your lover. You know, the suitcase you used to stay with Ivy for the week while I was at that conference months ago. You stayed with her because you didn't want to be alone in the house, or so you said. Now I know it was just a story to make fucking your side piece an easier lie to hide from me," he says, venom coating every word. "You must have found a new hiding spot for the rest." He glares at me and motions to the destroyed room.

My brows furrow in confusion as I try to process what he's saying.

He closes his eyes and takes a step back. Then he hands me the note. I look up at him before I read whatever this paper says, knowing that this is why he is so furious with me.

It's a small white envelope, and it's addressed to me, but the address on them isn't mine, it's Ivy's. I don't recognize the handwriting, and I'm positive I've never gotten a letter at her house before. I pull the letter out to read it, my eyes widening in disbelief as I skim through it. What the hell is this?

Florence,
I can't stop thinking about you. As I write this, I wish I was laying in your bed with you and holding you in my arms again. I dream of the day that we can be together, and not have to hide in the shadows in fear of your husband finding out about us. I need more than a few hours of having you, tasting you, loving you, hearing you gasp my name in his bed. Meet me at our spot tomorrow at noon after he leaves.
Yours forever. X

I look up and see Ronan walking into the closet. I drop the letter and follow after him. He's throwing clothes hastily into a bag. I step up to him and place my shaking hand on his arm. He takes a deep breath before he turns to look at me. There are tears in his eyes and something inside of me breaks.

I reach out and grab his face and bring it to mine, our foreheads resting against each other. "Ronan…" I feel him shaking against me, trying to hold his tears in. "I swear this isn't true," I say softly, a hot trail of tears streaming down my face.

"Why would someone write that and go through all the trouble of making sure I fucking found it?!" he hisses out, and I watch as a tear escapes down his cheek. "Don't lie to me. You know I can always tell when you lie."

"I have no idea who that letter is from, but I swear I've never seen it before. I could never do this to you. Somebody is playing a sick fucking joke on us, and I don't know why. But I swear on my life, on our child's life that it isn't true. I've never seen that letter before. The only spot I have is the one I share with you in our forest and you know that. I need you to believe me. I would never do anything to rip our family apart. Never."

He reaches down and places his hands around my stomach. "You'll swear it on our son? That you are only mine?" His expression turned hopeful. Like he really wants to believe me.

"I have never seen that letter before. You are the only man I've ever shared myself with. I would never cheat on you. I swear that on everything that I am, and everything we are. I swear it on the life of our son, and the love we both have for him. I love you both so much, more than my own life."

He takes another deep, shuddering breath before he crushes his lips to mine. I can taste the salt from his tears on my lips as I kiss him back with all the love I have for him, like I can't breathe if his lips aren't on mine. I pull him down to the closet floor, and we undress one another as quickly as we can. Our joining is fast and merciless as both of us are desperate with need to claim each other.

We are both left panting and gasping for breath while staring into each other's eyes. He reaches up and tenderly strokes my face before he leans down and kisses me. "I love you so much," he says into the kiss. Suddenly, he grabs *my face hard and forces me to look at him,* "But if I find out you are lying to me, I swear, I will kill you both."

—

My heart hurts as I remember the beginning of the end of us. I was so grateful at that moment that he actually chose to believe me instead of the lies that some stranger wrote down. I never found out who wrote the note, but I truly believed that our love was strong enough to survive anything as we laid tangled up in each other's arms on the closet floor.

Two weeks later, he left me on the forest floor to die.

Chapter Twenty-Five

THE SUN IS SHINING brightly through the window, creating streaks of dust motes in the air around me. I look over and smile at Silas, who looks insanely adorable with his hair a mess and mouth slightly parted as he sleeps soundly next to me. We got back to his house late last night, so I don't want to wake him. I quietly get out of bed and grab my robe out of my bag of non-paint smeared clothes that lays by the door. I turn to look at him one last time before I sneak out of the bedroom and close the door quietly behind me.

I make my way into his kitchen and start a fresh pot of coffee, inhaling deeply as the smell of it percolating brightens up my morning. I glance around the tidy kitchen as I wait for the coffee to get finished brewing, admiring how neat and tidy he keeps everything.

Ivy and I are both a mess in the kitchen, and there's almost always something sticky on the countertops. When the coffee is ready, I grab a plain black coffee cup from the dish rack next to the sink and find creamer in the fridge. I see that he has eggs and bacon and decide that I'll make us breakfast once I've finished my coffee. It's the least I can do for him after what a disaster last night was.

After I realized that Ronan was looking for something in my room, I felt like I needed to be alone to go through it all. I needed the space to sort out what was missing, and what may have been added. After all, it only took one note from a stranger to ruin my life. I refuse to let that happen again. I won't let Ronan ruin the happiness that I've found with Silas. And as much as I appreciate and trust James, letting him go through all my belongings with cop eyes and hands just felt too personal to me.

So instead of going through it all last night, Ivy and I packed up what we could, and decided to stay somewhere else for a few days. Silas offered his home to both of us, but Ivy didn't want to take Lola around Duke when she was already so shaken up from being locked in the room with Ronan. Instead, she took Lola and they both stayed at James's house. Part of me wonders if there is something going on between them, but I know Ivy will tell me when she's ready. She's always been fickle with lovers, and even more fickle with sharing the details. She won't share it unless she deems it real. I silently hope that maybe she has found someone to make her as happy as Silas has made me these last few weeks.

I hated leaving her last night after everything happened, but I know when she needs some space to sort through her own feelings, instead of feeling like she has to hover over me and mother-hen me through this. Staying with James gave her that space last night. And as much as I missed having her right down the hall from me, I am glad that she has him to lean on.

After very little debate last night, we all decided to part ways and get some much needed rest. We are supposed to meet back at the house today at noon so we can all go over the scene with fresh eyes. James says that once it's light outside, he may be able to find more evidence on the outside of my window. It all feels a little like a CSI episode to me, but I'll do anything at this point to catch Ronan and keep him out of my life for good.

I wander into Silas's spacious living room with my mug of coffee and slowly take in all the little things I missed while we were here yesterday. God, that feels like a million years ago...was it really only yesterday? He has so many little knick-knacks on his bookshelves. I see a little wooden bird near the bottom of the shelf and pick it up carefully. I close my eyes and clutch it carefully to my chest as I let the grief over missing my son wash over me.

Duke is watching me from his bed in the corner of the living room. He stands up and walks over to me and lays his head on my knee. I put the bird back and then focus on giving Duke some much needed love. He must know that I'm in no mood for his tackling shenanigans because he licks my hand before rolling over and giving me his belly, calm and content as ever. He really is the sweetest boy, even if he loves to knock me on my ass more often than not.

One minute I'm petting his belly, and the next minute I'm jumping back while trying not to spill my coffee. Duke jumps up barking, his tail wagging excitedly and runs towards the front door. A second later there is a firm, but quiet knock on the front door. I look towards Silas's bedroom, wondering if he heard the knock, or at least heard Duke barking. But when moments go by and the bedroom door doesn't open, I know he is still dead to the world. I put my coffee on the counter and walk to the front door to peek through the peephole. I sigh a breath of relief when I see that it's just Ted. I open the door for him.

"Well hi there, Flor. I didn't know you would be here this early," he says warmly, before noticing my attire and giving me a small knowing smile. "I guess my grandson is still asleep since he missed our morning Bullshit and Breakfast," he chuckles.

I raise an eyebrow at him. "Bullshit and Breakfast?" I say, while opening the door wider and letting him inside. Duke darts out the front door before I can close it behind us. "Is he okay out there without someone?"

"Oh, yeah. That dog rules this land and we all know it. He'll go missing for hours and come back barking at the door covered in mud with a giant smile on his face." We both watch as Duke runs into the trees and disappears.

Ted makes his way to the kitchen, and that's when I notice he's holding a casserole dish covered in foil. "Anywho, Bullshit and Breakfast, also known as B and B is something my late wife came up with." He turns to the oven and sets it to preheat before turning back to me. "She always said if you get all the bullshit off your chest in the mornings, then the rest of the day would be alright. Nothing is better than venting out all the crap of the day before while eating a delicious breakfast surrounded by your favorite people."

"I actually kind of love that," I smile at him as I rummage through all the cabinets to find another mug so that I can pour him a cup of coffee.

"She always said it's better to wait until morning, that way you can't ruin your evening by coming home pissed off. All baggage was checked at the door until B and B time." He graciously takes the coffee from me and brings it to his lips before closing his eyes and taking his first sip. "That's some good coffee, Flor. Not too strong, but not too weak either. Sometimes, Silas makes his coffee so strong I feel like I'm going to have a heart attack after my first sip." He lets out a big belly laugh that makes me laugh right along with him. His good mood is contagious, and I can't help the smile that is plastered all over my face when I'm with him. The oven beeps, letting us know that it's preheated and ready, and Ted puts his casserole dish into the oven and turns the timer to 25 minutes. I still can't tell what's in the dish, but I'm guessing that it's another type of casserole.

I jump when hands sneak around my waist from behind me. "Good morning, beautiful," Silas says as he pulls me against his chest and nuzzles my cheek.

I blush and look over at Ted who has a shit-eating grin on his face as he watches us together. "Hi, handsome," I whisper back before I pull out of

Silas's arms to fetch him a cup of coffee. I walk back over to him and hand him the mug then lean back against the counter beside him. He kisses my head and then takes a drink, sighing in contentment. "I missed you while you were sleeping, but Ted kept me company. I learned all about this Bullshit and Breakfast thing you guys have, and honestly, I think it's kind of genius."

Silas chokes on his drink, and Ted starts to burst out laughing as he hunts down a paper towel to hand to Silas. "I completely forgot about B and B," Silas says as he wipes his face off with the paper towel, "And now I feel like an even bigger ass since it was my turn to bring breakfast." He walks over to Ted and gives him a quick hug before he starts pulling plates out of the cabinet.

"I figured when I saw your truck pull in well after midnight that you were going to forget, and I had all the ingredients for that tater-tot sausage casserole we used to love making. You know the one that Nan hated because we tried to make it for breakfast, lunch and dinner that one spring break." He huffs out a laugh and runs his hand through his thinning hair. "I was surprised when my sweet Flor answered the door though. Makes sense why you'd forget about breakfast when you have her keeping you company." He winks at me and I feel a blush spread across my cheeks. He lowers his voice and looks at me as Silas continues to carry different items from the kitchen into the dining room. "I'm really happy that he has you around though. He's always been kind of a lone wolf, even as a child, he never had many friends outside of me and his Nan. It makes this old man heart of mine happy to see the way he lights up when he's around you. He's a good kid, with a real big heart. So please be kind to each other, life is so short and you never know when the best times are going to end." He clears his throat and I can see the sadness in his eyes before he turns to the oven to check the food.

He turns and watches Silas fondly as he sets the table and starts to pull out a variety of fruit from the fridge. I can't help but smile at the two of them. I wish this was the type of relationship I had been lucky enough to have with my grandparents after my own parents passed away, but this was never my life. I am happy that Silas and Ted still make the effort to spend time with each other. As much as I have loved spending a couple of meals with the two of them, I also feel as though I'm intruding on their time and I feel like I'm going to burst into tears after Ted's words. So, I slowly make my way out of the kitchen and slip into Silas's bedroom, closing the door quietly behind me.

Chapter Twenty-Six

My body sinks to the floor against the door as soon as I'm alone. It breaks my heart that Ted has to live his life without his wife by his side. And I know that the emptiness that her loss has left in him will never truly go away. It's been a year, and the loss of Wren still burns bright and painfully within me every day. I bring my hand to my stomach and close my eyes, and let myself mourn the loss of the life I had before.

Ronan thinks he ruined me, but he doesn't know that I've only grown stronger through every loss I've experienced in my life. I survived the death of my parents, my grandparents, and my own son.

I will survive him too.

Because now I've found something to fight for after a year of feeling like the only escape to the loneliness of my life was my death. I've found Silas. And I refuse to lose him.

I wipe my face and stand up, feeling invigorated by my own fierce need to protect my people from Ronan. I dig through my purse at the end of the bed until I find my phone so that I can check on Ivy and James. Of course it's completely dead, so I plug it into Silas's charger and decide to take a shower while the guys do their B and B thing. I laugh to myself at the thought. What a fun woman his Nan must have been. I know I would have loved her instantly because even though she's gone, hearing the stories about her remind me so much of Ivy–that vibrant, care-free and sass for days attitude that just exudes happiness and kindness. Ever since the day I met Ivy, she's been my rock.

—

There is only one thing worse than being the new girl. And that's being the new girl with the dead parents. I didn't have many friends at my previous high school, but having to transfer in the middle of my freshman year is definitely not ideal. I already hate the idea of having to stand up in front of a whole new group of kids every hour and having to introduce myself. Maybe if I stick a post-it to my head that says "My name is Florence, and my parents died two weeks ago," then it might get the teachers to let me skip that 'shitty part of being the new kid' tradition.

Maybe, but probably not. I think it's part of the teachers handbook to try to make our lives as miserable as possible during this phase of our lives.

I've always wanted to be a teacher like my mom is...was. But I don't think I can do it without her being here to guide me through it and support me like she always had. I don't know how I'll ever be able to walk into a classroom full of kids and not think of her immediately. Hell, I don't know how I'll get through this day without feeling like I should see her standing at the front of every classroom with a bright smile on her face.

That's one thing that nobody warns you about when you lose someone. Their ghosts stick around. They are hiding in every nook and cranny. They haunt my every thought and plague every dream. A constant reminder of their death, haunting me, but this time I can't run to their arms and hide from the scary monsters.

They are the ghosts and monsters now. And I can't find comfort in them anymore.

I pull my hood over my head and walk through the quad towards my first class, letting the sounds of the other kids fill my mind so I can try to ignore the dark thoughts that always seem to plague my soul when it's too quiet. Usually my go-to free therapy is music, but after my parents died I can't seem to stomach listening to anything. All the lyrics remind me of them and how they should still be alive. But life is cruel and unfair and takes the best of us too soon. Because of course the drunk driver that hit them while he ran the red light going 75 in a 35 zone would survive the accident. He had nobody at home waiting for him. No kids, no wife. But I am an orphan now because of him, and it's not fucking fair.

 I feel the prickle of tears starting, and I decide to cut back across the quad and head to the bathroom before I fully lose my shit in front of everyone. My first period teacher will just have to understand if I'm late.

 Before I even make it halfway to the bathroom, something slams into the side of my face, causing me to lose my balance and fall into the grass. I bring my hand to my face, which stings and hurts so badly that I'm sure it must be bleeding. Someone comes running towards me and someone else is yelling somewhere near me, but the pounding in my face is making everything dull and unfocused.

 I look up and see a girl about my age kneeling down next to me. She has dark hair that's braided into a perfect fishtail and hanging over her shoulder. Her eyes are a deep hazel brown with flecks of gold in them, and she is wearing a leopard print shirt and a bright red leather jacket over it. The contrasting of colors shouldn't work together, but somehow this girl pulls it off. I bring my hand away from my face and look down at it. I'm actually surprised when I don't see blood.

 "Oh hun, I'm so sorry!" She starts to bring her hands to my face before I pull back. I don't want to be touched right now. She pulls her hand back and gives me a friendly smile before rolling her eyes and throwing her hands up in frustration. "I told my idiot boyfriend to stop throwing that fucking ball. But of course, like I said, he's an idiot," she explains to me as she shoots daggers at her boyfriend. Her voice is gentle, but also fierce. She reminds me so much of my mom in this moment and that's what finally makes me feel like I'm going to completely lose it in front of everyone.

I bite my lip hard, nearly drawing blood in order to force myself to stop the sobs that are trying so desperately to overwhelm my body. I don't want these people to see me crying, and I definitely don't want them to see me lose control of the leash I've been trying so hard to hold onto so tightly.

Her boyfriend comes up to us and asks me if I want him to carry me to the nurse. I shake my head no, and bite my lip harder as an onslaught of tears starts to stream down my face. I pull my knees up, so I can hide my face behind them. The girl says something to him, and he says that he is sorry again. I hear the footsteps of him walking away.

"I guess there are better ways to start your first day of school than taking my boyfriend's ball to your face, huh?" *I look up and see her smiling at me, and I notice that the quad is mostly empty now. The bell rings loudly around us, and I gaze back at her. She's playing with the grass, and she doesn't look like she's rushing to get to class. I'm actually relieved that she didn't leave me sitting here alone.*

I bring my hand to my face again, just to check one more time that it's not actually bleeding because it still stings. I rub my hands quickly over each cheek to wipe away the few traitorous tears that managed to escape. Then I turn towards the girl sitting next to me. "My name's Florence, and I'm not usually this much of a hot mess."

She looks up at me as I talk to her and smiles before reaching her hand out. "I'm Ivy, and I'm sorry my boyfriend sucks so much at soccer that he thought your face was the goal post." *I reach out and shake her hand as a laugh escapes my lips.* "He's a nice guy, but sometimes he's as dull as a box of chalk."

"Savage, Ivy. Savage." *We both look at each other and start laughing. I've known this girl for all of about ten minutes, and she's made me smile and laugh more in those ten minutes than I have in the last two weeks.*

Ivy stands up and holds her hand out to help me up. "I guess I'm just going to have to dump him now." *She links her arm with mine and starts to drag me towards the bathroom. "I can't date a guy who just tried to kill my new best friend with his flaccid soccer ball. Now can I?"*

I've never had a best friend before. But as I look over at her, I have this insane feeling that I've somehow known her forever, and I know that I'll go down swinging for this girl for the rest of my life.

I think I might end up liking this school after all.

—

I hurry out of the shower and rush over to my phone to see if it's charged enough to use it. Ivy and I have only been apart for less than 12 hours, and I miss her immensely. I'd feel a little pathetic if I didn't see the dozens of texts from her waiting for me after I turn my phone on. Instead of texting her back, I find her name in my contacts and press call. The phone rings and rings, then goes to her voicemail, which I don't bother leaving because I know she'll call me back when she can. My heart sinks when I text her instead and it goes unread after watching it for a couple of minutes. I know I'll see her in just a couple of hours. But I still miss her like crazy, and I can't help but worry about her since she's not answering.

I'm about to hit the call button again when there's a soft knock on the door. "Come in," I answer, knowing that it's Silas. I'm sitting on his bed in nothing but a towel, and I watch him open the door and cross the bedroom. He comes to sit next to me on the bed and offers me a plate of casserole. I look at my phone one more time before I sigh and place it back on the nightstand.

"You okay?" Silas asks me gently. It amazes me that I've only really known him for a few weeks, and he reads my moods so well already.

I lay my head on his shoulder and pick at the casserole. I'm starving but my stomach is in knots about Ivy not answering. "I'm worried about Ivy," I finally tell him. "After Ronan called her yesterday...I can't help but think that he's going to try to use her to get to me. And if anything happens to her because of me..." I shudder and he takes the plate out of my hands and places it next to my phone on the nightstand. He wraps his arms around me, pulling me closer and into the same warmth and comfort that he offered me the first time we met.

"Ivy called my phone earlier when your phone went straight to voicemail. Her and James stayed up later than either of them planned to, and she said they needed to sleep in or she was going to murder everyone today," he chuckles and shakes his head against me. "So, they aren't meeting us at your house until closer to 3 o'clock."

My whole body relaxes, and I laugh against his chest. "Sorry, I'm sort of manic lately. My head just goes to the darkest places, and I feel this overwhelming need to make sure that everyone is safe. When Ivy didn't answer, I immediately started to wonder and panic that somehow Ronan had gotten to her."

He softly caresses my cheek before he pulls my chin up, so that I'm looking into his eyes. "You don't ever have to apologize for feeling the way you feel, and you sure as hell don't ever have to explain it to me or anyone else. You have gone through so much more than any person should have to, and you've survived it this long because of those gut feelings. If your mind goes dark, it's because you're already thinking of ways to fight back. You are a survivor, Florence. It's what makes you so damn beautiful."

He leans down and brushes my lips with his own, and I let myself melt into him. I let the towel that is wrapped around my body fall away and we spend the next hour learning every inch of each other's bodies. Unhurried and unrushed, but with just as much passion and love between us like our time together was at the bench.

Somehow, in the midst of all the heartache and chaos of this life, I found him. And for some reason only known to the fates, he loves me despite all my flaws and mistakes.

Chapter Twenty-Seven

We pull into the driveway right behind my orange slug-bug a couple of hours later. Ivy finally texted me and said that her and James were on their way, with boxes and extra cleaning supplies in tow. Silas and I get out of his truck and make our way to the front door in silence.

It feels almost eerie being back even though this has been my home for the last year. Just another thing Ronan has tried to take away from me. I'm more angry about him running Ivy out of her own home than I am about him breaking in and searching through my belongings as if he still has the right to do so. He lost the right to know me when he chose to believe a stranger over his own wife. When he took the life of our unborn son. When he left me on that forest floor to die.

He lost me, and it's his own fault.

Silas must feel the anger radiating off of me as I get lost in my thoughts, because one moment he is walking next to me to the front door, and the next he's standing in front of me and placing his hands on my shoulders. I look up at him and realize he's not trying to comfort me. His face is pale, and he is trying to push me back to the car.

"What—" He quickly puts his hand over my mouth, silencing me. His eyes are wide with fear and begging me to understand the seriousness of whatever has just happened. We back up to his truck and he pulls me down to the concrete before he finally risks talking.

He's whispering to me in a hushed, but urgent voice. "There is someone in the front window. I thought I saw something when I pulled into the driveway, but when I looked again it was just the curtain," he says quickly. "As we were walking up, I saw someone standing there in the window. But they had their back to us, and I only realized it was a real person when they walked away. Back into the house."

"Ronan," I say, shock and fear pouring into my body as I think about how close he is to Silas right now. If Ronan sees us together, I know he'll stop at nothing to destroy Silas. He'll do it just to hurt me and punish me again.

Silas nods his head. "You need to call James and Ivy, and tell them not to come here. I'll call the cops."

"Yeah, yeah, okay," I respond back automatically. My brain is going a million miles an hour at the moment. I need to get Silas out of here, but I know he won't leave me alone. And I can't leave because I need to catch Ronan. I need proof for James, and for myself, so we can finally get the cops to take me seriously. I need Ronan behind bars where he can never hurt anyone I love ever again.

Silas is slowly opening his truck to get his phone out of the car, and moments later he is laying across the passenger's seat and bringing his phone to his ear. I can't stomach the idea of losing him too. I gaze at him one last time...fully committing every single thing about him to my memory.

Then, I take off running from behind his truck and into the side yard where the gate is unlocked.

It's time I finally face Ronan.

Before I make my way to the back door, I pull my phone out of my pocket and send Ivy a text warning her not to come home. I know she's going to kill me for this. But I need to know that she is far away from him and safe. I see the bubbles of her responding pop up, and I silence my phone quickly and say a quick prayer that she listens to me. Before I reach the backdoor, I remember that I left some of my paint supplies out–which means my palette knives are still sitting on the table…the table on the furthest end of the patio from where I am.

I crouch down and run from the back gate to the nearest window. My heart is pounding fiercely in my chest, and I'm drenched in sweat within seconds. Fear shows itself in the most disgusting ways sometimes.

I try to silence my pounding heart and listen hard for any type of noise from inside the house. I don't hear anything, but I know Ronan, and I know he is completely fine with lying in wait in silence. Instead of taking my chances, I pull my phone out of my back pocket and turn my camera app on. Pressing record on the video option, I slowly bring it to the window, turning it slowly in multiple directions before pulling it back down. I open the video and watch it several times to see if I can see Ronan standing anywhere near the back of the house. Nothing shows up on the video except for our kitchen and the hallway to our bedrooms. Maybe he's back at the front of the house, and that scares me even more.

What if he sees Silas?

I leave my safe hiding spot and rush to the other side of the patio and grab three of my palette knives before I run and hide against the other side of the house. There isn't a window on this side, but the back door is right around the corner from me and I know it's not locked. Ivy couldn't find her house keys last night in the chaos of everything, so James recommended leaving the backdoor unlocked before we all left. It wasn't like we were scared of someone breaking in again, because who would be stupid enough to try it twice in a row?

But Ronan isn't stupid. He's determined. And that's so much more terrifying.

I look down at the three palette knives in my hand. None of them are exactly sharp because they are made to blend and spread paint, but

I grab the sharper of the three and put the other two in my back pocket just in case. It's not a weapon that will be of much use, but I'll take any protection I can get. This time I will fight back even if it kills me. I pull my phone back out of my pocket and turn the video mode on again. I take a deep, settling breath and press record. Then I round the corner and slowly open the back door and enter my house, silently closing the door behind me.

At first glance, I don't see anything. I quietly tiptoe my way through the kitchen and into the living room. I take a couple of steps into the living room and realize I should have traded my paint knife for a real knife, so I slowly turn around in an attempt to do just that. I make it three steps into the kitchen and put my phone on the counter in order to wipe the sweat off of my palms before I grab a knife from the butcher block.

His voice stops me cold in my tracks.

"Hello, Florence," Ronan purrs my name out in a tone that means nothing but violence. "I've been waiting for you to finally show back up."

I close my eyes and let the fear of hearing his voice make its way through my body, the way it always has when I hear this tone from him. Then, I shut it down and clutch the palette knife harder in my fist. He's tormented my every thought for over the last year, and I'm tired of being this weak little fawn that he thinks he has control over.

I turn around to face the man I used to love with every part of my existence. He's standing in the middle of the living room wearing a black hoodie that's covered in red paint. He has both his hands tucked into the pockets of his blue jeans. His hair is a mess, and it still looks like he hasn't slept in weeks. When I finally meet his eyes, all I feel is rage and disgust towards him.

"Hello, Ronan," I answer back calmly, without an ounce of fear in my voice. His eyes widen at me in surprise before anger washes over his face again.

"I see someone thinks she's all high and mighty now. Is it because of this Silas fellow? Because you know that isn't going to last. He may treat you nice, but he doesn't know you the way I know you. He can't possibly please you the way I can. Or punish you, the way I know you crave," he smirks before he chuckles knowingly under his breath. I feel nothing but fiery rage burning through my veins as I hear Silas's name come out of his mouth.

"He would never lay a hand on me the way you have," I spit out at him. My whole body is shaking in rage, and I've never felt this overwhelming need to hurt him back. "You hurt me, and controlled me because you hate everything about yourself. You couldn't stand the failure you saw in the mirror every morning. So you chose to become the monster I saw every single fucking day."

He glares at me from across the room as I continue to finally unleash all the words I've wanted to tell him for years. "You had the perfect life with me, Ronan. We were happy! Then you got passed on one promotion and you turned to drinking, instead of talking to me. And after that you turned into someone I didn't recognize anymore," I take a deep breath as I watch him. "You got that promotion a few months later though didn't you? The one that meant so much to you that when you got denied it the first time, you came home and got so drunk that you tried to force yourself on me? Or do you not remember that?" I'm glaring at him and letting all those horrible memories wash over me, strengthening my resolve. "After that I wouldn't let you touch me for weeks because I was so disgusted with you. I begged you to get help with your drinking, but you just ignored me and tried to get me to fuck you every single day instead." I've never stood up to him like this before, and it's invigorating.

His eyes widen in shock as I continue. "But I refused you every time. Until the day I came home from work, and you accused me of sleeping with one of my students. You twisted yourself a perfect little story to get what you wanted from me. You used my love for you, and my need to make you feel loved as a weapon against me," I shake my head angrily. "That was the first day you put your hands on me and purposely hurt me in order to keep me in your grasp." I feel the hot trail of angry tears sliding down my cheeks. "And I fucking *let* you."

—

I'm standing in the kitchen making dinner when I hear the front door open. I'm surprised that Ronan is home early. He was supposed to fly in tomorrow morning from yet another work conference.

I peek my head around the corner, and I can tell from the set of his shoulders that he's already in a mood. We've had such a hard time getting back to normal after our huge fight last week.

My blood boils at the thought of someone trying to prank him with a note like that. I would never be unfaithful to him, but these days it's getting harder and harder for me to keep trying to prove that to him. But I will keep trying, because I know on his good days that Ronan is worth all of the dark days. When this baby comes I know he will finally start believing me, and that our family is going to be what brings the light back into his eyes when he looks at me.

I rub my hands across my stomach, smiling to myself as I feel the strong kicks of our son. How can I love someone so much that I've never even met? A little less than three months, and we will finally get to meet him face to face. I already can't wait to kiss his little nose every single day.

I look up as Ronan finally makes his way into the kitchen. I watch him as he pulls the whiskey bottle from the freezer. He opens it and takes a long swig before he puts it down loudly on the counter, making me flinch involuntarily. When I finally meet his eyes they are glaring at me. He reaches into his back pocket and hands me a piece of paper.

My stomach drops, because I know exactly what this is.

I look down at the paper in my hands fully expecting to see another folded up note. Instead, I see that it's actually a small envelope. The type of envelope a thank you card would come in. The envelope has his name typed on the front, along with the address to the car dealership.

His expression darkens as he watches me open the envelope and pull the small piece of paper out of it. "I decided to come home early from the conference to surprise you, but I had to stop at work to drop some paperwork off. When I got to my office, that envelope was sitting on my desk."

I unfold the paper and look down at it. On it is one sentence, hand written in large letters. Terror rises in my gut as I read it and reread it, Fully knowing that no matter what I say now, he won't believe me until our son is born and he can prove that this one sentence is a lie.

"Care to explain yourself, wife?" *I look up at him in fear.* "Is that what you've been doing ever since you left your job? Waiting until I had to leave town and finding a new hobby to fill your time? Is that what you were doing today when I called? Fucking him again?! I bet you both just laugh and laugh over the fact that I was fool enough to believe you last time."

"This..." *I gasp out.* "This is a lie. Ronan, you have to believe me that this is a lie. I don't know what kind of sick joke this is, but it's not true. I was with Ivy today, I swear it!" *I plead out. He grabs the whiskey bottle and takes the steps two at a time as I try to catch up with him.*

I follow him into our bedroom as quickly as I can. "I went to the school to have lunch with her and then came straight home. I swear it on our child!"

His expression hardens as he looks down at my stomach and then back up at my face. He reaches into his back pocket and throws a handful of envelopes at me. "And I'm sure all of these are lies too? All these love notes I found hidden in OUR FUCKING BEDROOM TODAY, FLO-

RENCE?!" *His voice cracks.* "How could you do this to me? To us?! I let myself believe you when I found the first note from your lover hidden in my suitcase. But this time, I'm done. I'm so fucking done with you."

Ronan walks into the closet and comes out with an already packed suitcase.

"No! Ronan, please don't leave me. I love you! You can't leave me, we're about to have a baby!" I cry out as I watch him look down at me in pure loathing, before he turns and walks out of the bedroom door, slamming it behind him loudly. I've never seen him look at me like he did this time.

My legs give out, and I sink to the floor, clutching this lie in my hand, knowing that all the promises and pleading in the world won't change his mind. Whoever sent him this note, they just destroyed us. I've never given him a reason to doubt my love and loyalty to him, but he's always been jealous and insecure, even with him owning my entire heart and soul. I've cut off everyone in my life aside from Ivy to prove to him that I only belong to him. But this is the first time I haven't been able to make him believe me. This is the first time he's walked away. This is the first time I have wished he would have just hit me in order to bring us back together again.

I hear the front door slam, and my heart cracks in two. He's left me, he has actually left me. I look down at the note in my hand...

"IT'S NOT YOUR BABY"

This lie might as well have just killed me, because I can't live without him.

Chapter Twenty-Eight

RONAN STEPS TOWARDS ME while pulling one of his hands out of his pocket like he wants to comfort me. His eyes soften the way they used to when I thought the real danger was over. But it was always there under the surface of his skin, waiting to strike out at me when he thought I deserved it most. I am not scared of him anymore, and he has no power over me. I have too much to fight for now, and I refuse to let myself fall for his tricks ever again.

I take a step back and raise the small paint knife up. "Don't you dare come any closer to me," I hiss through my teeth. He stops in his tracks, his eyes glued to mine as I see him breaking apart right in front of me. "You know what the worst part of all of this is though, Ronan?" I keep the knife up as I step closer to him. I am fueled by rage and power, and I am not afraid of him. "You got yourself so twisted up in an effort to control me and keep me. And that's what broke us. I loved you more than I had ever loved anyone in my entire life. You had my whole heart and soul. You didn't need to make up stories, or send yourself fake notes in order to keep me. I was always yours."

I continue to walk closer to him until finally we are an arms length apart. We are both breathing heavily, and as much as I hate it, I can feel the same pull towards him that I've felt since our first kiss in the forest.

He opens his mouth to say something. "The notes were–" I bring my finger to his lips to silence him. He doesn't get to talk now, just like he didn't give me the chance to talk before he took everything away from me on that fateful and terrible day a year ago.

I close the small gap between us and move my hand to caress his face. He brings one of his hands out of his pockets, and I feel something soft fall onto my sandals. He closes his eyes and sucks in a shuddered breath as he places his hand over my own. His forehead dips forward to lean against my own, and I swallow hard against the sobs I know are ready to burst out of me.

I've missed this version of him almost as much as I've always feared the dark version of him. I think a broken part of me will always love this man. An even more broken part of me wants to forgive him for everything he's done to us…and give into the feelings that I still have for him.

I lift my head up and place my lips gently on his before I pull away and bring them to his ear instead. "I know now that I'll always love you Ronan," I whisper in his ear. I feel the tear that escapes his eyes slide in between my fingers. "Instead of believing me when I said there was nobody else, you killed our son." His hand presses my hand against his face harder as he cries into it. "And for that, I will always hate you more than I ever loved you." I hear the gasp that escapes his lips at the same time that my hand holding the palette knife feels the small trickle of warm liquid spreading across it.

His hand falls away from my own, and we both pull slightly away from each other. Not far enough to pull the small palette knife out of his side, but enough to where we can stare into each other's eyes. His eyes are lined with tears and betrayal as he stares down at me. I look up at him and smile, knowing that even though my small knife wound won't kill him, I still won. I hurt him back.

"Now you'll have a scar that matches mine," I say triumphantly as I listen for the sound of police sirens getting closer to the house. "And as you rot away in a jail cell for the rest of your life, you'll always have that reminder. The reminder of what you did to your own child."

He stares at me in shock before he looks down at the knife sticking out of his side before I yank it out forcefully. The only thing that could have made this moment better was being able to stab him with the same knife that he used to kill our son.

"You made a mistake by coming back into my life. You can't control what I do anymore, or who I date. I don't belong to you anymore Ronan. You broke us."

An emotion I can't place crosses his face before he takes a step towards me again. He reaches out and grabs my arm and pulls me close to him again. "I didn't come back because I wanted to win you back," he whispers urgently in my ear, making goosebumps spread across my skin. "I came back to protect you from *him*." I pull out of his grasp and stare into his eyes in confusion. "I couldn't risk him finding out what I know about him," he says quickly. "I understand that you hate me, Florence. There aren't enough ways to say that I'm sorry for what I did to you...and to our son. I know there's no future between us anymore. You deserve the world, and a better man than me." He reaches forward and pulls my face to his, kissing me deeply before he lets me go. "But I will always love you, and I couldn't just leave until I was certain that you were safe from him. You need to go *now*, before he finds you."

I've known him for what feels like my entire life. I'm looking into the eyes of the man I used to love, and right now he isn't lying to me. He isn't trying to manipulate me. Right now, he's telling me the truth, and I've never been more scared.

"Safe from who, Ronan?! What the hell are you talking about?!" I scream at him as he tries to push me into the kitchen and towards the backdoor. I yank myself away from him and turn around to face him. "Wait, just wait!" I yell at him. "Who are you talking about?! You can't drop all of this on me and then expect me to just leave! What is going on?"

Before he can answer me, there's a loud bang at the front door and we both jump. Ronan grabs me and pulls me behind the island in the kitchen.

"Florence, are you in here?!" I release the breath I didn't even realize I was holding in and sigh in relief. It's just James. I go to stand up and Ronan grabs my arm and pulls me back down, covering my mouth with his hand quickly as he stares into my eyes pleadingly...just like Silas was staring into them when we got here and he saw Ronan in the window.

I reach up and pull his hand away from my mouth and grip it tightly with my own. For a moment, I forget that I'm supposed to hate this man sitting next to me and I shake my head, reassuring him that I'll stay quiet. After everything he's just told me, it's hard for me to know who I can trust.

James's voice calls out again, "Florence, please tell me you're in here? Ivy is outside with Silas freaking the fuck out over the text you sent her." I hear the telltale creek of the front step and I know that he walked back outside. "Hey, I don't see her or anyone else inside. I'm going to do a quick sweep. Keep trying her cell!" I hear him shout across the yard at someone before I hear the creek of the front step again.

James shuts the door behind him and we listen as his steps come closer to the kitchen. He must stop somewhere in between the living room and the kitchen because I can't hear his footsteps anymore. I turn to Ronan before I pull my hand out of his and try to tell him with my eyes that I'm going to take a peek to see where James is. Once I see James go into the hallway, I can get Ronan out of the house using the back door.

I slowly creep from our hiding spot and make my way to the edge of the island and peek out. James is kneeling in the middle of the living room, and it looks like he has some type of paper in his hands. Just then my phone vibrates from on top of the kitchen counter where I left it and James looks up, and I freeze when his eyes meet mine.

"Florence, holy shit do you know how worried we've all been?!" He stands and starts towards me. I can't let him see Ronan, so I stand up quickly and walk to the other side of the island to cut him off. He looks me up and down and his eyes land on my hand. Which is still holding the palette knife and is covered in Ronan's blood.

"What's that you got there?" James's voice has changed, and he starts to back away from me, quickly taking in the room and looking down the hall. "Is he here with you?" he asks me as he reaches around and pulls his gun out from behind his back.

I feel the panic rising as I watch him bring the gun up, his finger laying just above the trigger. I force a laugh out as I bring the knife to the sink.

"Oh this is just paint! It's such a nice day out that I figured I'd try to get some work done." I set the knife down in the sink before turning back towards him. "I forgot my phone inside so I came in and that's when I heard a loud bang at the front door, and I dove behind the counter thinking it was Ronan."

James looks at me like he doesn't believe a word coming out of my mouth, but he starts to lower his gun to the floor. "Well, let's go tell Silas and Ivy that you're okay so they stop worrying." We start to move towards the front door when there is a loud knock at the back door. I turn around and my stomach drops as I see Silas standing there, and he's looking towards the floor next to the island.

To where Ronan is still hiding.

James turns towards the knock, and as soon as he sees Silas's expression, he brings his gun back up. Before I can say anything, Silas is throwing open the back door and at the same time Ronan stands up from behind the counter.

Ronan looks my way first, and his mouth drops in shock when he sees the gun in James's hand, and then he looks back at Silas. "Florence..." Ronan says calmly. I look over at him, then my eyes dart to Silas who is still at the back door. I know James is still behind me because I can hear him breathing heavily.

One moment I'm in the middle of a twisted triangle between the three of them, and the next, Ronan is ducking and running towards me. He reaches me and grabs my hand as he yells "RUN!"

Before I can do anything, I hear the gunshot and let out a strangled scream.

I'm tackled to the floor. The last thing I remember, aside from hitting my head hard against something, is someone whispering into my ear, "You can't trust him."

Then the world goes black.

Chapter Twenty-Nine

My feet are running fast beneath me as I chase someone through the forest. I can't see past the bright lights that are pouring out from behind them. All I can see is the dark silhouette of the person I'm running towards.

Who is it?

I open my mouth to ask them, but before I can, I'm being pulled by a force in the opposite direction...making it impossible to reach the person.

"Who are you?!" I yell out at them.

A voice that sounds vaguely familiar answers me, "You can't trust him."

The dark silhouette I've been chasing suddenly stops and slowly turns around to face me. I gasp when I recognize my father.

This must be a dream. All I want to do is run into his arms. I try my hardest to fight the current that is pulling us apart.

But it's no use.

I can't fight against death.

"I LOVE YOU DAD!" I cry out before I'm pulled back into reality.

—

My eyes fly open and I'm instantly blinded by the bright lights above my head. I try to bring my hands to my face to cover them, but they feel heavy. I try fighting against the invisible restraints while blinking rapidly. I need my eyes to adjust to what's going on around me. Every blink brings more of my surroundings into focus. I must be in a hospital because

I can see glimpses of the monitors, and I can smell the antiseptic that permeates through the hospital walls. I look to my left and right and all I can see is the faces of people that I don't recognize.

I look around at the large room I am in. None of the doctors running around are paying much attention to me. I lift my head up and a sharp pain shoots through my skull and down my spine. I gasp out in pain.

A woman in teal scrubs hears me and comes running to my side. "Shh, just try to remain calm. I know you must be confused right now, but you're going to be okay, sweetheart," she says. Her voice is gentle and reassuring. "Let's go get you to your room, and I'll have the doctor explain everything in just a bit. You woke up a lot faster than we expected, but that's a terrific sign!" She claps loudly next to me, making me wince as pain shoots through my skull again. Her overly cheery voice at the end makes me want to punch her in the face.

I try to open my mouth to ask her what's going on, but my throat is extremely dry. She gives my arm a quick squeeze and then walks away, leaving me alone again in this personal hell. I can't move, I can't speak, and I have no idea what's going on right now. My body feels so heavy.

The only thing I can remember is trying to reach my father in my dream.

"You can't trust him," he said. His voice sounded exactly like I remember it.

Can't trust who?

The cheery nurse comes back and checks the monitors that are hooked up to me. I watch as she pulls a syringe out of her pocket. I try to shake my head no, because I don't want to go back to sleep. "Sorry, sweetheart. Doctors orders." She plunges it into my IV without ever looking at me, and within seconds I am falling asleep again.

·····•·····

When I open my eyes this time, I'm in a different room. This one looks like the same patient room I woke up in after I lost Wren. It takes a moment to still my pounding heart as all the memories of that day rush to the surface. I run my hand over my stomach on instinct like I do any time I think about him. I search through my blankets for the remote that moves the bed up and down. When I find it, I slowly press the "up" button and wince slightly when it jerks into motion.

Now that I'm sitting up, I take stock of the room. It's not the exact same room as last time, and I don't know if that makes me sad or grateful. That day was the hardest day of life...learning that not only had my son died, but I would also never get to see him. I'd never get to gaze upon his face and kiss his little nose like I dreamed of doing every day while I was pregnant with him.

My thoughts are interrupted when there is movement at the door. I watch as the handle turns and the door slightly opens.

"Is there any update on him yet?" Ivy's voice floats into the room from the hallway.

"He is still in surgery, but it shouldn't be long now." The door to the room starts to open and a middle aged man wearing a white doctor's coat with a stethoscope around his neck walks in. His brown eyes meet mine, and his eyebrows raise in surprise before giving me a small smile and closing the short distance from the door to my bed.

"Hello, Ms. Samuels, my name is Dr. Connell. How are you feeling?"

I stare at him while I try to assess how I'm feeling. "Umm. I'm honestly not really sure what's going on. I just know that I woke up to an overly peppy nurse who stabbed me right back to sleep instead of explaining anything to me."

"Well, she seems like she's just fine to me." Ivy walks out from behind Dr. Connell with a smirk on her face. I roll my eyes at her before she lunges at me for a hug. "Florence Renee Samuels, if you ever try to do some stupid shit like that to me again I will freaking murder you myself! How could you do this to me *again*?!"

I clear my throat and look at the doctor who has an amused smile on his lips. "Ivy, I love you, but my whole body hurts like I've been run over by a tonka truck." She pulls back quickly and apologizes, then moves to the chair next to the bed. She reaches out and grabs my hand, just like she did the last time I was here. I swallow the memories quickly and give her hand a tight squeeze before I continue. "I also have no idea what you're talking about. What happened?" I don't miss the alarmed look that Ivy shoots Dr. Connell. "What?" I look back and forth between the two of them as they look at each other. "What aren't you telling me?"

"Ms. Samuels, what is the last thing you can remember?" Dr. Connell asks me while pulling out a clipboard from the end of my bed.

I close my eyes and try to remember the last thing I did. "I remember driving back to our house with Silas. And then I snuck into the backyard and through the backdoor..." I try to sort through all the twisted memories, but it feels like I'm trying to wade through mud. "Something happened...and I had blood on my hands. And the gunshot was so loud." I open my eyes wide and look at Ivy as it all comes rushing back.

The gunshot. Oh my god. Ronan. And Silas. And James.

Deep down in my gut, I know the answer already, but I ask anyway, "Ivy, who is in surgery?"

She brings her other hand to the bed and squeezes them both around my own. "James tried to shoot Ronan when he tried to attack you, but he missed and hit Silas instead."

I pull my hand out of hers, so I can use both my hands to cover my face as I try to keep breathing. No, no, no. I can't lose him too. Everything I tried to do today was to keep him safe and out of Ronan's way, and I failed him. Just like I failed my son when he needed me to protect him the most.

No. No. No.

But if Silas is in surgery, then that means he's not dead.

I pull my hands away from my face and look at Dr. Connell. "Is Silas going to be okay?"

"I cannot give you full details because you aren't a family member." He looks over at Ivy and I hear her scoff from next to me. Obviously they've already gotten into this argument. "But I can say that as of now everything is going in the direction we are all hoping for."

Okay. That's not bad news, but it's not reassuring news either. "What about Ted? Silas's grandfather, is he here?"

"Yes Mr. Hale is in the waiting room down the hall. I told him I would ask you if you were okay with him coming to see you once you were *allowed* to have visitors." He narrows his eyes at Ivy, and I have to swallow a laugh, knowing damn well that she must have broken every one of their rules to be in here with me...or given them so much sass and attitude that they finally just gave her what she wanted.

Dr. Connell comes closer and looks through the chart on the clipboard again. "You came in today with what seemed like a major head injury," he explains to me without looking up from the chart, "But when I got into the procedure room to take a look, all you needed was a few stitches. Head wounds tend to bleed a lot, so it looked a lot worse than it actually was. You'll have some discomfort for the next couple of weeks at the site, and you can expect to have some tenderness and headaches for the first few days." I watch him as he pulls a pad of paper out of his coat and starts writing on it. "I'll prescribe some Naproxen for the swelling and pain. You need to come back in later this week to get your stitches looked at to make sure they are healing correctly. We'd also like to keep you here for the night to monitor for a concussion."

"I guess I can't really say no to staying the night. Can I?" I look at him hopefully. All I want to do is go check on Silas and see how he's doing.

Dr. Connell shakes his head and gives me an apologetic smile before he finally leaves the room.

"Okay, so I need you to tell me everything that happened." Ivy pleads with me. I look over at her and scoot over, giving her room to lay in the bed next to me. "I'm serious, Florence. I've been waiting hours for somebody to explain anything to me. James left to go back to the station as soon as the ambulance came and picked you and Silas up. I've tried calling him a billion times, but he's either ignoring me or his phone is off because it keeps going straight to voicemail." She takes a giant breath and then lays her head on my shoulder. "So, please, just tell me what the hell is going on."

I start at the beginning. I fill her in on everything that happened, including the bits that happened between Ronan and me. I'm embarrassed and ashamed that I started to fall for his crap again, but I also can't shake the feeling that he was telling me the truth about trying to protect me. I don't understand why he started stalking me though. Or why he tried so hard to scare me, like he did at the arcade. Those pieces of his puzzle just don't make sense to me, and I don't have the energy to figure out how to put them back together. Yet.

"Right. So obviously, Ronan has to be talking about either Silas or James. Because what other man have you gotten close to in the last year? And please don't tell me Ted is the stalker now. Because that's just ridiculous."

I smile to myself at Ivy's response to the whirlwind of a story I just gave her. This is why she will forever be my favorite human in the world. On the hardest days, or during the most stressful moments of my life, she always manages to make me smile while still being heard. She always trusts me for my word and has never once made me feel like I'm insane for some of the idiotic choices I've made.

"I know it can't be either of them," I finally answer back, "And I'm not not even sure what Ronan was talking about. You didn't see him, Ivy. He's a mess. I think it's very possible that he's suffering some kind of psychotic break. One minute he's ready to hurt me, and the next he's acting like he still loves me. I just can't be sure until the cops can perform some type of mental wellness check or something." Is that even a thing? I feel like that has to be some type of way for the cops to know if someone is losing their mind.

"They have to catch him first," Ivy huffs out next to me.

"What do you mean?"

"After James accidentally shot Silas and you passed out or whatever happened, Ronan got away." She chews at her nails nervously. "I was in the front waiting for the cops like Silas told me to do, and when I heard the gunshot I—I just froze. I swear it felt like I was frozen to that spot for an hour but didn't *see* anything. He ran right by me and I didn't even realize it was him until James came chasing after him and screaming at me to call an ambulance. I'm so sorry, Flo. That monster is still out there, and it's all because of me."

"No, no, no. None of this is your fault." I squeeze her hand tighter. "*I'm* the one who believed his lies again. Silas is hurt now because I didn't stop Ronan when I had the chance. When James came in the first time I could have told him right then and there that Ronan was hiding behind the island. But I didn't, because I desperately wanted to believe that there was still good in him. It's my fault we are all in this mess right now, and I'm going to do everything in my power to fix this."

"Like hell you are!" Ivy snaps back. "*We* are going to fix this. I'm not letting you out of my sight again, woman. Unless it's to let you and your new beau go do the horizontal tango." She wiggles her hips against me and makes me laugh. "That's definitely way beyond my best friend duties."

Chapter Thirty

I WAVE GOODBYE TO Ted as he pulls out of the driveway. I was discharged from the hospital this morning, and Ted offered to drive me home while Ivy is at work. He came to my room to see me after Ivy left last night and filled me in on everything happening with Silas.

As of this afternoon, Silas was still in the ICU, where he's been ever since he got out of surgery. They won't let me see him until he's moved back to a regular room because I'm not family...which infuriates me to no end. The doctor told Ted that they should be able to transfer him to his own room by tomorrow as long as he doesn't have any major complications. He was shot in his left shoulder, so he'll be in pain for a while. He'll have to do months of physical therapy once he's healed, but he's alive, and that's all that really matters in the end.

If James would have missed by even a couple of inches, then Silas would be dead. I can't stomach the thought of losing him. Not when we just found each other again.

But, I can't let my mind go to those dark places right now. I wanted to come home so I could clean up the mess I know we left behind after everything happened. I unlock the front door, step inside, and inhale deeply when the normal homely smells of mine and Ivy's hit me. Ivy always jokes that every family has their own "unique scent." Today, I'm glad for it because I was more than just a little nervous to come home.

I didn't want our home to feel tainted with the ugly memories of what happened between Ronan and I.

Now that I'm here though, I feel nothing but happiness to be home again and to be enveloped in this safe and comforting place. The first thing I want to do before I start cleaning anything is to take a shower. Or maybe I want a nice hot cup of coffee first. I feel gross and grimy after being stuck in the hospital for the last day. Though I also crave the kick of caffeine that the watered down coffee from the vending machine did not offer.

Coffee first, shower after. Cristina Yang would be proud of my decision.

I go to the kitchen and start the coffee and see that my phone is still sitting there by the knife block. I press the home button, and of course it's dead after sitting there for over a day. I plug it into the charger we keep in the living room and throw myself down on the couch as I wait for the coffee to finish brewing. I can't stand the silence that permeates throughout the house right now so I grab the remote and turn on reruns of Grey's. It reminds me too much of the last time I sat in my house in nothing but silence.

—

It's been six days since Ronan walked out on me. He hasn't called. He hasn't texted. The silence of the house without him is deafening.

The only thing keeping me together right now is the fact that I need to stay strong for Wren. I went almost an entire day without eating or drinking anything after Ronan left. Then, I felt my son kick and it finally woke me up enough to remember that he needs me more than I will ever need Ronan...even if the idea of raising our son alone is devastating. He's only been gone for six days, and I feel like my entire world has shattered. How am I going to survive the rest of my life without him?

I've been sleeping uncomfortably on the couch because I can't bear to be alone in our bed knowing that he's not coming home this time. I still don't understand where everything went wrong. Why would somebody write such vicious lies on those notes? Is somebody angry at Ronan? At me? I can't think of any reason why someone would want to hurt us like this. But whatever their reasons are, they succeeded at breaking us.

My phone lights up from the coffee table alerting me that I've gotten a text. I don't rush to grab it because I assume it's Ivy. It certainly won't be Ronan. He hasn't texted me back all week or answered any of my calls. I haven't answered Ivy's because I haven't told her what happened and if I tell her, then it becomes real.

I'm not ready to face that truth. My husband walked out on me while I'm carrying his unborn child. The love of my life chose to believe the lies written on some pieces of paper instead of trusting me.

At some point, I know he'll have to come back and face me because our son is due in a couple of months. But what if he really believes that this baby isn't his? If he believes that then I know there's a chance I may never see him again. My heart constricts in pain at the thought, and I feel like I'm being crushed from the inside.

My phone flashes again, and then starts ringing. I jump up immediately and grab it because it's Ronan's ringtone. I press the green button and take a deep breath before bringing the phone to my ear.

"Hello?" I answer. Relief courses through my body as I hear his breathing on the other line. "Ronan, is it really you?"

"Meet me at our spot," he responds quietly. His voice gives away no clues as to how he's feeling right now. "One hour." Then he drops the call.

I can't help the giant grin that spreads across my face. I know if he wants to meet there, at the spot that began our love story, then he must be willing to work this out. I knew deep down that he couldn't truly believe the lies of some stranger trying to tear us apart.

For the first time in six days, I feel hope bloom in my chest. I rub my hands over my belly as I whisper to our son, "Let's go bring your daddy back home where he belongs. With us."

How could I have been so stupid to have trusted him again? What is it about Ronan that makes me throw my gut instincts out of the window? But the moment he shows me just a little bit of his vulnerable side I forget all the horrendous and evil things he did to me.

He killed our son.

There is nothing he can ever say or do to earn my forgiveness, and right now I am vowing to myself to never give him my trust again. Yesterday was a slip up that almost cost me Silas. I cannot let that happen again when Ronan tries to come back. Because I know that he will. If he is as twisted up as he appeared to be, he will keep coming back with his excuses of doing it to protect me from some unnamed villain.

Ronan is the only villain in my book, and I'll be ready the next time he comes back.

The coffee finishes brewing, and I force myself up from the couch and pour myself a mug. I bring the cup to my lips and savor the first sip before walking back to the couch. After the shitshow of the last 48 hours, I deserve to watch one episode before I go take a shower and start tackling the mess of the house. A loud crash comes from somewhere down the hall. I jump up and set my coffee down, causing hot coffee to spill all over my hand and the table.

I bite back a yell as the coffee burns me. I grab my phone to call 911 and want to scream when I see that it's still dead. I silently slip into the kitchen and grab the biggest knife I can from the butcher block, mumbling a quick prayer under my breath to Sky Daddy. I pray that maybe it's just an open window, and not Ronan forcing himself back into my life again. All the doors in the hallway are open except Ivy's. I hold the knife out firmly in front of me, ready to attack whoever the intruder is and slowly open her door.

I scream and almost drop the knife when Lola comes running out from under Ivy's bed like a bat out of hell before she takes off down the hall. What is with these animals and trying to give me actual heart attacks lately?!

As I glance around Ivy's room, I notice that Lola has pushed her food and water dish completely off the bathroom counter. Well, that explains the loud crash I heard. It isn't the first time she's done this while in a huff about being locked in the room. I walk to the windows and check to make sure they are still locked and that the window alarms are turned on. I've watched one too many scary movies, so I give Ivy's room one last sweep by checking the closet, under the bed and behind the shower curtain before finally deeming the intruder to be Lola.

When I walk back to the living room, I see that the fluffy culprit herself is laying in a ball in my spot on the couch. She's lucky I love her so much. I decide the shower can wait as I pick Lola up and lay down with her on the couch before throwing the cuddle blanket over the both of us and pressing play again, letting the over the top drama of the show take over my brain for a while.

Chapter Thirty-One

I'M IN THE LOBBY of the hospital, staring at the elevator door, waiting for it to open to take me up to the third floor. My heart is pounding hard with excitement and nervousness while I fidget with the necklace Silas gave me as I step into the elevator to go up.

It's been a week since I've seen Silas, and it's felt like the longest week of my life. He was supposed to be transferred to his own recovery room the day after I was discharged, but when he woke up after surgery, he was panicked and confused and decided to pick a fight with the nurses and doctors. He ended up ripping his stitches open and tearing part of the muscle in his shoulder in his struggle against them. The doctors took him back into surgery, and today is the first day they've allowed him to have visitors that aren't relatives.

I really, really loathe that damn rule.

I have so much to apologize for. He wouldn't be here in this mess if it wasn't for me. And a part of me thinks he only woke up in such a panic because he was worried about me. The elevator stops at his floor, and I am full of butterflies as I walk up to the nurses station to sign in. They direct me to his room down the hall, and when I reach his door I have to wipe my hands on my jeans because I'm so nervous.

Don't be a coward, Florence.

I knock twice before I hear him answering for me to enter. God I missed his voice. We texted back and forth most of the week, but it's nothing compared to hearing him talk to me. I open the door and close it behind me once I'm inside. As soon as I look up and see him sitting up in his bed, I feel the weight of the guilt that I've been carrying lift off of my heart.

He's actually okay, and he's safe. Well, mostly okay. He's still in the hospital from being shot on accident by our friend. His eyes meet mine and the smile that lights up his face is one of the most breathtaking things I've ever seen.

I close the distance between us as quickly as possible and make my way into his one outstretched arm, because the other one is wrapped up in a sling. I lay down next to him on the small bed and curl myself around him as carefully as I can as he puts his one good arm around me.

"I missed you so much," I whisper to him as I snuggle closer into his warmth.

"I can promise you that I missed you more," he chuckles back while kissing the top of my head and making me smile like an idiot against his chest. "I can't believe it's only Monday and they won't let me out until Friday. Is it overly clingy and pathetic if I beg you to come have lunch with me every day until Friday?"

"Only if I'm allowed to be pathetic and overly clingy by coming for both lunch and dinner." I turn my face towards him so I can finally get a real good look at him. He looks so tired, but also so damn happy while he looks down at me. His eyes still are as bright and mesmerizing as ever. I reach my hand and let my fingers play with the facial hair he has started to grow over the last week. It makes him look older, but still ruggedly handsome. Still like a lumberjack, but with the short beard this time.

"I'm so glad you are okay. I've been going out of my damn mind all week in this room just waiting to be able to talk to you. Being able to text you when the cell service decided to work was the highlight of my days. Well, that and all the photos you sent of Lola."

"Well, you could have seen me a week ago but someone decided to try to go all Hulk on the hospital staff," I smirk at him and lean in to kiss him. He reaches up and grabs the back of my head gently and pulls me even closer to him, deepening our kiss in a way that makes me melt against him and sends small shock waves throughout my body. All of the nervousness I had about seeing him floats right out the window as I feel him smile against my lips. We break apart when there's a knock at the door. I sit up and smile widely at James when he walks in.

James came over to the house the day after I got home and took my statement of events. He was all official and business-like until we were done, and then he apologized profusely for everything that happened. I reassured him that I didn't blame him for anything. If *anyone* is to blame for the awful events that happened between all of us, then it's me.

I told him about everything that happened between Ronan and I before he got there, and how I purposely tried to hide him because I was scared of anyone getting hurt. While that part wasn't exactly a lie, it wasn't the full truth either, and I hate the way the omission makes me feel.

I purposely left out the part of Ronan claiming to be back to protect me from some unknown person. Because while I know it's probably just another tactic he's using to control me and pull me back to him, I still can't shake the look in his eyes when he said it to me. There's a small part of me that might believe him.

James explained that he went to the station after the ambulances picked us up, and finally got the other cops to believe that Ronan is back. He said they're back on the lookout for him and won't stop until he is caught and behind bars this time. I cannot explain the overwhelming peace of mind that it gives me to know that they finally believe me.

I know from James that he and Silas have talked about the accidental shooting when James came in to get his official statement. There seems to be no hurt feelings on Silas's end, but since I haven't been able to talk to him all week aside from a few texts, I can't really be sure. I'm still a little salty that James got to break the "only family allowed" visiting rule because he was able to flash his badge and got all the nurses to swoon over him. When I begged him to take me with him, he wouldn't budge because it was "police business."

There's another knock on the door, and when James opens it, Ivy comes blazing in and pushes past him. She's holding what looks like two take-out bags from Lucene's Pasta & Pizzeria. I'm already drooling over the smell of the breadsticks. I give Silas's hand a squeeze before standing up to help them pull the chairs and the small end table over to his bed.

"You guys know I can stand up, right?" Silas says as he pulls the blanket back to get to his feet. "Let's go eat in the cafeteria down the hall. We don't need to pretend that this room isn't filled with a definite funk, and I could definitely use a change of scenery." He stands up and crosses the room to grab his robe from the hook in the bathroom, giving the three of us a very clear shot of his completely naked ass.

We all stand around in silence trying to avoid looking at each other. Each of us trying to stifle a laugh when he turns back around and looks at us. "What? Did you want to take a picture before I put my robe on?" Ivy is the first one to break with the ugliest snort of a laugh, which, in turn, causes us all to laugh uncontrollably, breaking the awkward silence in the room.

"Hey! No photos allowed. This one is all mine." I walk over to Silas and wrap my arms around him again. It's hard for me to be away from him now that I can finally see him and touch him again. I know I still need to talk to him and tell him everything that really went on between Ronan and me. But I'm just not ready to darken such a happy and care-free moment between the four of us after such a stressful and agonizing week apart. Right now, I'm going to let myself enjoy this afternoon and eat lunch from one of my favorite restaurants with some of my favorite people.

And I'm going to try like hell to push Ronan out of my mind during all of it.

"Alright, you disgusting love birds," Ivy rolls her eyes at us. "Let's go eat before this pasta gets cold. And James, quit gagging at them, you're killing my appetite."

James responds to her with a death glare and then shrugs at Silas and I. "You guys are pretty gross sometimes. Too many googly eyes." He gags at us before Ivy yanks him out of the room behind her.

Silas tugs me back when I try to follow them out, and I turn to face him. "What's wrong?" I ask when I see how serious his face has turned now that we're alone.

"Nothing whatsoever. I just wanted to tell you that I love you." He runs his hand across my cheek, making my breath hitch and my heart thump rapidly in my chest. "And that I really, really can't wait to have you all to myself."

A blush spreads across my cheeks as an ache of longing builds between us. "This door does lock..." I respond. My voice comes out huskier than I've ever heard it. His eyes burn with desire as we stare at each other. It feels like there's a silent dare between us as we are both waiting for the other to make the move.

"LET'S GO LOVE BIRDS!" Ivy's voice yells from the hallway, making us both jump and walk swiftly towards the door.

Before we walk out, I feel Silas's breath next to my ear and he whispers a promise that makes my toes curl in anticipation. "When I get out of here on Friday, you're all mine." I bite my lip when I look up at him and nod my head as we follow the others down the hallway. The next four days cannot fly by fast enough.

Chapter Thirty-Two

FOUR DAYS LATER Ivy, Duke, and I are walking along the trail in the forest. After pouting religiously for two days, I finally convinced Ivy to come with me to visit Wren. We've been friends since we were in high school together and she's never been here before. She said this place has too many of my ghosts here, and she didn't want to intrude. I know a bigger part of it is that this forest has always made her nervous. She can't get over the fact that there could be hundreds of different eyes watching her while she walks through the forest, and she can't see any of them.

I glance over at her and she has her arms crossed tightly around her body as her eyes watch the trees in every direction. She has one hand balled in a fist and the other clutching onto a small bouquet of carnations to leave for Wren. I chuckle under my breath as she jumps when Duke brushes against her legs. I reach down and pet his head just before he goes running down the trail ahead of us. Silas asked if I could take Duke with us since he's been driving Ted crazy with restless energy. I'd never say no to letting my furry savior tag along.

"Thank you for coming here with me today. I know you hate this place and the heebee jeebees it gives you." I couldn't stomach the idea of coming here alone, especially knowing that Ronan is still out there and not in his right mind.

She reaches out to shoo a bug out of her face before running her hands through her hair and blows out a long breath while she looks over at me. "It shouldn't have taken me this long to come here and I'm sorry I haven't sucked up my heebee jeebees before today. I should have come to visit our boy a long time ago." She wipes a tear away then continues, "But you do have to admit this place is creepy and I just want to jump out of my skin every time I hear a branch break or see the leaves move around us."

I look up at the trees and breathe in the comforting scents of this forest. We chose to come early in the morning so Ivy could drive to work afterwards. The sun has just started to peek above the tree line, and it's filled the forest with the sunny steaks of magic that I used to love as a child. The earthy aroma of the dirt under our feet and the crisp smell of the fresh air surround us. It has always welcomed me back with a hug. This place is the one place in the world that makes me feel close to my parents again.

"Well, you're here with me now and that means more to me than I can actually express without dissolving into a disgusting puddle of tears. The last couple of weeks have been so damn hard. Being back at that hospital just brought up all those feelings and memories right to the front of my brain again." Not that I'll ever forget anything about Wren, but the worst moments of that day have been weighing so heavy on me all over again. It's like my tragedy is stuck on repeat, and I can't figure out how to skip to the next part.

Ivy smiles a sad, but knowing, smile at me and we continue walking the trail in silence. Duke stops anytime he gets too far ahead of us and waits for us to catch up. Silas has trained him so well and I'd be lying if I wasn't glad to have him here with us. Ivy brought her pepper-spray, and I have one of Silas's pocket knives folded in my jacket pocket, but having Duke here makes me feel safer than any of those options do.

We get to the part of the trail that lies parallel to the spot, and Duke turns off the path and darts through the trees like the spot-finding pro he is. Ivy looks at me questioningly before I explain to her that we have to go through a few trees before we're there.

"Even if this bench is made of gold, I'm still not sitting on it," she mumbles under her breath as she follows me through the dense and damp trees. I giggle back at her and blush. Maybe I shouldn't have told her about the bench sex. But honestly how could I not. It was sort of epic.

"It's not made of gold, but it really is perfect in its own magical way."

"Yeah, because it has Silas's ass prints all over it."

"Ivy!" I chastise her while trying to hold back a laugh. I stop before we can take the last step out into the small clearing and turn towards her. "Seriously though, thank you for being here with me. This place is so special and personal to me and having you finally coming here feels like a giant moment for me. My parents and my son are both here. And they all would have loved you just as much as I do. I truly couldn't have survived this life without you by my side, Ivy. So, really, thank you."

She just nods as she tries to keep herself from crying, and I throw my arms around her and hold her tight. "I love you most. Now dry it up because there's no crying allowed at the sex bench," I joke as we pull apart and both wipe our eyes.

"I could say so many crude and hilariously inappropriate things right now about that sentence. But I want your parents' ghosts to like me."

I roll my eyes at her and we both step into the clearing. I stop short as I gaze at the mess of wood that has been thrown haphazardly across the area. It takes me a moment to realize what I'm looking at, and then I see that Duke is sitting next to a small pile of broken wood where the bench used to be. I bring my hand to my mouth in shock as I take in the scene of the destroyed bench around us.

"Who–who would do this?" I say out loud. Even as I say it, I already know the answer. "Ronan must have seen us here together. Silas and me." I look over at Ivy and her face is a mix of shock and anger.

"I swear to Sky Daddy, Florence. We are going to catch this bastard and make him pay for every single thing he's done to you."

I nod my head in agreement and walk over to where Duke is sitting, petting him softly on his head. "I can't believe he took this away from me too. I can't believe I almost fell for his bullshit again. How can I be this stupid, over and over again?" I say in disbelief.

"You aren't stupid. You loved him and trusted him. It isn't a switch that you just get to easily turn off after giving your entire self to him for that many years. I watched you both fall in love with each new version of yourselves over those years. And I know that there is a small part of you that must love this twisted, evil version of him, because you've loved every other version of him from the moment you met him."

"I wish to God I didn't. I wish I could just hate him and be done with him forever. I've met this amazing guy who truly cares about me. All I want to do is let myself enjoy this. The whole falling in love again and finding happiness thing with him. But I can't do that when I know Ronan is out there just waiting to ruin it. He will destroy everything I love until he's the only one left. Just like he did to this bench. I don't know why I'm even trying to fight against this anymore. Maybe Ronan really is what I deserve."

"Oh no. Don't start that shit with me. We aren't going to let that happen. You deserve to live your life without his shadow plaguing every good thing to happen to you. We are going to fight him every damn step of the way until you get your happy ending. And I know that sounds really ridiculous and cliche, especially right now." She takes a deep breath and continues, "But I don't know anyone who could have gone through the hell you've gone through in your life and survived it. I'm so proud of you every single day for just waking up in the morning. You are the strongest woman I've ever met and I'm not letting you give up the fight now." She stands up and wipes her hands on her leggings then holds her hand out to me. "Now stand up so we can take pictures of this place and report it to the cops."

I take her outstretched hand and let her pull me to my feet. "Thanks for always being my rock when I need some solid sense knocked into me." I pull my phone out of my purse and start taking photos of the entire area, making sure I get all the broken pieces of wood thrown around the clearing as well.

Ivy slides up next to me before I put my phone back in my bag. "Now turn it so we can take a selfie. Proof that I finally came and met your parents." She puts her chin on my shoulder and smiles big as I click the selfie button. I love her always, but I love her extra hard in this moment right now. "Wait let me see it, I don't want my wrinkles showing." She snags the phone out of my hand as I roll my eyes at her.

"You don't have any wrinkles, you hag."

"I know. I just wanted to send it to myself before you disappeared with lover-boy and ignored all my texts for hours. Wait, why do you have a 30 minute video on here? Please don't tell me it's a sex video because I'll literally die laughing."

I yank my phone back from her. "Oh my gosh it's not a sex video, you nasty!" I find the video and press play, turning the volume up so we can hear whatever it is.

"What is that noise?" Ivy reaches over and turns it to the max volume.

We're both quiet as we listen to the video, the screen is black, but there are definite noises on the recording. We hear a thud, and then it's quiet again. My heart stops as I hear Ronan's voice.

I quickly press pause on the video. "Oh my god. Ivy! This is the video I took when I snuck into our house to try to catch Ronan. That way I'd have proof for James to give to the department."

"Okay, first off, that's really freaking smart. Secondly, are you sure you want me to listen to this with you? I know you and Ronan talked before James showed up. I'd understand if that's something you'd rather keep to yourself."

"No, I want you to listen to all of it. Maybe you can actually help me make sense of it all." She nods her head in understanding, and we both sit down again in the dirt before I press play again.

We sit there listening to everything. All the lies Ronan spoke to me, and all the words I said back to him. Hearing the anger and defiance in my voice while I talk to him gives me that same rush of power again. My voice comes out so powerful, that I can't believe it's me that I'm hearing. We get to the part where James banged on the door and the video gets quiet again.

"This must be when me and Ronan are hiding behind the island." We both jump when the yelling starts. It's hard to decipher whose voice actually belongs to who because everyone was yelling so loudly. But I know the gunshot is coming next. I grab Ivy's hand for support. Even though we knew it was coming, the gunshot is louder than we anticipated it to be over the video and we both yelp in surprise, causing Duke to start barking.

I press pause and I call him over so we can pet him and calm him down. "It's just the tv, buddy," Ivy coos at him. "We'll protect you." I roll my eyes at her again and press play once Duke is laying calmly between us.

I don't know what I expected to hear after the gunshot, but hearing Ronan and James whisper back and forth was not it. Ivy and I share a look, both of us confused as to what we are hearing. We both lean closer to the phone and listen.

"What the hell are you doing?!" Ronan's voice yells out over the phone. "You could have shot her!"

"I wasn't going to miss...believe it or not, I know how to aim, asshole. Now, tell me what the fuck are *you* doing here?" James's voice calmly replies to him, "I've done everything to keep you off the radar, and yet here you are trying to ruin everything. So I ask again, little brother, what the fuck are you doing back here?!"

Brother? What is he talking about?

"You know why I came back. Don't pretend like you don't. It's taking everything in me not to fucking crush your skull in right now," Ronan's voice seethes out, anger clear as day even through the recording. "I know it was you."

"What are you talking about, Ronan?"

"I know that you're the one responsible for all of this, *brother*. I found the notes. I know it was you who ruined EVERYTHING!" We hear another loud thud from the recording. It sounds like a hand being slammed onto the counter. "I just don't understand why you did this to us. Was it jealousy or do you really hate me that much? When we both saw her in the school parking lot that day, I knew you wanted her to look your way just as badly as I wanted her to look mine. But I thought once she chose me that you'd move on and be happy for me. I was dead wrong. Instead, you left and never saw me again."

My brain is filled with a million questions as we continue to listen to them talk. My stomach is twisted up in knots. I'm finally starting to realize that Ronan wasn't lying when he told me he came back to protect me.

"Is that why you refused to come to our wedding even though I begged you to come officially meet the woman I loved? Because some twisted part of you loved her too? It was you, wasn't it? The notes? How long did you follow us? How could you sit there and watch me kill my son?"

I hear Ronan's voice crack, and I feel a small part of myself break for him. Break for us.

"No. You've got it all wrong. I—I can explain the notes, they aren't what you think. I swear, it's not what you think—" James's voice pleads with Ronan.

"I don't want to hear anymore of your fucking lies! I want you to leave and never come back. If I catch you around her again I swear I will kill you without a second thought. You are the only family I have left, and that is the *only* reason you are still breathing right now. But I will not let you hurt her anymore."

"It's not what you think!" James exclaims. "This is coming out all wrong. Fuck! Just let me explain! Please!"

"No." Ronan's answer is final. His tone is lethal. "Leave, James. Just leave."

My jaw drops as I hear my own voice from the recording next. It's low, but it is definitely me. "Silas. Don't leave me too." I don't remember anything before I woke up in the hospital, but my heart does cartwheels when I hear that I was calling out for Silas in my unconscious state.

"Go check to see if Ivy is still outside, and give me five minutes to call an ambulance for them. Once this is all cleaned up, I'll go out the back and you won't see me again. But mark my words James, I'll never stop watching you. You better fucking run, and never come back here." Ronan says it so calmly, but there is something deadly about the way he says it that goosebumps travel across my arms. We hear footsteps through the speaker and then the phone screen lights up with Ronan's face. He looks exhausted, and his eyes are haunted and lifeless.

"Florence, I know nothing I do will ever make up for what I've done to us, but please, please trust me when I tell you that you can't trust him. If you see this, and he comes back, please look in your notes. I will always love you, and I'm sorry for all of the pain and destruction I've brought into your life. I'm sorry that I broke us. Stay safe. And remember, you can't trust him."

Then the video ends, and the world I thought I knew comes crashing down all around me.

Chapter Thirty-Three

WE BOTH WALK BACK to the parking lot in stunned silence with Duke leading the way. I don't know how to wrap my head around everything I just heard. How could James have been the one sending the notes? I hadn't even met James until after Ronan attacked me. But according to what the recording said, he had seen me years ago on the day I met Ronan. It doesn't make any sense. All I want to do is curl into a ball and pretend I didn't listen to the video.

Ivy is the first one to break the silence. "I'll drop Duke off at Ted's on the way to work. You need to go get yourself cleaned up and go see your man. I know you love me most, but right now he's the shoulder you need to lean on. And I know he can't wait for you to pick him up." She opens the back of her car and Duke hops right in. "Just remember he only has one good shoulder for now, so be gentle with him." She wiggles her eyebrows at me suggestively. I love that she always keeps that sassy sense of humor of hers around even when life is literally falling apart around us.

"Thanks." The thought of being held by Silas is the only thing keeping me going right now after everything we just learned. "Wait, Ivy. I'm sorry about James. I don't know what exactly has been going on between the two of you, but I'm sorry."

She's never had a hard time finding someone to have fun with because she claims that she's just not ready to settle down, but I will still hate myself if whatever might have been going on with James was something serious.

"Oh god, no. Nothing happened between us. I literally slept in his tiny ass guest room with Lola when we stayed over. I just wanted to give you and Silas some time to be together without me being the creeper in the background. Seriously, there has never been anything going on between James and I, we stayed up talking about you actually…" Her eyes go wide as she looks back at me. "Oh my god, we literally talked about *you* the entire time. He was asking everything about you and Ronan, like when you two met…and he asked me about the wedding. He wanted to know how you were coping now that Ronan was back, and if you were going to be safe staying with Silas. We only called it a night when he asked if Silas was the real deal, and I told him yes."

She pauses for a moment before she continues, her face going pale. "I figured he was just tired, but now I think he was upset about you and Silas. They were all just random questions that I didn't think much about until now. I thought he was just asking because his cop brain didn't know how to shut off for five minutes. Now, I think maybe he just wanted to know everything there is to know about you." Her whole body shudders next to me. "I think maybe Ronan might be right about this. I hate to ever agree with him, but it's all starting to make sense now. Look at the timeline and the facts of everything. James only came into our life after Ronan was gone. He got himself added to your case and we met him when he came to the hospital to get your statement. Then, when you saw Ronan in the grocery store, *James* was the one who came. He was at the arcade when Ronan showed up, fuck…maybe he even turned the security cameras off in order to keep Ronan under the radar. He said in the recording that he's been doing everything he could to keep the cops away from him."

"Holy shit. I think you might be onto something." As I listen to her, it all starts to make sense. Everything she is saying can lead back to James possibly being the one who sent Ronan the notes over a year ago...the notes that ruined everything between us.

"Right? Just think. Every time something involved Ronan, James was there right after. And he never had a partner with him to listen to any of your statements. He wormed himself into your life with his promises of believing you when no one else did, essentially gaining your trust, and then placed himself right in the middle of everything going on! That way he would know when Ronan came back and could stop him from telling you the truth."

"What if James never actually reported anything to the department? Because now that I think of it, there's no way that the cop involved in an officer-related shooting would be the one to take the statements from the witnesses and victim. Right?" Uneasiness fills my stomach. I rush to the trash can nearest to my car and heave up my breakfast.

I feel Ivy's hands pull my hair away from my face as I continue to painfully dry-heave. "We are going to get through this. We will." I nod my head and use my sleeve to wipe my mouth before we both walk back to our cars.

"Yeah, you're right." A wave of nausea washes over me again, and I feel like I'm going to pass out as I reach the door of my car. I can't believe this is my life. I just want to hide from all of it. "I have to tell Silas though. I can't keep hiding things from him." I already feel so guilty over everything I've kept from him so far.

Ivy nods her head in agreement. "I know everything is totally fucked and upside down right now, but let's not do anything rash. If James really is the one responsible for all of this, then we need to find proof. How about you bring Silas to dinner at the house? Then we can brainstorm on what to do next. We can't just rush to the cops with this, obviously he has them in his pocket if this is true. Right?"

"Right. I just can't believe it's possibly been James this entire time. How are we ever going to face him again knowing what we know?"

"We'll figure that all out later. You go and get Silas and enjoy some much needed alone time with him. You deserve to have a few hours of happy bliss with that gorgeous ass of his."

"Ivy!" I smack at her playfully then she pulls me into a long hug. I promise her that I'll be home for dinner tonight so we can figure all this mess out together, then I get into my own car and head towards the hospital to finally bring Silas home.

·····•·····

I pace around Silas's bedroom with nervous energy while he takes a quick shower. The moment I saw him I wanted to blurt everything out, but I forced myself to not say anything until we got back to his house. Plus, I figured it would be better for us to be away from prying eyes and listening ears especially since there isn't anyone besides Ivy and Silas that I can trust with all of this.

I stop pacing when Silas opens the bathroom door in nothing but a towel wrapped loosely around his waist. I feel my mouth go dry as I look him up and down. All thoughts of today slip from my mind as he takes a step closer to me. Somehow, his injured shoulder wrapped in the dark blue sling makes him look even sexier, and all I want to do is rip the towel away from his body and have my way with him.

I step forward to do just that when he stops me with a look of concern. "Hey, are you okay? You've seemed kind of off ever since you picked me up." My libido grinds to a quick and pitiful stop as I process what he's just said.

"Umm, yeah, no." I shake my head in frustration as he steps forwards and brings his hand to my face. I lean into it without hesitation, savoring the feeling because I know that after he listens to the recording he may not want to touch me like this again. "No, I'm not okay. I actually need to show you something."

"Okay, just give me one minute." He walks into the closet and comes out with loose flannel pants on. A big part of me sighs with regret, and I'm internally chastising myself for not taking advantage of no-pants Silas one last time before things turn to actual shit.

He moves to the bed, and I grab my phone out of my purse before I join him. I sit opposite him and leave a wide space between us. He furrows his brows in confusion as he looks at me.

I take a deep breath, and then place the phone in the space between us. "Okay, so," I pause again as my stomach turns sour with anxiety. I do my best to swallow down the nausea and continue, "Alright, so Ivy and I went to visit Wren today and when we got there, the bench you made was completely destroyed."

His eyes widen in surprise as he reaches across the gap and tries to take my hand. I pull my hand back and hate myself for the flash of hurt that crosses his face. I need to tell him everything before I allow myself to be comforted by him.

"When I took my phone out to take photos of it so we could report it, we found a video saved to my phone from the day you got shot." I reach forward and open my phone and pull the video up. "I started recording this as I snuck into the house. I wanted proof that it was Ronan." I hand Silas the phone with the video waiting to be played. "Please, just listen to the whole thing, and then we can talk about it afterwards, okay?"

He takes the phone and presses play.

My eyes don't leave Silas's face while he listens to the recording. I want to crawl into a hole and die when we get to the part between Ronan and I. Silas surprises me when he finally looks up at me because I expect to see disgust in his eyes. Instead of looking at me in loathing and betrayal for trusting Ronan again, he eyes are full of understanding. He reaches back across the space between us and grabs my hand in his own, rubbing his thumb back and forth over my knuckles in comforting circles. I want to cry in relief when he doesn't push me away after hearing the horrible things I said and how unremorseful I sounded when I stabbed Ronan. The palette knife was so small that I doubt it'll leave much of a scar, but I still hate that Silas is listening to how dark I went while I was lost in the moment .

That person isn't me. I've never had that kind of evil in me until that moment when I was looking into Ronan's eyes and I wanted to hate everything I still saw in him that made my heart race. If I'm being honest with myself, I wanted to turn that small knife around and stab my own heart for still loving a part of him. Dark and twisty must love dark and twisty, right?

The guilt that washes over me as I watch Silas smile when we hear my voice saying his name on the video makes me want to puke again. How can I sit here across from this amazing man as he holds my hand while I think about Ronan? Then, I hear Ronan's voice again, speaking directly to me at the end of the recording, and it feels like a sucker punch to my heart.

The recording ends, and the silence between us is deafening.

"You loved him for a long time..." Silas's voice is quiet as he speaks. "It's okay to feel however you feel, I would never judge you for anything." He moves the phone to the nightstand and inches closer. "Just please don't shut me out."

"I hate myself for still feeling the way I do about him." I chew at my lip, unable to look up at him. "He destroyed me in every way possible. I should hate him. I *do* hate him. But there's a broken part of me that also remembers loving the man he used to be."

I reach up, and brush my hair out of my face. "That broken part of me doesn't care that he killed our son, and I know how totally fucked up and wrong that is. Believe me, I know that. And I hate myself everyday for not being able to cut that part of me away." I finally look up at Silas and all I see is understanding in his eyes.

"After everything that you've gone through...I don't think you're broken for feeling that way. I think it makes you stronger for still having the capacity to care about him. Especially after everything that man put you through. You have such a big heart, and that doesn't make you broken. It makes you a damn saint for being able to look at him and not only see the things you hate. I'll hate him enough for the both of us if you want." He lets out a small laugh as he says that last part, which makes me smile at him in return. "And I'll love every part of you that you think is broken. As long as you'll let me."

"How did you come out so perfect? Are you even real?" I reach out and pinch him in the leg and make him laugh. "Seriously, I'm waiting for the other shoe to drop because there is no way I am this lucky." I climb into his lap and close the space between us.

"I think it's helped that I was raised by two people who were madly in love with each other. They showed me what love is supposed to look like and I waited until I could find that with someone. And then I found you." I lean in and his lips meet mine half way, placing a whisper of a kiss on them. "...And now I'm never letting you go."

I moan as he releases the tension between our lips and slams his onto mine, claiming me entirely. It's been weeks since the last time we were able to lose ourselves in each other, so every touch he places on my body feels like fireworks are going to explode out of me. I let my hands roam all over his chest, silently thankful that he didn't bother to put a shirt on after his shower. He groans when I reach his waistband, and I tease him by skimming the top of it back and forth. I laugh as he tries to use his one good arm to take my shirt off, and it gets stuck over my shoulder.

"Hold on, let me." I stand up and finish taking my shirt off for him. His eyes look my body up and down, and I melt when I see his tongue come out to wet his lips. He starts to stand, and I push him back onto the bed, careful not to hurt his shoulder. I smirk at him as I reach down and unbutton my jeans slowly, letting the sound of the zipper echo throughout his bedroom. I push my pants down, and step out of them, leaving myself bare in my matching green bra and underwear as I look at him.

Silas moves himself to the edge of the bed and reaches out and hooks a finger into the lace underwear I'm wearing and pulls me closer to him. My breath is coming out in fast pants and he's barely even touched me. He stands up from the bed and when I look up at him he bends down and brushes his lips against mine. Then he kisses a trail down to my neck, biting me softly in between kisses as he makes his way down my body.

Once he's on his knees in front of me, he starts to pull my underwear off with his teeth, the entire time maintaining eye contact with me and making every cell in my body hunger for him. He places kisses against both of my scars, and then drags his mouth down towards the very core of my desire. I moan out his name loudly and grab a hold of his hair roughly as he uses his tongue in tantalizing ways to bring me over the edge as waves of pleasure soar throughout my body.

Once the waves subside, I urge him onto the bed behind him and climb on top of him. We both gasp as I lower myself onto him slowly. I reach up and grab his face, forcing him to look at me. "Don't ever let me go."

"I won't," his voice answers, husky and sexy as hell. "You're mine." He growls into my ear before his hips slam into me over and over again. I meet him thrust for thrust until our bodies are covered in sweat and I detonate around him as I feel him find his own release. My body collapses onto him as we both struggle to catch our breath.

I slide off of him and snuggle into his side, resting my head on his chest. I smile when I feel his arm wrap around me. He caresses my back softly as I listen to his heartbeat. I feel more grounded in this moment with him than I have in the last week. It's like some part of my soul couldn't relax until I was back in his arms again. Now that I'm here with him it finally feels whole again. My heart feels full and content as I let myself drift to sleep in his arms.

Chapter Thirty-Four

"Y'ALL NEED TO GET those cheesy 'I just had the best sex of my life' smiles off of your faces," Ivy says while glaring across the table at Silas and I, "or I'm going to throw this casserole dish at you both. Like frisbee style. Right to your heads." I can't help but smile even wider when my eyes meet Silas's. "Oh my gosh. STOP!" She starts pretending to gag and I can't contain the ugly laugh that comes out of me.

"Okay, okay, sorry." I try my best to not smile as I look at her. But then Silas's hand grips my upper thigh. I yelp in surprise and the goofy grin overtakes my face again.

"I swear I'm about to get Lola's spray bottle and start spraying both of you." She throws her hands up in exasperation. "Hormone riddled teenagers, the both of you!"

Silas stands up and starts to clear the table, winking at me while grabbing the casserole dish from Ivy's side of the table first. He taught me how to make his and Ted's pizza casserole dish at his house before we came over because I've been craving it nonstop since the first time I had it.

We all move to the living room and as soon as we all sit down we just know that the playful and fun part of the evening is now over.

"How much did you tell Silas?" Ivy asks me, all seriousness in voice.

"I told him everything. He listened to the recording, and I filled him in on all your theories about James."

"From what Florence has said, it sounds like you might be dead on with these theories. I think we need to find some type of proof before we take this to the cops. We don't know how many of them will take your story over his." Silas rubs his hand over his face in frustration. "I just can't believe we didn't see it. He seemed so...normal. And he seemed even more angry when Ronan broke in and destroyed your room than any of us did. It just doesn't make sense."

Ivy and I both nod in agreement before she asks me, "Did you ever figure out what Ronan meant about the note?"

"What note?"

"Whatever note he talked about on the recording at the end? The part where he said if you needed to get in touch with him? Didn't he say something like that?"

Silas and I look at each other and shrug, neither of us sure. I pull my phone out of my back pocket and replay Ronan's message. Silas grabs my hand as soon as Ronan starts talking.

"Florence, I know nothing I do will ever make up for what I've done to us, but please, please trust me when I tell you that you can't trust him. If you see this, and he comes back, please look in your notes. I will always love you, and I'm sorry for all of the pain and destruction I've brought into your life. I'm sorry that I broke us. Stay safe. And remember, you can't trust him."

"He just said 'look in your notes,' nothing about trying to get ahold of him," Ivy says once the recording ends.

I stand up and walk to my room and grab the only box of notes that didn't get ruined when he broke in. I carry it back to the living room and place it on the table between the three of us. "These are the only notes

I can think of that he's talking about, but I've looked through these a million times and nothing weird has stood out."

"Maybe he's trying to remind you that he loves you and his message has nothing to do with James. Maybe it's his way of making sure you don't fall for James," Ivy shrugs and then throws her hands up again. "No ignore that, even as I said it I knew it was stupid and made no sense."

Lola saunters in from the hallway and jumps right into Silas's lap. I can't even feel betrayed by her because his face lights up like a kid on Christmas morning when she starts purring.

"Well, it's official, you're part of the family." Ivy's smile is huge as she looks at Lola. "Lola hated James. Maybe we should have known he was bad news the second she ignored all his pleas for attention."

"What if Ronan meant the notes app on your phone?" Silas says after a minute of petting Lola.

We all look at each other, and I grab my phone from off the table and find my notes app. My breath hitches when I see a note that was created the same day as the shooting. Instead of a title, it has an emoji of a bird. I click the note, and the only thing in it is a phone number. I show Ivy and Silas and then put my phone back down.

A phone number to get ahold of Ronan isn't really helpful. I hate the backflip my heart does when I realize that I can contact him now.

"What if he knows something that we can use against James?" Silas finally asks. "I know we don't want to trust him, but so far he's been right about James. At least as far as we can tell by piecing our own knowledge together."

"I don't want to call him," I confess to them. "I don't think I can handle speaking to him right now after everything." Lola moves from Silas's lap and into my own, and I pull her into my arms and cuddle her close.

"I can use my phone to call him," Ivy offers.

"No, I'll use mine. I don't want to put either of you back in his path if we don't have to," Silas states. "If that's okay with you both?"

Ivy answers before I can come up with anything, because truthfully, I hate the idea of either of them talking to him.

"Yeah, I'd be okay with that. But ground rules: You only talk to him while one of us is there, and no going off all Batman style and trying to take all this on by yourself. I swear I'll bring you back to life myself if anything happens to you...just to break the casserole dish over your head."

"Jesus, Ivy," Silas mutters. "You're sort of scary when you get all violent like this."

"I just don't want Florence to get hurt again," she answers back casually while looking at her nails...like she didn't just threaten him with violence for the hundredth time since meeting him. "And if you get hurt again, it'll hurt her even worse. So, no Batman shit. Deal?"

He nods his head and she walks over to him. They shake on it before she walks to the kitchen and disappears.

"I don't like the idea of you talking to him. What if this is just another way for him to try to control my life again?"

"He won't know that it's me if I just text him, right? For all he has to know, you got a burner phone to text him. Maybe let's start with that and see what he has to say about James."

"Alright, let's do it. Text the number."

Ivy comes back with three open beers and puts two of them in front of us. Silas grabs his and they clink their bottles together before both taking long swigs. Ivy raises her eyebrow at me, and I just shake my head at her. I've felt off all day today. And right now my stomach is full of knots while I watch Silas add Ronan's number into his phone. If I drink anything right now I know I'll just puke it back up.

"What should we say?" Silas looks up from his phone and glances between Ivy and I.

"I'll do it." I reach out, and he hands me his phone.

> Silas: I want to believe you, but I need proof.

I hand Silas his phone back and within seconds, it pings with a new message. My heart lurches in my chest as he hands it back to me to read.

> Ronan: I know this isn't Florence or Ivy, so it must be Silas.
> Look in the guest room. The proof is in the wooden box in the closet.

I look up at Silas and Ivy and read the text out loud for them. All of us are wondering what the hell it means as I re-read it again.

"Does he mean the office?" Ivy stands and walks down the hall. We can hear her rummaging around in the closet for a few minutes. She walks back into the living room with her hands empty. "Well, the only thing in that closet is our crap. And an overabundance of fluffy blankets."

"Could he be talking about your house?" Silas askes me. "The house you shared with him, I mean."

"I don't think so." As soon as I moved in with Ivy, we found a couple to rent the house from me, knowing I couldn't afford to live there with no job. And there was no way in hell I wanted to be in that house alone after what Ronan did to me. "The renters living there know that the cops are looking for him, and I don't think that he'd be stupid enough to go back there," I respond while tugging at the holes in my jeans with frustration.

"I do have a key to James's house. He gave it to me when I was staying there just in case he got called into work, and I needed to leave," Ivy admits. "Ask if he means his house."

Silas picks the phone up and sends Ronan another text.

> Silas: Are you talking about James's guestroom?

We all stare at each other in agonizing silence as we wait for the response. I look down at the phone when we see it light up on the table.

> Ronan: Yes.
> Don't get caught.
> Keep her away from him.

"Okay, let's go. James is on shift tonight, so this is the best chance we are going to get." Ivy stands up and walks to the door and grabs her purse and keys as Silas and I stay seated on the couch. "Also, Florence has to drive since she is the only one who didn't chug their beer."

"Are we sure this is a good idea?" Silas asks. I watch as his knee jumps up and down next to me with nervous energy. "What if James comes home and catches all three of us lurking around in his house? I can't imagine that it will go over well, and we don't know what he's truly capable of. I mean, he admitted in the video to pretty much shooting me on purpose."

"We can say we came to surprise him. Grab a few beers from the fridge and *if* he comes home, I'll say that pizza is on the way. Easy peasy. Now let's go!" Ivy huffs as she opens the front door and walks out without waiting for us.

Silas stands up and reaches his hand out, pulling me off the couch and into his chest. I lay my head against him and let the gentle thumps of his heart beating ease the anxiety and fear I feel trying to flood their way into my body. I don't want to leave the cocoon of safety that I feel as I wrap my arms around him, but I reluctantly pull away from him. We walk hand in hand to the door to follow after Ivy.

I pray with everything in me that this absurd plan of ours goes off without a hitch.

Chapter Thirty-Five

WE ARE PARKED A few houses down from James's house. Far enough away to not be noticeable, but still close enough to see if he comes home.

"One of us should stay here and keep look out just in case. " Ivy suggests. It's a smart plan, but I know that all three of us are going to argue over who is going inside.

"I think Silas and I should go into the house," I tell them and hold my hands up as Ivy tries to argue. "No, just listen. If James comes home, you will be the one person he won't be suspicious of if he sees you." She glares at me from the passenger seat as I continue. "You can get out of the car with the pack of beer and make an excuse about needing to get away from Silas and I and our 'love bird' ways. You know it's plausible and it would give us a chance to sneak out the back before you guys get inside."

"So you'll just leave me with the maybe psycho stalker?"

I glare right back at her for even thinking I'd do that to her. "No, dumbass. I'll call you once we get back to the car. I'll pretend that Silas and I got into a fight or something and say that I need you." I look back and forth between them and Ivy cracks a mischievous smile. "See, I'm basically a genius. Now give me the key and keep your phone ready to call me if he gets home. Silas and I will be in and out as fast as we can."

Ten minutes later, Silas and I are standing in front of the guest room closet. My heart is beating so hard I feel like it's moments away from flying out of my chest. Every small noise around us makes me jump and I'm riddled with nerves as I grasp Silas's hand with my own.

"I'll check the top, you check the bottom?" I nod to Silas and start sorting my way through various items and boxes all piled at the bottom of the closet floor. There are a pair of cleats along with all sorts of different sports equipment. But I don't see a wooden box anywhere. I stand up to help Silas check the top. There's a large blanket thrown onto the top of the closet, and I reach up to pull it down so Silas doesn't agitate his shoulder too much. I almost yell with joy when I see a wooden box hidden under it.

Silas reaches up with his good arm and brings the box down, handing it to me. My hands shake as I start to pull the top off, and then we both freeze when we hear the front door slam. Silas grabs me around the waist and pulls me into the cramped closet with him as I reach out and quietly shut the door, closing us both in.

His hand is gripping my waist tightly, and I can feel his heart racing as he pulls me closer into him. I still have the box clutched in my hands and I wish I had brought my purse in so I could have my hands free. I feel Silas's hand move from my waist, then feel him pulling my phone out of my back pocket. The screen lights up and blinds us both, causing him to drop it with a very noticeable thump as it hits the floor.

We both freeze when we hear the guest room door open. I swallow a scream when the back of the door hits the closet doors. I can't see anything from inside the closet, but I can hear footsteps pacing around the room. Silas grabs me again when we hear James start to slide open the closet door. If he catches me with this box in my hands, I don't know what we will do. Before I start to really panic, we hear someone pounding on the front door and then we hear Ivy's voice.

"James! I know you're home!" She bangs on the door again loudly. "I brought booze, let me in!" James curses under his breath before walking out of the bedroom and slamming the door behind him.

"We have to get out of here," I whisper to Silas and slowly slide the closet door open. I hear Ivy talking to James from somewhere in the house. Her voice gets louder as I open the bedroom door. I take a step out into the hallway and remember that Silas dropped my phone in the closet. I turn and push him quickly back into the bedroom and dive to the closet floor to find my phone.

"Look Ivy, right now just isn't a good time. I'm actually getting ready to head out of town for a couple of weeks." James's voice gets closer to the door as he walks down the hallway.

"Boo! I'm so sick of the lovebirds right now, and I was hoping we could hang tonight. Where are you going?" Ivy's voice comes out whiny and extremely convincing.

"It's just a, uh, work trip. I have to go to San Francisco for a case."

"Oh my gosh you suck! I've always wanted to go, but just haven't found time. You better bring me a souvenir." We hear them both walking back down the hall and past the guest bedroom. "Hey Jay, before you go, do you think I could stay here just for tonight? I really don't want to hear what I know is going on in my house right now."

We hear the front door open again, and I try to quiet my breathing as I listen for his response. "Actually, yeah, that'd be great. Can you check the mail for me while I'm gone? And maybe water my plants?" He sounds so sincere. The conversation between the two of them is just so natural and friendly. My heart cracks when I realize that this man who I've seen as a friend for the last couple of months could really be the reason why my life fell apart.

"Of course. You have a safe trip and I expect a selfie of you in front of the Golden Gate Bridge!" She yells, "And don't forget my souvenir keychain! Actually get two so I can give one to Flo!"

I hear the front door close, and I run over to peek out the window that faces the driveway. Silas and I watch in silence as James throws a duffle bag into the trunk and then get into the driver's seat. I feel the panic leaving my body as we watch him pull out of the driveway and disappear down the street.

Silas and I reach the bedroom door just as Ivy is opening it.

"Holy shit, guys!" Ivy exclaims loudly. "I cannot believe that just happened. And that we pulled it off. I swear to Sky Daddy my heart felt like it was going to explode out of my chest when I saw him drive up. He ran inside before I could even pick up my phone to text you."

"You did great, Ivy," Silas says with pride in his voice.

Ivy beams up at him and then looks down to the box I'm holding. "Is that it? Is it the proof Ronan said it was?"

"I don't know. I didn't get a chance to open it before we heard James." I look down at the small box in my hands and slowly lift the lid up to see what's inside.

My body goes cold as soon as I recognize the blue post-it note with Silas's handwriting on it. The one that I thought Ronan had stolen from my car. My hand is shaking as I pick up the post-it and I gasp when I see the small white envelopes underneath it. The same envelopes that Ronan found hidden in our things that ruined everything a year ago. I close the box loudly and fight off the urge to puke.

Clutching the wooden box tightly to my chest, I push my way out of the room and out the front door without saying a word to either of them. All the exhilaration and adrenaline goes rushing out of my body as I run across the street. I throw the box into the car just before I turn and throw my dinner up into the bushes.

Everything Ronan said about James is true.

Chapter Thirty-Six

FIVE DAYS LATER, SILAS and I are sitting across from a burly looking man named Detective Phillips. I debated back and forth with Ivy and Silas for days about whether or not I should go to the police about James. Who's to say they would even believe me? Especially since I don't know what James has hidden from them over the last year. But, every time I flipped open the wooden box and read the notes inside of the small white envelopes, I knew I needed him to pay for what he did.

He may not have plunged the knife into my son himself, but he was certainly the catalyst that led to my son's death.

Now that I'm here though, I think this might have been a huge mistake. Detective Phillips has sat here across from us and listened to my entire story and hasn't said a single word in the last two minutes. The look on his face is not the look of someone who believes me.

He runs his hands down his face in exasperation. "So you guys are telling me that James, I'm sorry, Detective Olsen, has been the one stalking you for over a year now?"

"Yes, that's what I'm telling you. He is the one who was sending my husband letters like these in the past. He's openly admitting in the video recording that he shot Silas on purpose to protect Ronan."

"Detective Olsen never said anything about your husband being present at the time of the shooting. In his report, he said that he was at your house and you both thought someone was breaking in. He told the intruder multiple times to stop or he was going to get shot. The intruder didn't stop, so he fired. He didn't realize it was your new boyfriend until afterward." Detective Phillips flashes Silas a smug smile. I clench my hands into fists under the table and try to remain calm.

"That's not what happened. We both filed reports, and I guarantee they both match one another, and not James's," Silas explains in an irritated tone.

"I wish I could believe you. Unfortunately for you, there were never any reports filed about the incident other than Detective Olsen's."

"But it's him on the recording. He admits it!" I yell. Calm and quiet demeanor be damned. I knew coming here was a mistake.

"There's no evidence to prove who the two voices on the recording are." I continue to glare at him. "And, according to your own admission, you both broke into Detective Olsen's house and stole property from him." He points at the wooden box on the table between the three of us. "So, really, I should be interrogating the two of you. Not waiting for Olsen to get back from his trip to throw half-cocked stories at him." He stands and opens the door across from us. "Now, get out of here before I decide to throw both your asses in cells until he gets back."

I grab the box and my phone from the table and leave the room with Silas hot on my heels. Before I walk out of the front door, I turn back to Detective Phillips. "When one of us ends up dead like my son did, it'll be your fault for not believing us."

We let the door slam loudly behind us. I walk back furiously to my orange slug bug, refusing to acknowledge the knot in my throat and tears building in my eyes. I knew this was going to happen. I fucking knew it, and I still let myself believe that they'd actually do something to help. I'm such an idiot. Silas reaches my side quickly and ushers me to the passenger side.

"You aren't supposed to be driving with your bum shoulder," I protest as he rolls his eyes and opens the door for me.

"I think it's safer if I drive when you're seconds away from exploding into a red hot rage." He leans down and kisses my forehead before shutting the door for me. My eyes follow him as he makes his way around the front of my car and into the driver's seat.

"I just hate how they still act like I'm the bad guy! Like I chose to let all these horrible things happen to me." I swallow the rage that's building in me and let out a defeated groan. "I don't know what to do anymore. I can't just wait around for James to come back. How am I supposed to ever look at him again? I can't keep walking around feeling like I have to look over my shoulder every day for the rest of my life." I give up trying to keep myself together and let the angry tears fall. "I just can't live like this anymore. One day it's Ronan, the next day it's James. When will it end, Silas? When do we just get to enjoy our lives together in peace?"

"Hey," Silas pulls my face to his and attempts to give me a stern look. "We are living our lives together right now. I don't know about you, but I am enjoying every minute I get to spend with you." He gives my nose a kiss and then flicks it with his finger making me gasp out a choked laugh. "We're going to figure the rest of this out. And if that means I stay wherever you are until James and Ronan are both out of our lives, then that's just freaking gravy, baby."

"Gravy, baby?" I can't stop laughing as I pull the seatbelt across my lap and wipe at my eyes. "Did you really just say that?"

He flashes me an adorable smile and puts my car into gear and drives away from the station. I'm smiling widely back at him and I feel my bad mood dissipate before we pull out of the parking lot.

"I'm supposed to have dinner with Paw before I head to work. Do you want to join us?" Silas asks me.

"Not today. I told Ivy I'd go shopping with her once she got off of work today. We'll probably just grab something while we're out. You need to go spend some time with Ted without me tagging along every time."

"You know he loves you more than he loves me. He's just going to ask about you nonstop. 'Where's my Flor? How's my Flor doing?'" He rolls his eyes like he's annoyed at that, but I can see the smile playing at his lips as he does it.

"You know I've known him for a hell of a lot longer than I've known you. So maybe I should start calling him 'My Ted?'"

He narrows his eyes at me, and I deadpan him back before he shifts his eyes back to the road. "Ha. Ha. Ha. You're hilarious. I'll be sure to never invite you over for B and B or any type of casserole night ever again."

"That's okay. I'll just wait for My Ted to invite me over for a date," I sass back as he pulls my car into the driveway and parks in the spot next to his truck. He shuts the engine off and I can feel him shooting daggers as he stares at me. I risk looking over at him and see that he has a huge shit-eating grin across his face, which totally catches me off guard.

"What are you smiling about?" His mood is completely contagious, and I feel a matching smile spread across my face.

"I just love you," he answers, "And I love how much you and my Paw love each other."

A blush spreads across my cheeks as I smile wider at him. I unbuckle my seatbelt and drag myself across the center console of the car. I plant a happy kiss against his lips. "I love you too."

I kiss him again. "Seriously. Thank you for turning such a crappy day around by just being you." I feel him smile against my lips as I go in for a third kiss. A groan escapes my lips as I force myself to get out of the car. He follows right behind me, and I open his truck door for him. "Now, hurry to work so you can hurry back. I already miss you."

He tucks a piece of hair behind my ear and gazes down at me. "I'll be home before you wake up."

We kiss one more time before he gets into his truck and drives away. I watch his truck until I can't see it anymore, then make my way into the house to spend another day waiting for him to come back.

I sigh as I grab my overnight bags from the back seat of my car and force myself to enter the empty house. I started counting down the minutes until Ivy gets home from work as soon as Silas backed out of the driveway. I'm nothing but a pathetic mess of co-dependency now. Being alone in the silence of my thoughts is crippling, and I hate every minute of it.

I've been spending my time going back and forth from staying at Silas's house, to going back home with Ivy. During the nights Silas has to work, I stay with Ivy. It's been so nice to just have some old fashion girls nights with popcorn, candy and an abundance of horror movies and chick flicks. We've always watched a horror movie first, then we finish the night with a fun chick flick so we don't have nightmares.

But, anytime I'm home without Silas, as soon as the movies are over and it's time to call it a night, I lay in my bed and stare at the ceiling, jumping at every noise I hear around me. I check every night that the window alarm is set. Silas cut me a wooden stick that fits right into the space between both windows so nobody can slide it open.

It's been a week since we broke into James's house and found the notes, and I still can't shake the feeling of constantly being watched. Ivy has texted him several times to see when he's coming back home, but every text and phone call has gone ignored. I'm hopeful that this means he listened to Ronan and decided to leave. But I still can't shake this feeling in my gut that the other shoe has yet to drop.

I practically leap with joy when I see Ivy's car pull into the driveway. I run to the front door and throw it open for her. "Did you miss me as much as I've missed you? Because I missed you a whole lot."

She rolls her eyes playfully at me as she steps inside. "I always miss you, but I'm glad you have been getting to spend some time with tall, dark and handsome. Plus it's literally only been two nights that you've been gone. Me and Lola got some massive snuggle time in since she couldn't ditch me for you while you were gone."

She bends down and scratches Lola behind her ears. "I know I'm last on the Lola-love totem pole, but I'm a glutton for punishment and can't help but forgive her every time she has to choose me." We both watch as Lola walks away from Ivy and heads down the hall and into my bedroom. "That furry fracking traitor," Ivy mumbles under her breath.

"Come on," I laugh as I tug her out the door with me. "Let's go to Target and then get something delicious and greasy to eat so we can come home and watch Scream."

"Yes and yes," Ivy says excitedly, "But only if we can watch 10 Things I Hate About You afterwards."

"Always."

Chapter Thirty-Seven

I CATCH IVY UP on everything that happened at the station earlier today while we browse the Target makeup aisles at a snail's pace. I still want to hulk out in rage every time I think about that detective's smug face.

"Honestly, it doesn't surprise me that they didn't take you seriously. I hate it, but if history has taught us anything, it's that a woman's voice will never be as loud as a man's, especially when it comes to shit like this." She looks at an eyeshadow palette before putting it back on the shelf. "If a guy went into that station saying that he was being stalked and harassed, they would have opened the case right then and there. But a woman saying she's being stalked by a 'male friend?' Nope. It just sounds like you're on the wrong side of the friendzone, and it's horseshit." She huffs out an angry breath beside me. "I'm sorry that you had to sit in that room and deal with that. Again."

I look over at her and flash a weak smile. I know that everything she's said is right, even if I don't want to believe it myself. I don't think it has anything to do with me being a woman. I think it has everything to do with the fact that James has gas-lit me to his cop friends for over a year, and now, they all think I'm crazy. Why would they believe me after all the falsified reports and lies he's shared with them about my life?

Ivy turns towards me and grabs her stomach with a pained expression on her face. "Our Cycle Sisters powers failed us this time. She's finally here. A week freaking late," she groans out. "I need to get some tampons, chocolate, and Midol before we leave. Unless you have some left from yours last week?" she asks while grabbing the cart from me.

We start walking that way, and I stop short when I fully process what she just said. Last week? My eyes widen in a mixture of surprise and shock. "Ivy..." I croak out quietly as she walks next to me.

"What's wrong?" Her face turns to concern as she looks over me.

"I'm late."

"Late for what? I thought you were staying with me tonight?" She starts to walk away, and I grab her. She turns back towards me reluctantly with an annoyed look on her face. "What happened to *Scream* and Heath Ledger?! You can seriously ditch me every other night, but not Heath Ledger night."

"No...Ivy." I bring my hand to my stomach. "I'm *late*."

She looks down at my hand, then back up at my face, and I see it click in her head. "Oh shit. Okay. Okay." She dances up and down on the balls of her feet. "How late?"

"I guess at least a week now," I answer, trying to mentally do the math while also trying not to panic in the middle of Target. "With everything happening, my period cycle was literally the last thing on my mind. We haven't exactly been careful..." I'm mentally kicking myself for not being smarter about using protection.

"Alright, so I'll get the tampons, chocolate, and Midol. You grab the expensive pee sticks and maybe some prenatal vitamins..." I open my mouth to tell her that I can't be pregnant but she cuts me off. "You'll feel better if you have them *if* you need them. And if you don't need them, then one day you might." She gives me an encouraging smile and we both link arms and head towards the pink tax aisle.

There's a little tiny voice in my head that keeps telling me that we'd be okay if the two pink lines showed up. There's an even louder voice that keeps reminding me how horribly I failed at protecting my first baby and that maybe I can't handle this again. Maybe I shouldn't be allowed to be a mother.

·····●·●···

Ivy and I are both staring at the plastic stick in front of me as we listen to high schoolers getting murdered in the background by Ghostface.

Ivy ripped the box open and threw me a stick as soon as we walked in the door. I couldn't let myself look at it, so I placed it face down on the coffee table as Ivy set the 3 minute timer. My stomach is twisted in knots as we watch the timer tick down.

Do I want this test to be positive? I'm not sure.

Will I be upset if it's negative? I think I might be.

What is Silas going to say? I don't know, and that scares the hell out of me.

The timer goes off and makes me jump out of my skin. Ivy grabs my hand hard as I reach forward to turn the test over. I take a deep breath, close my eyes, and then flip it over on the table.

"I can't look at it," I tell Ivy with my eyes squeezed shut. "What does it say?"

"Do you really want me to tell you?"

"Yes. No." I let out a shaky breath, "Yes. Tell me. Please."

"Okay, two things," she says. "One, you'll be glad I bullied you into the vitamins."

My eyes fly open and I reach out to pick the test up and bring it closer to my eyes. Two pink lines stare back at me. My eyes fill with tears as soon as I look and see Ivy holding back her own happy tears.

"Second," she sniffles and pulls me into a hug, "You need to go talk to Silas and tell him he's going to be a dad."

I pull out of the hug and look back at the test in my hand. I still can't believe what I'm seeing. "What about Heath Ledger night?" I ask her while still staring at the positive pregnancy test in my hand.

She pulls me to my feet and laughs at me with happy tears in her eyes. "Tonight is definitely more of a 'Florence and Silas made a baby' night. Go get your bag, and I'll drive you to the forest. I don't want you driving when you're this worked up and emotional. It's not good for our baby."

"I can't stay there when he's working. Ted would kill him!" I protest.

"I don't think Ted is going to care about you guys breaking some stupid rules once you tell him he's going to be a great-grandpa," She teases. "Now go take a quick shower, and pack your bag! And don't forget to take your vitamins."

"You are such a mother hen!" I smile brightly at her as I walk down the hall and into my bedroom, "But I love you to death and couldn't survive without you!" I yell before closing the door behind me.

I hop into the shower and do my best to wash away the fears and anxiety about this baby. But it's no use. Within minutes, I'm curled up on the shower floor and biting back sobs so Ivy doesn't hear me and rush in. I feel so guilty for being excited about this baby. How can I be happy about this when I let Wren down in the most horrible way possible? I failed as his mother before he was even born. What right do I have to try to do it again? How am I supposed to protect this baby when I can't even protect myself from the monsters who have been circling me for the last year?

I let myself cry over the loss of my son and the guilt over the little life growing inside me until the water runs cold. Then, I plaster a smile on my face and tell myself this time will be different. This time, I'll do anything it takes to protect this child.

Anything.

Chapter Thirty-Eight

My heart is racing as Ivy pulls into the familiar parking lot of the forest. She pulls right into the empty spot right next to Silas's blue truck and turns the car off before looking over at me.

"How are you doing?" she asks. "You've been extra quiet on the drive over."

I sigh, pulling my knees up to my chest and laying my head on them. "Honestly, I feel like I'm going to throw up. And I can't tell if it's the nerves or actual morning sickness." I glance over at her and continue, "I don't know how he's going to react and right now, that's the scariest part," I answer truthfully. "We've technically known each other for a year, but we've only been together for a few months. Obviously, this is us moving at the speed of light," I say as I point at my stomach and let out a nervous laugh.

"He loves you...like so much it's disgusting. He's going to love this baby you guys made together just as much."

"I hope so." I look out the window towards the trail that leads toward the ranger cabin. "Will you come back if he reacts badly?"

"How about I just stay right here until you call me and tell me you are okay?"

"I can't ask you to sit here in this parking lot waiting on me."

"I seriously don't mind. And it would make me feel better to wait until I know you're okay." She reaches into the back seat and grabs something from her purse. "See? I even brought my kindle, and I have some much needed smut to catch up on."

"I love you. Seriously. I don't know what I'd do without you in my life, Ivy."

"I love you too. Now go!" She unlocks the car, and I take that as my cue to get out. "Call me as soon as you tell him so I know you're going to be okay. Promise?"

I grab my bag from the back seat and walk to her side of the car as she rolls down her window. "I promise. Now please be safe and lock the doors. You don't know what kind of freaks are out here at night."

"Right back at you," she scoffs. "Wait. Here. Take this." She reaches into her purse again and pulls something out and hands it to me through the open window. When I look down I see that it's her pepper spray and smile at her before turning towards the path to go see Silas.

It isn't long before I stop hearing the hum of her engine, and start hearing the nocturnal noises of the forest. I love being here at night. I love seeing the glow from the creature's eyes staring at me from the protection of the trees. I love the pitter patter of the small animals going about their business while the moon shines brightly above. I love listening to the leaves crunch under my feet as I walk down the path.

I can't wait to be able to take this baby here one day to experience the magic of this place like I did with my parents. I place my hand over my stomach and whisper a prayer, praying that this baby is the one I get to hold in my arms. And then, I whisper a promise to Wren that this baby will never replace him in my heart.

There is no replacing what I've lost.

Grief is a constant ghost that makes itself known in so many ways. It's impossible to escape, and I think that's okay. I don't want to ever lose the piece of Wren I will always hold in my heart. He can't be replaced and he will never be forgotten. Instead, I'll make room right next to him in my heart for this new life growing inside of me.

I see the ranger cabin ahead of me and the terror I thought I'd feel once I got here isn't there. Instead, I'm filled with excitement and joy as I walk faster to the cabin door. I knock quietly. I hear Duke start barking immediately and moments later, Silas opens the door and slowly peeks out. When he sees me, he pulls me in as Duke runs past me and straight into the forest.

"Will he be okay out there?" I look back towards the trees where Duke disappeared.

"Yeah, he'll be fine," he answers back quickly and shuts the door behind us. "Florence? What are you doing here?" He smiles down at me. He's obviously confused, but happiness is clearly written all over his face too.

"I have something I need to tell you, and it couldn't wait until tomorrow," I blurt out quickly while pulling him into the small love seat in the tiny living room.

"Is everything okay? Did James come back?"

"Yes, everything is perfect. At least I hope it is." I bite my lip as I look away from him. "And no, James isn't back that we know of yet," I add quickly.

"What is it then?" His face is full of concern as he wraps my hand in his own.

"I'm pregnant." I'm still biting my lip as I look up at him…nervous to see his reaction, but excited at the same time.

He stares down at me and remains speechless.

"And obviously, it's yours," I add as uneasiness floods my veins. "I found out earlier today and I just wanted to tell you right away." I let go of his hand and reach into my back pocket to pull my phone out. "So now that you know, I'll go. Ivy is waiting for me in the parking lot. I'll see you tomorrow, right?" I stand up and head towards the front door. I forbid myself from falling apart in front of him.

I turn the handle to open the door but before I can open it, Silas presses his hand against the door. His body pressed so closely against my own that I can feel each breath he takes from behind me. I close my eyes and refuse to turn around to look at him. I will not cry in front of him over this.

"Florence..." he whispers into my ear, "Please turn around and look at me."

His hand moves from the door and I feel him place it on my hip before he gently turns me towards him. My breath hitches when that same hand releases my hip and reaches up to find my chin, prompting me to look up at him with a slight tug.

Our eyes finally meet and my heart swells when I see nothing but unfiltered joy on his face. I know at that moment that everything is going to be okay. I release all the emotions I've been stuffing down since the minute I stepped into this cabin with him. I lean into him and relish the sound of his heart beating in tune with my own.

When I pull back and look up at him again I see that he's still smiling. There's a slight glaze to his eyes as well, like he's trying to hold back his own tears.

"You're okay with this?" I ask him while pointing down at my stomach.

"Florence, I am more than okay with this." He drops to his knees and lays his head against my stomach. "This is the happiest moment of my life," he whispers as he looks up at me. "I love you. And I love this baby so much already." He places a kiss against my belly and I finally let the tears of joy erupt. "We are going to be a family. A real family."

"Yeah. Yeah, we are," I hiccup in between words and run my fingers through his hair while he places his head against me again.

He stands up again and pulls me to the couch with him. I lean my head on his good shoulder. "Are you okay with this?" He asks me while he plays with my fingers with his own.

"At first I wasn't sure, but I think I am now." I answer truthfully. "It's hard for me not to feel guilty about being so happy about this baby when I failed Wren." I bite my lip and try to stifle the tears that I've just managed to get under control again. "I love him so much and never got to see his face. I already love this baby just as much, and it terrifies me."

"I can't tell you what to feel, or what is right or wrong." He lifts my chin and kisses me softly, "But I do promise to be here throughout it all. Every bad day. Every amazing day. On the days where it all feels too heavy to carry, I'll carry it for you. We will get through this a day at a time, together." He wipes away a stray tear from my face and kisses me again.

This kiss brands me with promises for our future together.

I pull back from him before this kiss turns into something deeper. "I need to call Ivy and tell her that she can go home. She's waiting for me in the parking lot in case you weren't as thrilled about this news as I was."

"Remind me to buy that woman flowers for being so damn good to you." He stands up and walks into the small kitchen. I smile fondly at him as the memory of our first date comes to mind, and thinking about the pasta carbonara he made me makes my mouth water.

I press Ivy's number and bring the phone to my ear. It rings twice before she answers, and I am too hyped up to wait for her to speak.

"Hey, things are great. So I'm going to stay here with Silas tonight." I blurt out with a laugh. "But I love you forever for being here with me through all of this. I promise *Scream* and Heath Ledger tomorrow night. With lots of pickles and ice cream." The line stays quiet. I look at my phone, and it shows that the call is still connected. "Ivy? Are you there?"

"She's here, Florence. But she's a little tied up at the moment."

My heart stops in my chest when I recognize the voice speaking to me from the other end of the phone.

James.

Chapter Thirty-Nine

I stare at Silas in horror as he runs over to me and quickly grabs the phone out of my hand. He puts it on speaker and we hear James speak again.

"Now, I didn't want to do this to her, but I needed to make you listen to me. I need to explain my side of things. I need you to actually listen, Florence. Do you understand me?"

"Ye–yes," I croak out. Fear for Ivy floods my veins as I stare into Silas's eyes.

"What do you want, James?" Silas asks angrily.

"Oh no, no, no. This won't do," James chuckles into the phone. "This is between Florence and I. Silas, you are not invited."

"I'm not leaving her alone with you!" Silas shouts out.

"You will if you don't want me to hurt Ivy anymore than I've already hurt her," James spits out. "I want to meet with Florence, and Florence only. Anyone else shows up and this ends badly." We hear Ivy's muffled scream in the background. "Do we all understand how this is going to go? I will call back in two minutes and expect an answer."

The line goes dead.

"I can't let you walk into this on your own." I can feel his eyes on me, but I can't force myself to look at him. "No! Florence. You seriously can't ask me to do that! Not after you just told me you're pregnant with our child! Please. Let's just think this through," Silas is pleading with me but I already know it's no use. There's no way in hell I'd risk Ivy's life by bringing him with me.

"Do you have a gun?" I ask him calmly. I think shock might have taken over my body because I don't feel anything but the feral need to go save my best friend from this monster.

"You cannot go and face him alone!" Silas shouts back in response.

"If this is the only way to save Ivy, then yes Silas, I will fucking go alone and you will stay right here," I snap at him. He looks at me like I've grown three heads. I don't blame him. The person he fell in love with is hiding under her common sense, and all I can focus on is how to get my best friend out of the situation that I've put her in. I basically gift wrapped her and brought her right into James path by letting her stay in the parking lot alone.

I rub my hands down my face and take a deep breath before I meet Silas's angry gaze. "Now, do you have a gun or not?"

He looks at me for a long moment and then walks into the small bedroom. I watch him as he pulls out a small safe from under one of the bunk beds. He is walking back into the living room as my phone starts to ring.

"Hello?" I answer. My voice is completely void of emotion as I look at the gun in Silas's hand.

"Meet me at the spot in ten minutes. I already know you're at the ranger station. I don't think I need to remind you that if I see Silas or think anyone has followed you, then Ivy will pay the price." James's voice is full of hatred and anger. "Ten minutes, Florence. Don't make me wait."

The line goes dead again.

Silas looks like he's getting ready to argue with me again, I cut him off with a wave of my hand. "I can't have this argument with you again. I'm going on my own, and I swear to God I will fucking kill him if he lays one more finger on her." I watch his Adam's apple bob in his throat, and then he reluctantly hands over the gun.

"This is a 9 millimeter. Safety is here. Trigger here. And it's fully loaded." He points out everything to me and then shows me how to release the clip and replace it with a new loaded one. He places the extra loaded clip into my jacket pocket and then pulls me into a hug. "I won't follow you unless I hear the gun go off. I can be there within 3 minutes if I cut through the trees."

"I'll be okay," I say back automatically, and then head towards the door.

"Wait. Please. Just wait a second." He follows me to the door and pulls his phone out. I watch his face as he looks down at it. He types something and I hear the distinct sound of a text message being sent before my phone starts ringing in my pocket. I pull it out and see his name flashing on my screen. He reaches over and answers it for me and then puts it back in my pocket. "That way I can hear what's going on. Your little stunt with the video recording was genius. If the line disconnects I'm coming for you and that's final."

"Okay. I love you." I look up at him and give him a swift kiss. "Please don't follow me." Then I turn and walk out the door without looking back. I say a prayer that he listens and stays put. I can't risk James hurting Ivy for my mistakes.

This forest used to offer me a place of comfort and safety. Walking the trail to our spot used to make me feel giddy with joy and excitement, because that spot used to be special and full of so much love I felt like I would burst with it. Today this trail only offers danger and betrayal. A year ago I walked this same path to meet with the man I trusted with my entire heart and soul, only to have my entire reason for living taken brutally away from me with one flash of a knife.

Now I'm walking down this same path again while another person whom I love with my entire heart is in danger.

This time I won't be weak.

This time I will fight back with every single shred of bravery I have in me.

This time I'm going to win.

This time will be different because I refuse to lose the life of my best friend or the unborn child growing inside of me.

I pull the gun out of the back of my jeans where I tucked it after leaving Silas, and I load the bullet into the chamber by pulling back on the slide.

Then I step through the trees to face the monster that set all this in motion over a year ago.

—

I look down at my phone again in hopes of seeing a text from Ronan. I've texted him several times since he called me, but he hasn't read or answered any of them. He's been gone for what feels like forever and I can't wait to see his face.

Everything has been so messed up ever since these notes started. I can't wait to prove to the awful monster that has been sending them that our love and our marriage is stronger than a few pieces of paper with some scribbled lies on them.

Nothing can break us.

I reach down and run my hand over my belly, laughing out loud when Wren kicks against my hand. He's going to be so rambunctious and I can't wait to watch him and Ronan play together. My heart swells with unending happiness when I think of Ronan holding our son for the first time.

This forest has always been my favorite place in the world. I walk confidently through the bumpy path of the trail with excitement in my veins. I smile to myself when I see the small opening that leads to our spot and head that way. This small hidden path has always made me feel like I was entering a new land, like a magical land that only exists in fairy tales. I can't wait to bring Wren here and share this enchanting little spot with him one day.

I finally reach the end of the tree line and push through the foliage to see Ronan sitting by the creek. His pants are rolled to his ankles, and he has his feet in the water. I am breathless as I stare at him and take in how perfect this man really is. Even years later, I am still head over heels in love with him. I love him just as much, if not more than I did from the first moment I laid eyes on him in the parking lot of our school.

I take a step closer to him and his head turns my way when a branch snaps under my foot. I stop when I see the expression on his face. He doesn't look like the man I married. His expression is the same one that clouds his features when I've done something wrong. His brows furrow in frustration as he looks at me.

My mouth is dry, so when I try to speak to him from across the distance between us it comes out in a mumbled croak. That just makes him look even more angry at me. I swallow hard and clear my throat and try again.

"Hi," is all I can manage to force out. I'm getting nervous now as he continues to stare at me with that angered expression on his face.

He stands up and wipes his hands on his jeans and then turns his back to me and stares down into the creek. He still hasn't said a word to me since I walked through the tree line. The voice in my head is begging me to run and leave him to his brooding.

But why would he want me to meet him here if he was going to continue to stay angry at me over the letters from a deranged stranger?

He can be upset with me all he wants, but I know he still loves me and I'm not leaving here until he agrees to come home with us. I suck in a nervous breath and walk towards him. Each step I take closes the distance between us until I stop right next to him at the edge of the creek.

He stiffens next to me when I reach out and place my arm on his. He yanks his arm away from mine and I flinch in shock and hurt.

Tears flood my eyes as I look down into the creek in front of us. "You still can't be angry with me. Right? You know those letters are filled with nothing but lies from a psychopath who wants to see us tear each other apart."

I gasp and reach out to him. When he finally turns and looks at me, I see the tears streaming down his face. Before I can touch him, he throws himself back away from me. Again.

"Ronan, what can I do to make you believe me?! How can I prove to you that none of this is true?" I cry out while reaching towards him again as a strangled sob escapes his chest. "I can't stand seeing you this hurt. It's killing me!" I scream out at him as I close the space between us and grab ahold of his face with my hands. My heart cracks when I feel his tears against my hands. "I love you so much," I whisper as I lay my forehead against his. "I love you. I love you. I love you."

I cry harder as he finally touches me back. He reaches up and puts one of his hands over my hand that is still cradling his face.

"You will always be the love of my life, Florence." His lips press against my forehead roughly and another broken sob escapes him, "But I can't live with the fact that you've been lying to me this entire time." His hand leaves mine and he grabs my face painfully, covering my mouth completely so I'm unable to speak. "I can't fucking look at you while you are carrying another man's child," he spits out. His eyes glare at me with disgust and hate. Fear like I've never known before pools into my heart.

I know I'm about to die.

Tears continue to pour from his eyes, and his entire body starts shaking against me. "You'll always be mine, and I won't let this break us. I won't let another man's child tear us apart or give you a reason to think that you can just up and leave me and live happily ever after with him. I can't let this child be the thing that tears us apart. I won't let it."

His hand is still clamped over my mouth as he reaches behind his back with his other hand. "I love you. And I know that you'll survive this. You're the strongest person I know, Florence. I knew it from the moment you pulled that sandwich bag of ashes out of your backpack so many years ago. And I promise that one day we can be together again like we have always been meant to," he says.

He pulls me into him as the sharp point of the knife pierces my flesh.

He releases me and stumbles away from me. I see the shocked look in his eyes as he brings his hand up and it's covered in blood.

"What have you done?" I look down at the knife protruding out of my belly and into my son. I reach and put my hands on my stomach, and I know he's gone.

I should have fought harder to save him.

I should have listened.

I'm sorry.

I'm so sorry, baby boy.

My little bird.

Pain like I've never felt before paralyzes my entire body as I fall to the forest floor. The last thing I see is Ronan disappearing back into the tree line before I lose consciousness completely.

Chapter Forty

A MASSIVE CASE OF déjà vu hits me as I step out of the trees and back into the clearing. I force myself to shake the memories of that day so that I can focus on saving Ivy.

The moon is full and bright as it shines down on the forest from above. I can make out all the ruined pieces of the bench that Silas built me. They're still thrown haphazardly all around the area like they were the day we discovered it.

I turn when I hear a branch snap and see Ivy tied up against the broken legs of the bench in the middle of the clearing. I raise my gun and look around, turning in circles until I finally spot James. He's leaning against one of the trees closer to the creek. Ivy is directly between us from where we're both standing. Her eyes are wide with fear and there's a gag wrapped around her mouth.

I step closer to her, and James steps out into the open at the same time. Every step I take to get closer to her, he mirrors. Playing with me. Taunting me. But he doesn't get to win this time. I raise my gun towards him, and he just laughs and continues walking towards Ivy.

"Put the gun down, Florence." He reaches behind his back and pulls out his own gun. "Put it down, or I shoot her." He points the gun at Ivy's head and she screams into the gag, making my stomach drop. I stare at him for a minute longer and he steps closer to Ivy, placing the barrel of the gun right to the back of her head.

"Okay, okay. I'm putting it down! I'm putting it down!" I yell at him from across the clearing. I place the gun down in front of me without ever taking my eyes off of him.

"Now, back up 10 steps." He orders me as he brings his gun back down and walks towards me.

I back up and watch as he walks over to where I set the gun down. He picks it up and tosses it into the treeline. There's no way I can make it that distance without him shooting one of us.

"Just let her go, and then you can tell me whatever it is you need to tell me," I say calmly. "You don't need to do this, James." I take a slow step closer to both of them. "We can just talk. I promise I'll listen to you." My eyes keep flicking from him to Ivy. She looks so small and helpless tied up like this. But my best friend is a fighter at heart and her eyes are filled with fury and defiance as she glares into the back of his head.

"You don't understand. I did all of this for you guys." James says as he steps backwards towards where Ivy is tied up again. "All of this. I did it for him."

"For who? Who are you talking about?" I ask him calmly while I continue taking small steps closer to them. I don't know what my plan is. I just know that I need to try to get as close to Ivy as possible if I'm going to have any chance of getting her out of here.

I trip over one of the broken pieces of the bench and yelp loudly as I fall face first into the dirt. James rushes over to me and helps me up which just confuses the hell out of me in the process. "Are you okay?" he asks genuinely.

"James, why are you doing this?!" I scream at him and throw my hands up in frustration as he backs away from me again.

"I just wanted you to listen to me and believe me," he mutters under his breath quietly.

"Then tell me! Tell me what you're talking about!" I yell again. The anger about the situation he's put me in comes out in full force as I stand up quickly and start walking towards Ivy.

"Stop!" He yells and points the gun at me while I stalk furiously towards her. "I don't want to hurt you, Florence," he pleads with me. "So please, just stop! STOP!" He fires a shot into the air, and Ivy and I both scream. I look towards her. She shakes her head furiously at me, telling me with her eyes to stop and listen to him. I drop to the ground three feet away from her and nod my head at her as tears stream down her face.

He comes and stands a few feet away from both of us. I look up at him as he sighs loudly. "This isn't how I wanted things to be. I just wanted to keep you safe. I need to keep you safe." He uses the gun to scratch his head. "Ronan was supposed to believe me. He was supposed to believe both of us."

"Believe us about what?" I am getting even more frustrated and confused by the minute.

"That the notes were—" he's interrupted by a loud noise coming from the trees and points the gun at the tree line. Panic grips me as I realize that Silas must have heard the gunshot and is making good on his promise.

No. I can't let James hurt him, not when I've just found him. We are going to have a baby together. I can't lose him.

The noise gets closer to us, and I decide that the only way I can save Silas from being shot is by finding a way to distract James.

I open my mouth and let out the loudest scream that my body can conjure. I watch as James jumps and then yells loudly beside me before he throws himself down on top of me, dropping the gun in the process.

I'm still screaming when I look back towards the tree line and watch as Ronan comes barreling out of the trees.

"Ronan?!" I yell out in surprise as James's weight crushes me into the ground. Ivy is thrashing around next to us trying to untie herself as I'm trying to push James off of me.

"Get Ivy!" I yell at Ronan when I see him running towards me. He does a double take and looks from me to Ivy. "Help her!" I scream at him. I exhale in relief when he actually listens and throws himself down beside her to help free her.

"I won't let him hurt you again. He doesn't get to win this time," James mutters to himself while his body is still draped over mine. It's hard to tell if he's trying to protect me with his body or if he's only using his strength to keep me from trying to get the gun that he dropped.

I knee him in the thigh with as much strength as I can muster while being forced into the odd position he has me trapped in, and he yells out in pain. I want to scream when he doesn't shift his weight off of me at all.

I look over and see Ronan still struggling to free Ivy, so I try to throw another knee into James's thigh, but he screams out in pain before my knee ever reaches him. I look up at him confused as I watch his face contort in pain. Then I look down and scream with joy when I see Duke biting into his leg and trying hard to pull James off of me. An angry growl comes out of him as he thrashes his head back and forth with James's leg trapped between his teeth.

I love this damn dog.

I look up and see Ronan and Ivy running towards me. "No! Get her out of here! Please, Ronan! Get her to safety!" Ronan's eyes meet mine and I silently beg him to listen.

"I'm not leaving without you, Florence!" Ivy screams back at me as Ronan grabs her from behind and starts to drag her into the safety of the trees. I almost laugh when I hear her constant string of curse words directed at him.

He saved her. He actually listened to me and saved her. A relieved sob escapes my lips now that I know Ivy is no longer in danger because of me.

Duke tugs hard at James again, causing him to shift his weight off of me momentarily so that I'm able to push myself out from underneath him. I stand up and look around for the gun, but it blends in too much with the dark earth. I get down on my knees again and search for it with my hands. I search frantically and freeze when I hear Duke cry out in pain before the forest goes utterly silent, the nocturnal animals hold their breaths as this unfolds in their sanctuary.

I continue my search for the gun, swiping at the ground in quick motions while praying that Duke is okay. I finally feel the cold metal of the handle and a sob escapes my lips as my fingers wrap around it. Suddenly, it's being pulled out of my grasp. I look up in confusion and then fall back onto my hands in alarm when I see that James has the gun pointed directly at me.

Chapter Forty-One

"I TOLD YOU THAT I really don't want to hurt you, Florence," James pants, completely out of breath after his fight with Duke. "But you both need to listen to what I have to say! I have to tell you both the truth! You've got it all wrong! It's not me! I'm not the person who wrote those notes!"

My eyes are wide with fear as I look at the gun shaking violently as he keeps it pointed directly at me. I keep backing up with my hands, trying to put as much distance between myself and his gun until I hit something hard. I use my hands to feel around, hoping maybe it's a weapon I can use against James. But I only feel a pair of shoes. I look up and see Ronan standing behind me looking more enraged than I've ever seen him as he leers at his brother.

"Stay the fuck away from her," Ronan hisses, stepping around me and putting himself between James and I. My heart is trying to pump itself out of my chest as I look back and forth from James, Ronan, and the gun between them.

Sweat is pouring down James's face and contorts with different emotions as he looks from Ronan to me. He lowers the gun slightly and takes a step closer to us. "You don't understand, those notes aren't—"

"I DON'T GIVE A FUCK ABOUT THE NOTES, JAMES!" Ronan yells loudly, making the wild animals that have been hiding in silence in the trees surrounding us scurry away in fright. "You took everything from me! EVERYTHING!" He cries out in anguish as he turns to gaze down at me, then back at his brother. "I destroyed the only thing in this world that ever mattered to me because of your lies."

"It's not what you think. Please just let me explain. I was trying to help you!" James's voice comes out so pathetically small that it's almost a whisper. He lowers the gun and just stares at me like a broken husk of a man. I smile in satisfaction at his obvious pain. This man took everything from me, and then he tried to take even more. Ronan, Wren, Silas and now Ivy. He's a fucking monster, and he deserves to rot for the rest of his life.

Ronan ignores him completely and turns around to help me off of the forest floor. His hand is so warm against my own and all I want to do is let myself forget about everything that's happened to us and step into his arms one last time. But I won't let myself forgive him. James may have been the catalyst that drove us apart, but Ronan chose to murder our son and left me on this same forest floor to die. I can't let myself forget that. Even if I wish I could.

And right now, I have another child I need to protect from both of these men who have both ruined my life in so many ways. I let Ronan help me to my feet and then yank my hand out of his swiftly. I refuse to acknowledge the hurt that flashes across his face when I take a few steps away to put some distance between us.

He doesn't let me go far before he's angling himself between James and I, blocking James's direct path to me. I don't want to feel thankful for his protection, but I can't help but feel just a little bit safer with him as a buffer between me and the gun again.

"Are you okay?" Ronan asks me, keeping his body in front of mine while still keeping his eyes on James and the gun. "Did he hurt you?"

"I'm fine. And no, he didn't hurt me," I respond back to him. I'm shocked at how calm my voice sounds right now, because my heart is still racing a mile a minute. "But I can't say the same for Ivy." I turn around and look towards where Ivy ran into the trees. I'm glad when I don't see her hanging around. I hope that somehow she found her way through this dark forest and made it to Silas. Maybe they'll call the cops now that she's not in danger anymore.

"I didn't hurt her," James promises both of us. "I just needed you to pause long enough to listen to what I had to say."

"Well then tell me, James! Please explain to me what all of this is about!" I yell back at him in anger. "You stalked me, ruined my marriage, got my son killed, and kidnapped my best friend." Ronan flinches next to me, and it takes every ounce of willpower not to lash out at him too. "What could be so damn important that you had to orchestrate this entire crazy plan?! If you wanted me that badly, you did a piss poor job of making that happen." I glare at him and hope that he sees nothing but loathing for him in my eyes. "You know what. No. I don't want to hear anymore of your bullshit and lies. I've had enough of this. I'm done with both of you."

I turn towards where I last saw Ivy and start walking that way, leaving them both staring after me. To hell with this. If James wanted to hurt me, he would have already, and I don't owe Ronan another minute of my time when part of this is his fault. He didn't force his brother's hand, but he chose to believe all those twisted letters instead of me.

He chose to destroy us.

"Florence, don't walk away from me." I ignore him and refuse to stop when I hear James's voice reach me.

"NO!" I hear Ronan shout from behind me. "James, you can't do this! Don't. No, no. NO! Please don't hurt her!" His voice is laced with fear as he begs his brother. Every muscle in my body goes numb as I stop and

BIRDS OF A FEATHER

turn around slowly and see that James has the gun pointed directly at me again. His face is twisted in rage, and his body is shaking so furiously that I can see the gun trembling in his hands.

James laughs loudly as Ronan tries to move towards me again. "I'm surprised that you still care so much about her, seeing as how you murdered her first child because you thought it was fathered by another man." Ronan looks back at me in confusion at the same time that I instinctively move my hand to my stomach. "I wonder. Would you still be trying to protect her if you knew she was carrying another man's child right this minute?"

"How do you know that?" I gasp out at him as I watch Ronan's face crumble with pain in front of me.

"Ivy begged me not to hurt you. She begged loudly while I dragged her kicking and screaming through this forest right to this spot." His voice is full of mockery. I wish I still had Silas's gun because I know I wouldn't hesitate to use it against him for hurting Ivy. "Then when her bravado wore off, she pleaded with me as these big, giant crocodile tears streamed down her beautiful face. She told me I couldn't take another baby away from you. She begged me to kill her instead, because she wouldn't let you lose another one."

Tears of my own run down my face as I listen to him recount everything that happened between them. I have never loved her more than I do right now. I would rip my heart out ten times over to keep her safe from him.

"You're pregnant?" Ronan asks me quietly now that he's reached my side.

My heart does a backflip when I look up at his face, and I see that his expression isn't one of anger, instead he's smiling at me. *A real smile.* Like the smile of the man I used to know and love with my entire heart and soul once upon a time. Before the world conspired to ruin everything good about him. Before his brother corrupted his love for me.

"Yes," I whisper back, giving him a hesitant smile in return.

He reaches out and grabs my hand, clasping it tightly with his own. "I promise I won't let you lose this one too. I can't be the reason you lose another."

I look back to James and he is looking down at where our hands are clasped together with a sneer on his face. "So you're just going to keep choosing her? Even after she spread her legs for another man barely a year after you left her? When are you going to stop letting her tear us apart, brother? When will you finally choose me over her like you should have years ago?"

Ronan grips my hand harder as he takes a confident step towards his brother. "Florence and I are leaving. I will choose her every moment or every single day and nothing you can say will change that. If you don't want all of your dirty cop friends learning about the kind of disgusting human being you are, then you need to leave all of us the fuck alone. I mean it, James. Leave Florence the fuck alone or I'll shove a knife so deep down your throat you won't be able to scream when they torture you in Hell."

James says nothing as Ronan threatens him. He does start to lower his gun when Ronan starts to tug me away and towards the tree line. Ronan urges me to walk in front of him, and I pull him along with me, anxious to get both of us away from his deranged brother.

I stop when I hear something, or someone, coming back through the trees towards us.

"What's wrong?" He whispers into my ear, and I squeeze his hand harder while listening to the symphony of noises around us.

The hairs on the back of my neck stand up when I hear the tell-tale of the gun being loaded behind me. I turn to see James's face filled with fear and fury as he points it towards us again.

"THIS IS ALL YOUR FAULT!" He howls at us. "YOU DID THIS TO US!"

Everything happens so fast. I scream loudly and throw my hands over my ears when I hear two shots fired, one after the other. Before I know what's happening, I feel myself being slammed to the ground.

Chapter Forty-Two

When I look up, I see Ronan laying next to me. There's something off about him as he's staring at me. I sit up and gasp in horror when I see the blood spreading quickly across his chest. "No!" I cry and bring my hands to his chest, trying to stifle the blood flow. I know it's no use though. It's coming out too fast. I grab ahold of his hand with my own as I cry over his body.

"Florence..." he whispers out as I bring my face right up to his. "I'm so sorry..." he coughs, and I sob harder when I see the blood trickling out from the corner of his mouth.

"Shhh, it's okay," I brush my hand through his hair and caress his face as my tears mix with his own. "I'm here. I'm here," I whisper back to him.

"I couldn't let you lose this one too..." His breaths are coming out more shallow and I can feel each pump of his heart thumping slower. "You're going to be the best mom. I hope they get your eyes. I've always loved that your eyes matched the trees in this spot. So green..."

I feel the moment his life leaves him, and I scream in agony as I throw myself onto him and hold him tightly. I hated him. But I loved him too. He didn't deserve this, and I wish we could just go back to the beginning. I wish we could be those kids again who found love in this place.

My body shakes as gut-wrenching sobs escape my lips while I try to hold him closer to me, clutching at him and praying that I could take it all back.

"Florence..." I look up to see Ivy kneeling down on the other side of Ronan's body. "Florence, I'm so sorry." She reaches out and puts her hand over my hand, the hand that still has Ronan's clutched in it and squeezes it tightly as I cry over the man I used to love...the same man that just saved mine and my unborn child's life from the monster that destroyed his own.

I look up and see James's body laying crookedly on the ground. His eyes are lifeless as he gazes at the trees past us. The bullet hole in his head confirms that he'll never look at anything ever again.

I lick my lips and taste the salt from my tears. "What happened?" I ask Ivy. My voice is hoarse and raw from screaming as my body continues to shake uncontrollably.

"Ronan told me that I needed to get Silas as soon as he got me into the trees. He said Silas texted him that he needed his help because you were in danger." Silas trusted him enough to ask for his help. That must have been the text he sent out before he called my phone as I was getting ready to face James alone. The two men I loved put their differences aside and both saved me today. I look down at Ronan, and my heart breaks all over again as the tears flow freely down my cheeks.

"He told me that Silas was waiting for the cops to show them where we all were." Ivy's eyes linger on me as her voice cracks. "When I got to the cabin, Silas was heading to the parking lot to meet them. I couldn't just wait though, I couldn't leave you alone to fight him. So I ran back."

She swallows loudly and then continues, "When I found the small trail through the tree line, I found the gun that James threw so I picked it up and snuck my way through the trees until I saw you guys." Tears stream down her face as her hand starts shaking on top of mine. "I saw that James had the gun pointed right at you...and I couldn't let him take you from me. I couldn't lose you." She wipes at her face and gazes down at Ronan, "But I wasn't fast enough, and I'm so sorry." Her shoulders shake violently as she cries with me over Ronan's body.

I pull my hand out of Ronan's and reach down to close his eyes. I lean down and whisper all the things I never got to say to him before I place a shaky kiss on his forehead.

I stand up and pull Ivy to her feet and crush her body into my own, wrapping my arms tightly around her. "Ivy, you have nothing to be sorry for. You saved my life. And I'll never be able to thank you enough for coming back for me. Even if I also want to kick your ass for doing so." I hold her tighter as she cries harder into my neck. "Hell of a damn shot, Ivy."

She scoffs at me, "My dad taught me how to shoot when I told him I was moving away from home for college. He takes me to the range every time I go home to visit."

"Remind me to thank him for being such a father-hen the next time I see him."

We pull apart as the cops start walking through the tree line with their flashlights. Ivy leaves my side to go give her statement, and I do the same. Silas had already filled them in on almost everything. They were able to listen to mostly everything since my phone call was still connected with Silas's, so there wasn't much of a statement for me to add. I rehashed and explained again what had happened to me and Ronan last year, including the notes, and losing Wren. I glare at Detective Phillips, who refused to believe me earlier, and he looks away in embarrassment.

Ivy and I stand together in silence and watch as the coroners come to take away Ronan and James. More people show up with flashlights. All of them shine light on the awful events that have happened here today. I gasp and run over to Duke when I see someone's flashlight stop on him. I throw myself down and thank the world when I realize he's still breathing. I run my hand gently over his body and a whine escapes him when I brush over his ribs.

"He most likely has a broken rib, but he's going to be okay. The cops are calling someone to come help him." I look up and can't contain the uncontrolled sobs that start pouring out of my body when I see Silas standing there looking down at me and Duke.

I throw myself at him and unleash all the emotions of today while he holds me. His warmth envelops me in a cocoon of safety like he did the first time I met him, in this same spot, over a year ago.

"Are you okay?" I ask him, reaching up and grabbing his face, then grimacing when I see that my hands are coated in Ronan's blood.

Silas grabs my hand and brings it back to his face. "I'm sorry about Ronan." My eyes fill with tears again as I look to the spot where his body was. "I wish I was here sooner. I didn't know what to do after you left. I texted him to come help because I knew that some part of him would have done anything to keep you safe." His voice is shaking, and he takes a breath before he continues. "He sacrificed everything to keep you safe. I'll owe him a debt that I'll never be able to repay for the rest of my life." He pulls me closer to him, and I lay my head against his chest. "I couldn't leave until I knew that the cops could find you. Then they wouldn't let me leave. When Ivy showed up and told me Ronan had saved her, I knew you would be safe with him. But fuck, it almost killed me not knowing if you were okay. And I'm so sorry I wasn't here for you when I should have been. Maybe I could have saved him if I had fought harder to get here."

I shake my head against him. "No, you can't let yourself think that way. You helped me in the only way you could have, and I can't thank you enough for trusting me. And for actually listening to me when I asked you not to follow me. I couldn't live with myself if you got hurt again."

"Well, I was out of my mind with worry. So, I promise I will never let you go running off into danger alone again because I can't stand the thought of losing you." His hand brushes my hip. "Either of you."

I look up, letting our gazes linger between us, then I bring my lips to his. A promise of understanding and forgiveness wrapped into one soul crushing kiss as I press my lips against his again and again.

"We aren't going anywhere," I promise him as we break apart. I smile when I look down and see Ivy sitting beside Duke with his head in her lap. "None of us are."

Silas holds me tighter as I let my gaze linger over the place that has always been so magical to me. "Can you rebuild my bench when your arm is healed?" I'd love to have a place to sit while I visit my parents and Wren. I know that I'll bring Ronan's ashes here. I hope it will bring him peace.

"What if I build you a whole gazebo so we can all come together once in a while?" Silas looks down at me, then over at Ivy and Duke.

"I would love that." I hold him tighter with one arm and stretch my other hand out to meet with Ivy's. Pulling strength from the two people who mean everything to me, and the little one that I haven't even met yet but already love with my entire being, I can face anything this life throws at me with them by my side.

Today brought so much death and heartache, just like it did a year ago. But this time I didn't fail to protect the ones I love. This time, we won against the monster who tried to destroy us. Winning at such a steep cost though.

I'll never be able to thank Ronan for what he gave me today. He saved my best friend, and then gave his life to protect me and the little life growing inside of me.

He took it all away once, but today he gave it all back.

Epilogue

Silas
One Year Later

I'm smiling down at my daughter when I finally hear them. I look up and chuckle as I watch Florence and Ivy come barreling through the trees and into the small clearing. Both of them are giggling loudly and the hem of Ivy's emerald green dress is covered in mud from the recent rain. Paw shakes his head and lets out a deep laugh when he finally sees them.

"TURN AROUND SILAS!" Ivy yells loudly across the clearing. "You know you aren't allowed to see the bride yet!"

I gaze back down at my daughter and roll my eyes playfully before turning away from them. She inherited my one decent quality, my bright blue eyes. She looks just like her mother though. They have the same nose, luminous skin, and auburn hair color. She's beyond perfect, and I still can't believe this is my life.

I'm moments away from marrying the woman of my dreams in the gazebo I made for her, while holding our daughter in my arms. Surrounded by the two people who have loved us most in this world.

Life just doesn't get any better than this.

Duke barks excitedly as he strolls out of the other side of the forest and heads towards us. His emerald green bow-tie askew and tongue hanging out as he reaches my side. I'll never be able to thank this dog enough for being there for Florence on that fateful day when I couldn't be. He protected her when I wasn't able to and almost got himself killed in doing so. He's the best partner I could have ever asked for. That's why he's my best man today.

Paw clears his throat to signal that I'm *finally* allowed to turn around to see my soon to be wife. I'm shaking with nervous energy as our daughter coos happily in my arms.

The breath is knocked out of me when I turn around and lay eyes on Florence. She's radiant. Her auburn hair is loose and wild as it hangs over her shoulder. The only piece of jewelry she's wearing is the forget-me-not necklace I had made for her and it shines brightly as the sun hits it from above.

The yellow dress she chose to wear today makes her look like she's glowing as she walks confidently towards me with the biggest smile on her face. Her deep green eyes sparkling as she passes Ivy her bouquet of sunflowers and forget-me-nots.

Once she reaches the top of the gazebo she leans down and presses the lightest of kisses onto our daughter's cheek and my heart swells with so much happiness and pride as I watch her look down at her with nothing but adoration and love in her eyes.

Paw reaches out towards me and I place our daughter, Robin Ivy Hale, into his arms. I turn towards Florence and take both of her hands in my own, giving them a tight squeeze that makes her laugh loudly.

"Alright, are you guys ready to get hitched?" Ivy beams at both of us as Duke wags his tail happily by her side.

"Yes, yes, yes. A million times yes!" Florence says excitedly. "I've been waiting months for you to get this gazebo done just so we could have our wedding here! Now let's get on with it before I pass out from nerves!"

I smile widely at the amazing woman standing across from me. "You heard the lady," I say, laughing loudly along with the rest of them. "Let's get freaking married!"

I can't believe this is my life.

I can't believe that the woman I fell in love with many, many years ago is just a few vows away from becoming my wife.

I can't believe my plan worked.

—

The first time I laid eyes on Florence was when I was 11 years old. I was sitting in the back of the ranger station reading my Spiderman comic book when my Paw came in with a red-headed girl following him. She looked so angry at him. Her hands were balled into tight fists by her side, but the moment Paw turned around she acted like nothing was wrong and smiled sweetly up at him. I couldn't hear everything they were talking about, so I crept closer and I heard something about how she couldn't feed the animals Cheerios. Cheerios? She tried to feed the animals Cheerios? I remember laughing into my hands so Paw wouldn't yell at me for snooping. She promised him that she wouldn't do it again and he opened the door and off she went. I ran to the small window in the bathroom and watched as she looked around, and then opened her small backpack and grabbed something out of it.

I think I fell in love with her at that moment. When I realized she was sprinkling a trail of cheerios behind her.

—

Ivy is beaming at me, tears streaking down her face as she tries to compose herself enough to marry us.

"Do you, Silas Patrick Hale, take my beautiful and wonderful best friend, Florence Renee Samuels, to be your lawfully wedded wife as long as you both shall live?"

"I do." I reach up and wipe away a stray tear that's escaped Florence's eye. God she's so beautiful, even when she's crying. Even after all these years, she's still the most stunning person I've ever seen.

—

I didn't see Florence again for years, but not a single day went by that I didn't think of her. She plagued my mind and haunted my dreams. I begged the heavens to bring her back into my life, and prayed that she'd come back to the forest so I could see her again.

The next time I saw her I had just turned 18. I was manning the station myself as Paw went to make us lunch and she walked right by, with a guy around her age trailing closely behind her. I recognized her red hair and defiant attitude right away. I followed them until I saw them sitting by the creek. In a little spot that I didn't know was hidden back here.

That's when I learned that her parents had died, and that's why she hadn't been back. I finally learned her name too, Florence. And I knew I'd whisper that name in my sleep until the day I died. My body was fueled with jealousy and rage when he stepped forward and kissed her. I followed them out of the forest and watched as she got into his car and they drove away laughing. I vowed that day to do whatever it took to make her mine.

—

"Do you, Florence Renee Samuels, take this handsome hunk of a man, Silas Patrick Hale, to be your lawfully wedded husband for as long as you both shall live?"

Florence squeezes my hands harder and is bouncing up and down with excitement before she finally answers. "I do. I do. I do. I so freaking do."

"I love you so much." I say.

"I love you." She smiles up at me with tears swimming in her eyes, making her green eyes shine so brightly that it almost knocks the breath out of me.

How did I get so lucky to finally have her look at me like this?

—

I watched them come to this spot many times over the years. I watched as he held her close against this body as she kissed him back with the passion I felt for her. I watched as he stole her virtue here, and listened to the noises she made and pretended it was my name she was whispering. I watched as she said yes to his ridiculous proposal. Every time she looked at him, I could see the love and adoration shining brightly for him through her forest green eyes. I vowed that one day she'd look at me like that.

Each time I saw him with her I felt the monster come alive under my skin.

What was so special about this guy?

What did he have that I didn't?

He had her, and I needed to find a way to take her away from him.

—

"Okay, then I guess this is the part where I pronounce you guys husband and wife!" Ivy squeals out.

Florence and I are both smiling at each other, and I'm dying for Ivy to get to the next part. I can't wait to press my lips against my wife's for the first time. I lick my lips in preparation as I look over at Ivy, silently begging her to get to the next part so I can finally claim Florence as my wife.

"You may FINALLY kiss your bride!"

Florence and I meet right in the middle. I reach up and hold her face in my hands and I kiss my wife for the first time. I feel her groan in contentment as I kiss her with every emotion and feeling I've bottled up for her over the years.

DANIELLE MORRIS

She is worth everything.
All of the waiting was worth it.

—

I started following her over the years. I learned where they lived together. I found out she was a teacher and that her friend worked with her. It was easy to find out where the friend lived. And where her husband worked. I took meticulous notes of every detail of her life. She preferred the gas station near the Target, and she only shopped at the local mom and pop grocery store instead of the giant chain ones.

I liked to watch her, so any time I wasn't working, I sat in my car and watched her go about her day from afar. I learned that if I parked my car in the spot right behind the street sign on the opposite street, I could see right into her dining room.

One day, the husband came home angry. I had never seen him angry before and I worried for her safety. I forced myself to sneak closer to the house and listened at the window as he accused her of cheating with a student. I stood there at the window and watched helplessly as he physically hurt her. Fire burned in my veins as I watched her face turn from terror to pleasure as he fucked her loudly on their dining table. How could she let him treat her like that and then let him have his way with her? I would never put my hands on her. I would make sure her pleasure and happiness came first. Always.

I walked back to my car as hope filled my chest. I finally had a way to force the wedge between them, he was a jealous man, just like me. And I knew what to do to take her away from him. I just had to wait for the right moment. It could take months, years even.

But one day she'd be mine.

—

Paw and Ivy take Robin back to Ivy's house so that we can have some alone time here in our spot before we all meet up for dinner later.

Florence is leaning against my chest and my arm is wrapped around her as we sit here in the gazebo, listening to the sounds of the forest around us.

"What are you thinking about, husband?" she says playfully while pulling away from me. There's that mischievous look in her eyes that I've always loved so much.

"I'm thinking about how every minute of wanting you from afar was worth it. Worth this moment right here. Because now you're finally mine and you can't ever escape me."

She throws her leg around my body so that she's straddling me. This is my favorite way to sit with her because it reminds me of our first time, in this same spot.

"You never have to worry about me leaving you Silas. You are it for me. You're my other half, and I'll thank the world every single day for making sure that it was you who found me here and saved me. You've saved me again and again, and I'll never be able to thank you enough for everything. You have given me everything I've ever wanted. You gave me this wonderful life, and a beautiful baby girl. Nobody will ever be as happy as I am when I'm with you. So I promise I'm not going anywhere. Ever."

I have to swallow against the emotions that this woman brings out in me.

"I love you more than anything, and I'd burn down the entire world to keep you."

"I'm yours, Silas. Forever." She starts to tug on my tie and deepens the kiss between us.

"Mrs. Hale, are you thinking what I'm thinking?"

"Well..." She smirks at me and slowly unbuttons the top button on my shirt. "If you're thinking that this would be a perfect spot to consummate our marriage, Mr. Hale. Then yes."

I raise my eyebrow at her before we shed our clothing quickly.

—

Years later, I followed her and her husband to a prenatal clinic. I knew right then and there that any hope I had for keeping her was gone when she walked out crying tears of joy and carrying that little black and white photo and smiling at him like he was her whole world.

But instead of giving up, I realized that this ending wasn't mine. It was theirs. I knew this was the moment I'd been waiting for. This is what I was going to use to drive them apart.

He wouldn't be able to prove that the baby wasn't his until after that baby was born, and by then she'd hate him for not trusting her love for him.

I told myself this was the perfect plan as I walked into the store and bought the small white stationary that was going to ruin him. I smiled to myself as I typed out message after message that I knew would drive doubt into his head.

Then I waited until they were both out of the house and started planting them for him to find. Amongst her things, her drawers, her makeup bag. I even added one to the suitcase I knew she took to her friend's house, because I knew he liked to use that same suitcase when he left town.

All I had to do was sit back and wait for him to ruin his own life.

So I could finally pull her into mine.

—

We walk hand-in-hand back to the truck, just like we have so many times before. She might not realize it, but I'm slowly replacing each moment that they had together here with our own.

"I can't believe we are actually married." Florence says wistfully as her hand swings back and forth with mine.

"Believe it, baby. You're all mine now." I say back with a sly smile. "And that's never going to change."

She stops and pulls me to her, and stands on her tiptoes to place a kiss on my lips. "Well, that's just gravy baby."

I can't stop the deep laugh that bubbles out of my chest. "You are ridiculous, and I love you."

"I love you more."

I flick her on the nose and make her gasp out in surprise. "I doubt that baby."

She'll never know how much I really love her, and how hard it was to get us to this minute right here. If she knew everything I had to do to prove to her that she belongs to me, she'd never doubt the love I have for her.

―

It took a few more months for him to start finding the letters. I watched as he came home angry at her after he found the first one. I watched as he tore apart their bedroom, looking furiously for more. But even once he found them, he still kept going back to her. He still stayed. I knew his confidence was wavering though, and I couldn't give up. I needed him to leave so I could be there to pick up the pieces.

The thought of taking his wife and his child away from him became my new dream. I'd raise that child as my own while he got to stand on the sidelines and watch her fall in love with me, just like I've been forced to watch for years.

Florence became even more breathtaking as her belly swelled with the life inside her, and I fantasized that the baby growing was my own. I couldn't wait to be a father, and have her look at me the way she looked at her husband.

I needed to hurry this along, she only had a few months left before the baby was due. So I wrote the note that I knew he wouldn't be able to forgive, and when I wrote it I smiled. Knowing that soon that baby wouldn't be his because they'd both be mine.

I fucked up though and underestimated him, and when I found her laying there in the forest, frozen and covered in blood with the knife coming out of her and the baby, a part of me died. I stayed with her, and I hoped that she'd remember me one day.

I knew I'd spend my whole life making it up to her in every single way possible. But I knew I had to wait for the right moment to introduce myself to her. She needed time to heal after the insurmountable loss of her son.

I bided my time, but still watched over her once she moved in with her friend. I didn't know where her husband had taken off to, but I couldn't risk him coming back to claim her. I spent my days trying to figure out a way I could show her that I had cared about her and thought about her while she was in mourning.

I went to her spot often with Duke by my side and that's when it hit me. One day I knew she'd be back. She had to. This is where her parents were laid to rest, and one day, I knew she would come visit them. What better way to look like a man she could fall in love with than building a bench just for her.

She came back to this spot a year after the death of her son, and I was here waiting, just like I always had been.

I knew my plan had finally worked. Our lives finally lined up and I finally had her all to myself. She was mine, and I was hers and every moment I spent with her was exactly what I had always dreamed it would be.

Then Ronan came back and almost ruined everything. I caught that cop friend of theirs snooping around the storage unit that held all of the husband's old things. I watched as he found more of the notes I had hidden that the husband had never found. When I saw him hiding in the back of the coffee shop on the day I was supposed to meet Florence for our first date, I knew he was really just looking out for Florence. The guy really did care for her in his own way and I had seen him following her around many times throughout the last year.

But, that same night after Florence came to the cabin for the first time, I followed her out to her car. I knew a shortcut through the trees and got there before she did. When I got to the parking lot I saw the husband looking at the post it note I had left for her, and he was on the phone whispering angrily at someone. I got closer and heard him tell the person on the other line that he had seen him at the coffee shop, he called him Jay. I knew that he was talking to the cop that had followed me there, Detective James Olsen, and he was threatening him and telling him to stay away from Florence.

I smiled as I disappeared back into the trees because I knew exactly who to pin everything on, and I wouldn't give up until Florence believed it.

The rest of it fell into place much easier than I anticipated. James acted like he was my friend in front of the girls, but when it was just the two of us he asked too many probing questions. I knew he was trying to figure out how to prove that I was the one behind everything, but he didn't have any proof other than his cop gut telling him that something was off about me.

I knew how to cover my damn tracks.

I finally got my chance to turn it all on him when I watched James pick up the post-it that Ronan dropped before I got shot and put it into his pocket. I knew exactly where he'd hide it. And I knew all I needed to do was get Florence to sneak into James's house and find it in the box that he hid all the other notes in. The same box that I watched Ronan find a week earlier as I watched him from my car and through the blinds I had opened while James was gone. I knew the moment he opened that box in James's closet that he would believe that James was the one who had sent him the notes and in turn ruined his life.

I banked on the fact that Ronan still loved Florence and would protect her when I texted him that she was in danger because of James. I was able to watch as it all went down from my hiding spot after Ivy took off again.

I watched as she found the discarded gun and pointed it towards James. All I needed to do was get James to lift his gun again and I knew Ivy would finish this for me, choosing to save her friend rather than wait for any explanations.

So, I popped my head out of the trees when Florence and Ronan weren't looking and I made sure James saw my face. I smiled at him when he yelled that this was all my fault and then I bathed in victory as Ronan and James both went down at the same time.

James never found any real proof that it was me who had sent Ronan the notes. And as I watched him lie there with a bullet hole in his head, I knew he never would. Ronan dying in the process was just an added bonus.

Because now I really would have Florence all to myself.

—

A smile tugs at my lips and I lean down to kiss my wife again as we both watch our beautiful daughter sleep peacefully in her crib.

I look at my wife as she gazes down at our daughter with nothing but love in her eyes. This is my favorite version of her. She was born to be a mother and I'm so glad that I was able to give her that in the end. A day doesn't go by that I don't wish that Wren would have survived, and I whisper my own apologies to him every time I hold our daughter in my arms. I don't think I could have survived losing her. I'm not nearly as strong as her mother is and I'm thankful everyday to have them both in my life.

Florence bends down and gives Robin a soft kiss on her cheek before she grabs my hand and pulls me out of our daughter's bedroom and towards our own.

The love in her eyes when she looks at me almost brings me to my knees every time she gazes my way.

But that's how I know that my plan worked.

Every minute of pining for her from the sidelines.

Every time I had to watch her find comfort in his arms.

Every agonizing moment I had to spend without her...

It was worth it.

Because she's mine now and forever. And nothing will ever take her away from me.

We are soulmates, who share one heart, one soul.

One might say...birds of a feather.

THE END.

Acknowlegdments

WE DID IT GUYS! I can't believe I'm actually writing the acknowledgments for my first novel. This story has my whole heart and soul thrown onto these pages and I couldn't have done it alone. It took a village to write this, so prepare yourselves for an extra long and overly sappy 'thank you's.'

First and foremost, I want to thank my husband, Zach. I truly couldn't have done this without you. You cheered me on from the minute I brought up the idea of wanting to try my hand at writing a book. You kept the excitement of this dream alive during the darkest of days. The days where I wanted to quit and throw my laptop at the wall because I felt like this dream was unattainable. The days where the negative feedback almost crushed me. Thank you for brainstorming throughout every chapter, and telling me when I was going just a little too far out there with this story. You kept me balanced through it all, and cooked me all the best surf and turf when I was in my "don't talk to me because I need to get this scene out" mode. I love you most. I can't wait to create so many stories together in the future.

Annabell, you kept me going every time you came home from school and asked if you could color in the next word count box. Thanks for helping me choose names for my characters. You were the first one besides me to hold my book in their hands and didn't make fun of it. As a preteen, I know that mom becoming an author isn't all that cool, but thanks for not saying that out-loud, even if you won't ever read any of my books. I love you, Bug.

Cassian, you literally forced me to take breaks by dragging me to the snack cabinet any time I looked stressed out over a scene. Lucky charms and hot cheetos can be meals if you let them. You are only 2 and a half, so you won't read this until you are much, much older, but thank you for being the rainbow at the end of a very long storm. I loved all our extra cuddle sessions in between writing sprints. I love you baby bat.

To all the ones I lost too soon, thank you for letting me love you, even if our time was cut too short. You're all in my heart, my soul. This one is for you.

Dad, thanks for always being my rock during the darkest of days. You are the reason I fell in love with books as a kid, and the reason I can call myself an actual author today. Thanks for always supporting me through the ups and downs of this world, and making sure I get cute cat photos on a daily basis to make me laugh. I love you.

Mom, thanks for always asking how my book was coming along whenever we talked. It doesn't seem like much, but every time you remembered to ask meant the world to me. Especially on the days that I wanted to quit writing and give up on this wild dream of mine. Thanks for always giving me sage advice when I need it, that's why I named Dr. Angelica after you, lol.

Mom, I couldn't write a book without throwing a couple Braves references in there just for you. I hope they made you smile when you read them. I know Paw-Paw and Nanny are up there laughing about it. Did you know you were the first person in our family to hold my book? Well you were and I think that's pretty freaking awesome.

To my siblings, Aaron, Marisa, Adrian, Damian, Mathayus and Ayla: one day you'll see all your names in one form or another in all the books I write. There's a whole bunch of you so I couldn't fit you all into this one, but there's definitely a few first and middle names of yours floating around this book. Make sure you text me when you find them one day. I love you all and I hope I'm still your favorite sister after you read the crazy things my brain comes up with.

Nancy, Larry, Paul, Melinda, Sam, Peyton, Chris, Taylor, and Miss Mila-Mouse, thanks for raising the best guy ever. Every single one of you helped shape my husband into the amazing human being he is today, and I will never be able to thank you enough for that. This book wouldn't exist without him. Mila, you didn't raise him but here's written proof that you have the best uncle ever. It's in a book so it has to be true!

Brenda, my amazing editor, thank you for taking this project on. This book would be a dumpster fire without you and your gorgeous brain. You are truly a superhero and the bookish world is so lucky to have you. I can't wait to see our book in your little library!

Lorilea, Sarah, and Marisa, Thank you all for being the biggest hype women from the moment I spilled the beans and told y'all that I was writing a book. One day you'll all be characters in my books and our real life shenanigans will make for the best laughable scenes ever. Rom-com series, anyone?

Lindsey C, I truly, truly couldn't have done this without you. Your guidance when I finally took this plunge into the Indie-Author world was invaluable. Thank you for listening to my hundred voice-notes a day and for answering every single question I had, as stupid as they were! You are such an inspiration and I'm forever thankful to have met you through the Bookstagram community. Fingers gun forever.

Speaking of Bookstagram, this book wouldn't have been possible to write without all the kind feedback and unwavering support from so many of you. Thank you to every single one of you who have followed along with me on this journey. To every person who has shared, liked, or commented on any of my posts, you guys kept me going.

To my amazing beta readers; Mary, Amber, Kaitlyn, Stella, Nicole, Brenda, Haley and Esther: Thank you for being the first eyes on my hot mess of a first draft. Each of you helped shape this story into what it is today. I may never make the best seller list of any kind, but you all helped make this book the best version it could be. Thank you for all your honest feedback, your excitement and hype, your "WHY WOULD YOU DO THIS TO US" text messages and voice notes. You guys reading this book and not hating it was one of the highlights of my year and I'm thankful for each of you.

Haley, I have about a million things I want to thank you for, but the most important one is this; thank you for being my friend when I needed you most. Being able to go to you and being honest about how difficult it was to write a book meant everything to me. You never sugar coated it, but you always had the best advice and offered the greatest moral support. You are in the middle of writing your own novels and you still made time to read mine, I'll never be able to thank you enough for that kindness. I love you, and our ZA Trauma and Drama group. Esther really knew what she was doing when she basically forced us into each other's lives, even if she sucks and still won't read ZA 8. Also Team Tripp always and forever. Give Pedro the moon-man some love for me.

Esther, the other half of my dark and twisty soul. Are there even enough ways to say thank you for everything you've done for me, not just with helping me advertise the fluff out of this book, but in our entire length of friendship? Thank you for being my person, through thick and thin. The Grey to my Yang. The Petty to my Betty. The Reputation Era to my Lover Era. The Ivy to my Florence. You are the MVP of this story and the MVP of my life. I love you to the Moon and to Saturn. And thanks for giving me Duke. He may live with you, but he's the real hero of this story and I adore him, always. Enrique, Emma, and Little E, don't worry, you'll all be in a book one day too. Esther and Duke can't have all the fun!

Zelda Elizabeth, my fluffy feline companion who inspired my sweet Lola in this book. I have to write this because Annabell told me I had to thank you, so don't get a big head about it. You may drive me insane with your zooming zoomies and tendency to knock everything off of my desk at the worst times, but you're cute and cuddly when you want to be. I love your sassy, fluffy little butt and I can promise every book I write will have some sort of cat in it just for you.

Last but not least, let me say thank you to YOU as the reader. I am honored that you chose my book to pick up and read out of all the

DANIELLE MORRIS

billions of novels out there. I hope that some part of this story resonated with you, and I hope that everyone is able to find a small piece of themselves within these characters. I'd love to hear what you think about it, good or bad, though I hope it's mostly good things! If it isn't too much, please think about leaving a review wherever you write reviews! Reviews are so incredibly important for new authors like myself, and I would truly appreciate it!

Love always,

Danielle

Danielle Morris

has been an avid reader her whole life and always dreamed of one day writing her own novels. She loves reading and writing about complex and flawed, but highly relatable characters that make you laugh, cry, and feel all the things.
If she's not reading or writing she's likely spending quality time with her husband and two kids. She loves starting her day with a good cup of coffee, traveling, and being creative in other areas.

Birds of a Feather is her debut novel and you can connect with her online @daniellemorriswrites

Grandpa Ted's Pizza Casserole

prep time: 20 min | cook time: 45 min

INGREDIENTS

- 10 oz egg noodles
- 1 jar pasta sauce
- 3c mozzarella cheese, shredded
- 1 lb ground meat
- 1 package of pepperoni

DIRECTIONS

1. Pre-heat oven to 350°.
2. Cook noodles according to package instructions, until al dente. Drain water.
3. Brown ground meat and season to taste with desired seasonings. Drain grease.
4. In a greased casserole dish, spread a thin layer of sauce.
5. Then start layering by adding one ingredient at a time. Start with half of the noodles, next half of the meat, layer on half of sauce left, then half of the cheese, and top with a layer of pepperoni.
6. Repeat step 5 with the rest of the ingredients.
7. Cover with foil and bake for 30 minutes. Remove foil and bake uncovered for an additional 15 minutes.
8. Once done baking remove from oven and let rest for 10-15 minutes.

Printed in the USA
CPSIA information can be obtained
at www.ICGtesting.com
LVHW090300020923
755847LV00026B/139